The Question Is Murder

ISBN: 978-1-68313-224-0

Library of Congress Control Number: 2021930534

Pen-L Publishing
Fayetteville, Arkansas
Pen-L.com

First Edition
Printed and bound in the USA

Cover design by Jessica Slater
Interior design by Kelsey Rice

The Question Is Murder

By

Mark Willen

Other Books by Mark Willen

Hawke's Point

Hawke's Return

Hawke's Discovery

For Janet

Dear Mr. Ethics

Sam reads the email a second time, then a third, not sure whether to dismiss it as a prank or call the police. He prints it out and then reads it again, looking for some clue to the sender's frame of mind.

It's probably a stunt. Sam gets more than his share of cranks and weirdos. There's something about writing a newspaper column and calling yourself "Mr. Ethics" that attracts them. Some people just take offense at the notion of a guy sitting behind a computer trying to tell them there's a right way to behave.

He takes a deep breath and reads the email again, a blue felt-tipped pen in his hand. He studies the words, the grammar, even the sentence structure, looking for oddities or inconsistencies. Nothing jumps out.

He doesn't need this. Not now.

But then maybe he does. Maybe it's *just* what he needs. Something to take his mind off of Lisa, not unlike the migraine that makes you forget the sprained ankle, at least for a while.

He looks up from the sheet of paper in his hand and glances at the poster that hangs in front of him. It's filled with quotations on writing, and although it's the kind of thing a college kid would hang in a dorm room, he's always liked having it near. And he didn't have much else to stick on the wall two years ago when he was awarded his own office, a privilege he didn't especially want and still hasn't adjusted to. He loves the column, both for its intellectual challenge and for the feeling that he may be helping people, albeit in small ways, to make the world a better place.

He turns back to the email. He needs another opinion and knows it should come from his boss, but he doesn't want to lose control. Brenda would be cautious and call in the executive editor or a lawyer, maybe both, and that would mean days of delay. He's not going to use the email in his column, so whatever he does shouldn't come back to hurt the newspaper. He wants to help if he can, and he doesn't want anyone to get in his way. He's too old for bureaucratic games.

But he does want another opinion.

He gets up, grabs the printout, and walks down the hall to the newsroom. It's eerily quiet, nothing like the newsrooms he grew up in. Gone is the chaos of constant motion and loud conversations carried on from opposite ends of the room. Gone too are the ugly metal desks shoved together so close you can smell the whisky on your neighbor's breath, hear him belch or argue with an official or a source on the phone. Some had hated it, but Sam thrived on the synergy it produced, the bonds it created, the shared excitement of doing something he believed—still believes—is important.

Now, in its place he sees what the younger reporters view as high-tech paradise, with desks crowded with laptops and other electronic devices. The reporters and editors are stuck in a maze of mini-cubicles with three-foot high, sound-absorbing barriers to create a sense of privacy. They need to stand up to see another person.

He's acutely aware of how much journalism has changed in the thirty years he's been practicing it. Not that it was ever pure and not that all its practitioners had less than selfish motives. But many did. Now it's nothing more than a business, a fight for internet clicks or a spot appearance on TV, just when facts and truth matter the most because they're in such short supply. It's one of the reasons he was ready to give up reporting and editing to take on the ethics column, but that's not to say he doesn't miss the thrill of unraveling an important story.

He walks the maze, heading to Molly's corner. "Hey," he says as he comes up behind her.

Her right hand rises in a silencing gesture, and he realizes she's on the phone. One of those ear things hidden by her hair. How was he supposed to know?

While he waits, he glances up at the silent TV monitors on the wall and tries to guess why the weatherman is moving his arms around in a circle. After a minute or so, Molly ends the call and turns to him.

"What?" she asks, not unfriendly but not friendly either. *Busy* is the vibe he gets.

Sam was once Molly's editor and mentor as she learned her way around Congress, which was Sam's beat for twelve years. She still comes to him for advice, though not often, and he will seek her out when his ethics column needs the perspective of someone younger, or a woman.

He hands her the printout without speaking and watches her read it, biting down on her lower lip, a habit he's grown used to. He averts his eyes when she looks up and catches him staring at her. He glances around her cubicle while she finishes, then turns back to her, focusing now on her hands, which grip the printout on either side, as if she's worried he'll have second thoughts and try to take it back. He's never noticed how graceful her hands look, with long supple fingers, as though she was born to play the piano. Or type. The thought makes him smile.

Molly hands back the email and frowns. "So what's the question?" she asks.

"Do you think it's for real?"

She purses her lips and turns her head slightly. Her blue eyes, accented with eye shadow she doesn't need, seem to settle on a photograph of her and Kyle, her fiancé. They are wearing hiking gear and standing atop a boulder, Molly's bleached-blond hair blowing lightly in the wind. Their wedding is set for Memorial Day weekend, less than three months away.

"Look, Sam," she says finally, picking up her water bottle and taking a swallow, making him wait for what's coming. "Every woman has some rat-bastard in her past she'd love to blow to kingdom come, but they never actually do it."

"Some do."

"Not many. And probably only on the spur of the moment. More passion than planning, and never with advance notice."

"This is different. He didn't dump her. He's stalking her and she's scared. She doesn't see any other way out."

Molly tilts her head slightly and he's not sure what that means. She reaches for the moisturizer she keeps on her desk. He watches her squirt some in her palm and then rub it carefully on the backs of her hands. He feels himself getting annoyed. Since Lisa asked him to move out, he has less patience for everything and everyone. He reminds himself of that and takes a deep breath.

"I can't ignore it," he says.

"But what can you do? It's vague and anonymous. You can't use it in the column. Are you thinking of turning it over to the police?"

"No. I have to answer her. Reach out in some way."

"Tell me why. You always told me not to get involved in the stories I cover."

"I can't just let it go."

"What if you find out she's serious? Or suicidal?" she asks. "Then you'll have no choice but to go to the authorities."

The question annoys him. "Of course. But I don't have enough to work with now."

"I don't disagree, and if it's not a hoax, I feel sorry for her. But all you can do is tell her to go to the police."

"She says she can't," he says. "I want to find out why. This is a cry for help."

Molly shrugs, making it clear she doesn't agree. "If I came to you with this, you'd say reporters shouldn't get involved. I'd get your lecture on how our job is to shine a light on problems while staying above the fray, not try to make everything okay."

He doesn't know what to say. He can't argue with the journalistic principle she's quoting, but it doesn't apply here because he's not a reporter planning to write a story about the email. "I have to follow it up," he tells her. "I just do."

"Why'd you ask my advice if you already had your mind made up?"

He walks away without answering. On the one hand, he sees her point, but he's disappointed she isn't more concerned, more helpful. It surprises him that Molly isn't able to put herself in other people's shoes more often. Seeing the other side of an issue—any issue—is an important skill for a reporter. Call it empathy.

But maybe he's just annoyed because she doesn't agree with him.

Back in his office, he forwards the email to the IT department. He deletes the content, but they can analyze the IP address or whatever they look at to try to determine where it came from. He doesn't have much hope, but it's worth a try. Then he turns back to the email and rereads it.

> Dear Mr. Ethics:
>
> Is murder ever ethical? I hope so because I don't have a choice. An ex-lover is destroying me. I broke up with him and now he's

ruining my life. He got into my laptop, stole all my data and used it to stalk, embarrass, and almost bankrupt me. Now he's moved on to even worse stuff. He's killing my hope for any kind of normal life, so killing him is a form of self-defense. Justifiable homicide, right?

I can't go to the police for reasons I can't explain here. And I can't give you any more details because I can't risk you figuring out my name.

So can I murder him? And no, I'm not kidding.

Sincerely,
Truly Desperate

Sam jots down several notes. The tone strikes him as strangely calm and rational. She's making a logical argument, not what you'd expect from someone stressed and frantic. Or crazy. Is it a hoax? Maybe a college kid bored with her ethics class and looking for term paper ideas. Or an author concocting a crazy plot for a thriller. Or maybe someone pissed off at Mr. Ethics and hoping to draw him into a discussion that will embarrass him if made public.

But maybe not.

It doesn't matter. He has to answer her. Keep her talking, try to get more clues so he can stop her on the off chance she really is planning a murder.

He turns to his keyboard and after several false starts comes up with his reply.

Dear Truly Desperate,

I'm going to assume this is a not a prank because I have no way of knowing, and I want to give you the benefit of the doubt.

From the little you've told me, I can assure you that what you propose is not ethical. Justifiable homicide applies only when your life is in imminent danger, and you haven't convinced me that this is the case. I don't think you've convinced yourself or you wouldn't be asking me.

You need to go to the police. If you can't do it yourself, is there someone who can do it for you? If necessary, I might be willing to do that, depending on the details. And with the newspaper behind me, the police will feel obliged to take it seriously.

If you don't want my help, I suggest you talk to a mental health professional or a social worker or someone experienced in cases involving domestic partner abuse (which this obviously is).

If you'd like to talk about this more (and I will treat any conversations we have confidentially), you may call me at any time (cellphone number below).

Above all, don't do anything rash.

Regards,
Sam Turner (a.k.a. Mr. Ethics)

He sits back and reads the note again. He considers his offer to go to the police on her behalf, mindful of Molly's warning not to get involved. He wants to help her, but that's going too far. He eliminates that sentence.

He also cuts the promise of confidentiality. If she asks for it, he'll agree, but there's no need to offer it up front. And it might tie his hands unnecessarily.

He reads his response one last time and hits the send button.

A drizzle is falling in Washington when he leaves the office on 11th Street a little before five. He hasn't made much progress on this week's column, but he needs an early start to get to the University of Maryland in College Park, where he teaches a weekly seminar in journalism ethics.

On the ride along slow-moving Rhode Island Avenue, he keeps thinking about the email. He's hoping she'll call soon, but he knows there's a good chance he'll never hear from her again, never find out whether it was a hoax or whether she changed her mind or even whether she carried out her plan. There isn't much he can do but wait.

The ethics seminar is for graduate students in journalism, many of them in mid-career. He loves handing them a difficult problem and watching them wrestle with it, struggling to put ethics above the constant on-the-job demand to write attention-grabbing stories. The class is diverse in every way, split by gender, race, and background, a fact that makes for spirited discussions. His email doesn't pose a standard journalism issue, but tonight's topic is anonymous sources, and he wonders if he might find a way to work it in.

He arrives on campus in time to grab a sandwich that he eats quickly. When he reaches the seminar room, everyone is already seated. He unloads his briefcase, takes a breath, and begins.

"We've talked a lot about transparency in reporting and how important it is to limit your use of anonymous sources. You owe it to your readers to show what and whom your reporting is based on so they can judge its credibility. But sometimes granting anonymity is the only way to get information. When that's the case, it's crucial to set ground rules and stick to them. Let's run through some typical approaches. Who wants to start?"

He stands up and begins pacing while he waits for the answers.

"Question the source's motives and how that affects his information. Don't let him use you." The answer, a near verbatim quote from the Society of Journalists' Code of Ethics, comes from Danny Flores, one of Sam's favorites. He is in his late twenties, an earnest student who works as an editor on a TV news website, waiting for a chance for a real reporting job. Danny and Sam are the only men in the room wearing ties. Everyone else is dressed in jeans or shorts, with T-shirts or simple blouses.

"Yes," Sam says, "but I'd qualify that. Sources often have ulterior motives and that's not necessarily a problem. Just be sure you're aware of them and that the benefit to your readers justifies what you're doing. What else?"

"No personal attacks," another student says.

"Exactly," says Sam. "Never let someone hide behind anonymity to attack another person."

They continue through the list, Sam still moving around the room, waiting not so patiently for an opening. When he doesn't get one, he plunges in. "What if you find out the source has broken the law or intends to break the law?"

"That's not your problem," Danny says. "We're not cops. Besides, sometimes we need them to break laws. Like if they're giving you confidential information."

"Agreed. We're not cops and sometimes it works to our advantage if they break a law to reveal information," he says before stopping and running his eyes over the group. "But what if someone confesses to a crime? Say they offer you an exclusive interview to say how sorry or guilty they feel but won't let their name be revealed?"

"I'd take it," says Josh Glenn, an eager but not-too bright kid who works for an online political news aggregator and who once told Sam he didn't believe ethics should be a required course. That was right after Sam asked him not to wear his baseball cap in class.

"Why would you take it?" Sam asks.

"Great human interest story. And it would serve the public."

"How would it serve the public?" he asks, genuinely curious.

Josh doesn't answer right away, and Eliza Morado tries to come to his rescue. "If the person felt guilty and sorry, and the interview showed that, it might discourage someone else from committing a similar crime," she says.

Eliza is a thirtyish woman who writes a sports blog and is already lobbying Sam for a job with his paper. She's wearing too-tight jeans and a top with a plunging neckline.

"So you'd be doing it to discourage crime?" he asks, knowing he hasn't hidden his skepticism. "Do you really believe it would have that effect?"

"It might. And anyway, it'd make a great story."

He looks around the room to see if anyone else wants to comment. His eyes settle on Danny. They look at each other for a second before Danny speaks. "You don't know that it would discourage crime. It could have the opposite effect. It might encourage some nut case who wants his fifteen minutes in the limelight."

"You can't control that," Eliza says. "If you never printed anything that might provoke some nut job, you'd never print anything."

Others jump in and the discussion goes on until Sam worries that time will run out.

"Let me put another twist on it," he says, still moving about the room. "What if you became aware of a long-ago sexual assault case that was never reported to the police? Let's say the alleged perpetrator is a teacher who's still in the school system. The victim is now a married adult. You grant anonymity to the victim thinking she deserves it and you want to save other kids from a similar fate. Plus, you know it could turn into a major news story if it checks out. During the interview, the victim tells you she doesn't want to report it to the police because it's her word against his and no one will believe her. Instead she's contemplating killing the teacher."

It sounds implausible even to Sam, so he modifies it. "No, scratch that last part. Let's say she tells you that her husband bought a gun and she's worried he's going to go after the teacher."

He lets that float for a minute, turning from one student to the next as they take it in.

"You have to give the teacher a chance to comment before writing the story," one student says.

"Sure," Sam says, "but what would you tell him? You can't name the woman."

"If she's telling the truth, he already knows her name."

"Maybe," Danny breaks in. "What if the teacher's assaulted several kids over many years? He won't know which one is talking."

It's a good point, but it is steering the conversation away from where Sam wants it to go.

"Let's come back to the woman's fear that her husband is going to kill the guy. Would you go to the police with that?"

There is a pause while they think about it. "It's too vague," another woman offers, "and the police wouldn't take it seriously." The woman is Ariana Soto, a bookish, normally quiet and tentative student who has yet to break into journalism. Sam has seen Ariana and Danny arrive at class together and believes they're an item. He likes them both and, on some level, hopes he's right about them being together.

"Maybe you could talk to the husband first to see if the threat is real," Josh says.

Sam shakes his head. "Not unless the victim agrees. And even if you talk to the husband, how can you tell if he's a serious threat? You're not a shrink or a social worker."

"It will make him think twice about killing the guy if he knows you suspect him," Josh says. "He'll know he'll get caught."

Sam leans his weight against a wall as he considers that. "Is that your role? Why not go to the police? Citizens are required by law to speak up if they know a crime is about to be committed. Or do you think the First Amendment exempts the press?"

"The First Amendment is why you have to write the story," Eliza says. "It's not that complicated. You go to the teacher and say a woman is accusing him of assault. You don't need a name because he's going to deny he ever assaulted anyone. You let him comment and then print what you have. You don't use the woman's name, you don't mention the husband or talk to him, and you don't go to the police. Once it's public, the cops can sort it out."

"But if the woman doesn't want to go to the police, they'll have nothing to go on unless you tell them who she is," Danny says. "You're back to square one. And it's not right to print that kind of allegation from an unnamed source. It's not fair to the teacher."

"It's not fair to the woman to do nothing," Ariana says.

Eliza shakes her head and starts to respond, but Sam interrupts her. He is out of time.

"Let's make this an additional assignment for next week. Take the situation as I've outlined it and tell me what you'd do and how you'd justify your actions. Keep it to a thousand words. Be sure to include the threat from the husband and how you'd handle that. Is it your responsibility to do something or not? And if you think you should write a story, what would it say?"

He is tempted to tell them to email their essays to him within seventy-two hours, but he doesn't. Much as he'd welcome it, he can't expect his students to solve his problem.

When Lisa asked him to move out, Sam found a short-term rental, a furnished one-bedroom, hoping the separation would end soon. The apartment is on Massachusetts Avenue in an older building with a sparse, high-ceiling lobby, a perpetually annoyed doorman, and a chugging elevator that rattles on its way to the twelfth floor. It's a big step down from the colonial in Bethesda, which was spacious enough to raise three children and a dog named Dodger. He doesn't miss the house or the space, and the children are grown, but he misses Lisa. And he misses Dodger.

It is after ten when he opens his door, and he is still nursing a glass of bourbon, stretched out on a couch at midnight when his cellphone sounds. The screen says, "caller unknown," but he guesses who it is.

"Hello?"

"Mr. Ethics, I presume?" The voice sounds distant or maybe muffled. He wonders if she is trying to disguise it.

He takes a breath. "You can call me Sam."

"You can still call me Truly Desperate."

Sam stands up and walks over to the window, peeking behind the shade as if he expects to see her. "I'm glad you called."

"Why? Why do you care?" He can't tell whether it's fear or hostility that gives her voice an edge.

"You asked for my help."

"No, I asked for your advice on an ethical question."

"Well, I gave you that in my email and you still called me." He finds himself getting annoyed and isn't sure why. He tries to shake it off. "I'm not your enemy," he says. "I want to help if I can. If you don't want that, why did you send the email?"

"Truth is, I don't know why."

"Yes, you do. You said it yourself. You're desperate and you need help."

She is silent so he keeps going. "If what you say is true, you need to go to the police."

"You don't believe me," she says in a voice smothered with disappointment.

"I didn't say that, but you haven't given me much to grab hold of. If you'll trust me, maybe there's something I can do."

She doesn't answer right away, which he takes as a good sign.

"I can't deal with this much longer," she says.

"Why don't we meet somewhere? You can tell me the whole story, and then we'll try to figure out what to do."

"I can't let you know who I am."

"Why is that?"

"Because I really do have to kill him. It's the only way to make him stop."

"I don't believe that, and you don't either. You wouldn't have written me if you didn't want me to do something."

"Don't analyze me. I already have a shrink."

"Have you talked to him about this?"

"Her. And that's none of your business."

He sighs. He can hear the stress in her voice and wants to ease it.

"Look," he says as gently as he can. "I'd like to help, but I can't if you won't let me and won't talk to me. Why don't we meet? No strings. You don't have to tell me your name."

"And you won't try to follow me and find out who I am?"

"Of course not. I won't do anything you don't want me to do." She doesn't answer so he pushes on. "Just pick a place."

More silence.

"Are you near downtown Washington or can you get there?" he asks.

She hesitates and he takes that as encouragement. "Take the subway and get off at Metro Center. Exit on 13th and turn left. You'll see a Peet's Coffee shop. How about we meet there tomorrow? You can pick the time."

Now he hears her sigh. "Ten-thirty," she says. "How will I know you?"

"I'll wear a blue shirt and a red tie."

"Like that'll be different from everybody else in D.C.? Tell me what you look like."

"A fifty-five-year-old Prince Harry. But with a lot less hair. The usual paunch."

"If I'm not there, you'll know I changed my mind."

My Real Name Is Kelly

Can Mr. Ethics help? Danny and Ariana made me think he could, and he sounded genuine, if a bit too old to understand what I'm going through. But meeting him is awfully risky. In fact, it scares the hell out of me, though it's not like I have a lot of other options I haven't already tried.

The thought makes me dizzy and I sit down on the couch. As my head clears, I consider a cigarette, but going out on the balcony feels like more than I can handle.

I should never have let Ariana get involved. I know she's trying to help, and she thinks she's doing the right thing, but she and Danny don't understand. I've tried to handle it in a rational way, but there's nothing rational about what Wade is doing.

I wish I hadn't mentioned murder in the email. God, I don't even know where that came from. The truth is, the idea didn't crystallize for me, didn't really seem a possibility, until I started writing the email. I was just trying to get his attention and make some excuse for writing to an ethics advice columnist. How stupid of me.

Not that I don't have justification. Wade's destroying my life. I have every right to stop him and what other option is there?

Could I actually go through with it? I probably don't have the guts for it, though I'm desperate enough.

Oh, God!

I flop down on the floor and assume the yoga corpse pose, focusing on breathing, trying to relax. Lassie is immediately upon me, settling on my chest as if to check my heartbeat. For a cat, she's phenomenally caring and sensitive. I used to think she could tell my moods before I did, but now there is only one mood. And there's nothing hard about recognizing it.

Danny was the one who pushed me to contact the newspaper guy. But I don't see what Mr. Ethics can do to help. Danny says I'm wrong. That there are options I haven't thought of. But what exactly can he do that makes the risk of meeting him worth it? Danny has always had this highfalutin idea that journalism is something noble and reporters are supermen, somehow able to leap tall buildings at a single bound and fix problems or at least shine a light on them so somebody else will fix them. How ridiculous.

I don't know if I can go through with the meeting. I haven't even told Heather the whole story and she's my shrink. Oh, I told her the most important part. How I met Wade and how stupid I was and what he's doing to me. But not that I might kill him. Of course, I didn't admit that to myself until I wrote the email, though I guess it's always been in the back of my mind. Doesn't everybody daydream about killing the person who makes their life miserable? An evil boss. A sexual predator. A competitor. Your parents when you're thirteen.

I really do have justification. He's ruined my life. I can barely make it into work, and I have no life outside the office. Ariana and Danny are the only people I see, and that's only because they keep coming over and insisting I let them in.

Wade deserves to die. He really does. The credit card shit was bad enough, but the dating profile was vicious. And the threat with the pictures? I still remember the day I posed. How could I forget? I didn't want to do it, but he could be so persuasive.

And as bad as what he's done, I'm sure he's planning something worse. Who knows what he'll come up with next? That's why killing him might be the best solution. The only solution.

Lassie is purring. I guess she agrees with me. I rub under her chin and the purring grows louder. Her eyes are shut tight. I remember once purring in Wade's arms after having sex with him. It's hard to even imagine that happened.

I was so stupid! Did I ever love him? I thought I did. Oh, I knew it was crazy to let it go so far. And for so long. He'd never leave his wife, as awful as he claimed she was. And I always knew I loved him more than he loved me.

I remember when we met at that fundraiser. I was a volunteer helping check the guests in, and when he came over to thank everyone, he took an interest in me.

Yeah, I was flattered. Stupid me. When he came back later and pulled me aside to ask me what issues were most important to me—like he'd actually shape his campaign around my advice—I let him lead me on. I knew it was part of his political routine. They do that all the time with constituents to pretend they care.

But it worked. And when I told him I wanted to get a job in government policymaking, he said he could help. So how could I refuse an offer to have coffee that Saturday morning when he had to be downtown for a meeting?

I was surprised to see him walk into the shop by himself—no aides and no security. A week later he called to say he had a lead for me with a House member who was also from South Carolina. I was thrilled, but it didn't go anywhere—other than my bedroom, that is.

When he next called and suggested we get together, it was clear something else was developing, and when he said he had to be careful about being seen alone with me in public, I invited him over.

I know what he thought, and he had every right to think it. We never went anywhere else after that. It was always him coming over, usually late at night, for a drink and sex. At least he bought his own Scotch—he preferred the expensive kind—though for some reason he expected me to supply the condoms.

I know it sounds stupid, but for a few months, I was the happiest person in the world. And he kept getting me interviews for jobs, though none ever panned out. I thought I loved him. Maybe I did. He pretended to love me, but he fed me a pack of lies, especially about leaving his wife.

I began to resent it, and he started to get annoyed. It was gradual. We'd fight over little things. And over sex when he asked me to do things I wasn't at all interested in doing. It was on one of those nights when he was pressuring me that I finally agreed to the photos. I felt ashamed afterwards. That was the beginning of the end.

Although it wasn't the end. Not by a long shot.

I'm not sure how he got into my computer. When I took it into the shop, they found spyware. He could have planted it sometime when I wasn't there or fooled me into opening a loaded email. Does that mean he planned it all along? Or did he find some IT geek and give him some excuse for breaking into my computer? I know he has the resources to do that and anything else he wants to do. Unlimited resources.

Whatever, it's been horrifying. Each trick more devastating than the last. I've begged him to stop, but he denies it all, won't admit to anything. Claims it must be someone else. He was so convincing I even began to wonder if I'd been hacked by some thief.

Until the pictures. The pictures proved it was him, as I always suspected. Ariana says I should go to his wife and tell her. She'll make him stop. But I can't do that. I'm not strong enough, and why hurt her? It's not her fault, and who's to say she can stop him anyway?

No, there is no way to stop him.

Except one.

Maybe I should try once more to get through to him, but that will be his last chance. Mine too.

I better take a sleeping pill and hope it works for a change. I'll wait until morning to decide whether I want to keep my appointment with Mr. Ethics.

First Impressions

The morning rush has slowed by the time Sam reaches the coffee shop. He asks the barista for the smallest, least exotic coffee they offer and takes a conspicuous table facing the door. No one seated or standing in line seems at all interested in him, so he focuses on the new arrivals as they enter, trying to imagine what his caller will look like.

She'll be nervous, even scared, cautiously looking over her shoulder, probably young, strained from sleepless nights, maybe even a bit crazed. And fragile as a light bulb rolling around a tabletop.

Sam takes no satisfaction in being right on almost every count. The woman who arrives fifteen minutes late can't be more than twenty-five. She has a raincoat wrapped tightly around her, though no rain is forecast, and she wears a hat that hides her hair and sunglasses that keep him from seeing her eyes. She looks the part so well he almost wonders if she's faking it.

He watches as she looks around and finds him and then walks over to his table and sits down.

"I'm glad you came," he says, putting his doubts on a mental shelf.

"I'm not sure why I did."

"Maybe for the same reason you sent me that email."

She looks away.

"I'm glad you wrote," he continues, "and I'd like to help if I can."

"I'm not sure anyone can."

"But you need help. I'm just curious why you chose to ask me."

She shrugs.

"Why me?" he asks again as the silence continues. "You weren't really seeking ethical advice."

She turns her face toward him, but with the sunglasses on, he can barely see her eyes. Still his stare seems to get to her. "Let me get a cup of coffee," she says. "I'll be right back."

He wonders for a second whether she's going to skip out, but she gets into line and as he waits, he tries not to get impatient. As soon as she returns, he repeats his question.

"Why did you pick me to ask for help?"

She shrugs but doesn't say anything.

"I really wish you'd take off those glasses," he says.

She does, but instead of placing them on the table, she goes through an elaborate procedure of pulling a case out of her purse, putting the sunglasses away, and replacing them with a pair of rounded clear glasses, all of which gives her a chance to delay.

"I'd like to help," Sam says, "but if you're not going to tell me anything, you're wasting my time."

"We have a mutual friend," she says, placing both hands around her coffee cup. "He said you were a decent guy and could be trusted."

"Who?"

"It's not important."

Sam lets it go. "Tell me about the harassment," he says.

"It's more than that," she says and takes a sip of her coffee. Every move she makes seems aimed at stalling. So why is she here?

"You said you broke up with your boyfriend, and he's using your personal data to harass you." Sam stops and waits for her to look up so he can meet her eyes. The glasses give her a scholarly look and she isn't wearing any makeup, but even with the obvious stress and anxiety, he can see she is pretty. "Can you be more specific?" he asks.

"He got into my computer, planted some malware or something. All I know is he got into my accounts. I changed my passwords, but it was too late."

"So what did he do? Buy a bunch of stuff on your credit cards?"

"That's part of it. He bought airline tickets, booked hotels, bought concert tickets. Always picking expensive shit that was nonrefundable."

"But surely the credit card companies can deal with that. Your liability is limited."

"Yeah, but it's taking forever and meanwhile I have no credit." Her voice cracks when she says it. "But money isn't the worst of it. There were other things. Personal things."

Sam waits.

"Look, if we're going to talk about this, we need to get out of here," she says. "There's no privacy."

He considers asking her to his office, but he doubts she'll agree to that. "Why don't we take a walk and find a spot?" he suggests. "It's warm enough to sit on a bench, and at this hour, we ought to be able to get some privacy."

She nods and they leave. They walk slowly, not talking, up 13th Street to Franklin Square, where they find a stone bench behind the statue of Commodore Perry.

When they're seated, Sam turns slightly to face her, but she stares straight ahead, again unwilling to meet his eyes. At least she hasn't put the sunglasses back on. She's taken off the raincoat and is looking down at her sneakers, and he notices a nervous tremble in one hand. She sees him watching and clasps her hands together.

"What other things did he do?" he asks.

"You can't print this."

"I won't, but I need to know."

"First he signed me up for an online dating service, posting a ludicrous description that made me sound like a complete slut."

"But don't they protect your identity? They wouldn't have let him post your phone number or your email."

"No, only the agency had that and when I found out, I canceled it."

"So no real harm done," he ventures.

She turns to him and shakes her head as though he doesn't have a clue.

"It was a warning, and it was just the start." She takes a deep breath before continuing. "You see, I'd let him take some pictures of me. Dumb, I know. Real dumb. He posted one online. Topless and without my face, but he called my attention to it, a rather explicit threat of what might happen. He could post pictures that are much worse." Her voice breaks and she turns away again. He waits while she pulls out a tissue.

"You need to tell me all of it," he says, not sure what right he has to ask.

"Then he sent me a website for some prostitute. Asked how I'd feel if he created one for me with my pictures and my phone number and email. I've already changed them, but that won't help. He knows where I work and where I live."

Sam shakes his head. "I don't understand," he says. "This is a no-brainer. You know his name. You go to the police and prosecute."

"It would be my word against his."

"No, you've got enough detail and enough of an internet footprint for them to confirm it."

She shakes her head. "You don't understand. He's very powerful. The police won't do anything, and if he finds out I went to them, it'll only get worse."

"How powerful is he? What does he do?"

She shakes her head again.

"If he's that powerful," Sam says, "he probably has a lot more to lose than you if this becomes public."

"He'll deny it and no one will believe me. Remember the Kavanaugh hearings? It'll be like that—only a blip for him. But it'll destroy me. It already has."

"Maybe you can confront him and record it secretly. That way he can't deny it."

"He won't admit anything, not even to me. Says it must be someone else, but it can't be because no one else had the pictures."

Sam leans back and presses his fingers against his eyes, trying to absorb everything he's been told, but after a few seconds, she gets up.

"I've got to go," she says. "There's nothing you can do."

Sam reaches up to take her wrist but stops himself. "Not yet. Please."

She sits down slowly and scrounges in her purse for a cigarette, but before she lights it, she stops, shakes her head and puts it back in her purse. She leans back on the bench and sighs.

Sam does the same. He still isn't getting it. She came to him for help but won't let him provide any.

"What does he hope to gain by all of this?" he asks. "Surely he can't expect you to take him back after he's treated you this way."

"How many people in real power do you know?"

"A lot," he says without hesitation.

"Then you know how it gets in their head. They can't stand someone rejecting them, at least not on a personal level. If I'd had any sense, I would have arranged it so he was the one who broke it off."

"Just how powerful is this guy? Is he in the White House? A member of Congress?"

"I can't give you any clues."

"Is he married? Can't you go to his wife?"

She stands up again. "I better go."

"If the police know that my newspaper is sniffing around and interested, that could make a big difference. They will do something."

"You don't know that. I can't take the risk."

Sam doesn't like looking up at her, so he stands, although he's reluctant to end the conversation. "I want to help, and I think you want me to. You've told me a lot, but I need more."

"You need his name and that's the one thing I'm afraid to give you."

"At least think about it. It's a better alternative than trying to handle it yourself. That isn't getting you anywhere."

"I know. I guess I wrote to you hoping you'd have some idea I hadn't thought of. Obviously, you don't. I'll have to deal with this my own way."

Hard Questions

Sam takes a roundabout route to the office, replaying the conversation in his mind. Something about it doesn't jell. Well, a lot really. She needs and wants help but is incapable of accepting it. But it's more than that—something under the surface that he can't get hold of.

The frustration makes him think of Lisa, not that he needs much of an excuse to do that. Lisa has always been the person he could think aloud with. She always knew what questions to ask, when to probe, when to be silent, when to give advice. Nobody else comes close.

Lisa.

Sam knows their separation was a long time coming. Maybe that's why it was such a surprise when it finally happened. It's been seven weeks now, and he hasn't called or emailed. She wanted it that way, saying a complete break, at least for a few months, was what she needed. In a way that hurt the most. Maybe the fire went out long ago, but they never stopped being friends. Not from his point of view. He really misses her.

The kids are doing their best to help, staying in touch with him, and undoubtedly with Lisa, without asking too many questions or rendering judgment. How long will that last? They have lives of their own, out of town now, with jobs and families that keep them busy.

Can he call Lisa and ask to talk to her about this new problem? Maybe make it clear he just needs advice and doesn't want to force a conversation about their future. Or their past.

The worst that could happen is she'll say no, and that's no worse than wondering. Still, he puts off calling.

Sam feels agitated and gets up to walk around the newsroom, but before he reaches his door, his phone rings. It's the IT department.

"That email you asked me to look at? I can't tell you much. It came from a computer at a library in College Park. That's about it."

"From the university?" Sam asks.

"No, a public library. I can't get anything on it without the library's help or a court order. Is it a big deal?"

"Just an anonymous email that's bugging me. Thanks for taking a look."

Sam ends the call, sits back down, and starts scrolling through his email, searching for a question to use in this week's column, when Molly appears in his doorway. He looks up, and she smiles and gives him a cutesy wave of her hand, which holds her trusty water bottle.

"You okay?" she asks.

"Yes." He turns away from his computer, and she takes the seat at the side of his desk. Hardly anyone uses the one directly across from him.

"You were late this morning?" she says, putting a question mark on the end of it that he chooses to ignore. "What did you decide to do about that email?"

He looks at her and sighs. He doesn't want to lie, even by omission. One of the problems with writing an ethics column is that you feel a lot of pressure to practice what you preach. He often argues in his column that a white lie is okay under certain circumstances, and he could probably rationalize this one away if he had more time, but he doesn't.

"Yeah, I met with her this morning."

"Really? That was quick. How'd you track her down?"

"I answered her email and she called me."

"Is she for real? Who is she?"

"I don't know."

Molly waits for more, but he doesn't offer anything.

"Don't know what?" she asks. "Who she is or whether she's for real?"

"She doesn't want me to know her name. I wouldn't have met her if I didn't think she was for real, but she didn't give me enough to go on." He leaves it there, but of course Molly won't let it go.

"Don't be a tease. Tell me what she said."

Sam looks at her. He does want someone to help him sort through this, but he no longer thinks Molly is the right person.

"I need to keep the details confidential," he says.

"But you wanted to talk to me about it yesterday."

He nods. "I did, but you were pretty dismissive of the whole thing."

She pushes the hair back from the side of her face and runs her tongue over her lower lip, both signs of a mind in motion. "How old is she? You can at least tell me that."

"Mid-twenties."

"That's close to my age. You might need my point of view."

He smiles. "Maybe, but not right now. Besides, yesterday you told me it was a mistake to get involved."

"Yeah, and a lot of good that did. Did she at least tell you why she picked you to write to?"

Sam shakes his head. "She claims we have a mutual friend but wouldn't say who it was."

Again Molly pushes the hair off her face as she considers that. "Does she have a good reason for not going to the police?"

"I'm not going to play twenty questions with you."

"I'm just being a reporter."

"I know, but I'm not playing along."

She raises her eyebrows as if to say, "have it your way," and gets up. But then she hesitates and sits back down.

"Sam, this doesn't seem that complicated. She needs the police or a lawyer or a counselor, not an ethics columnist. There's nothing you can do."

"You don't know that. She's in a bad place and maybe I can help her."

"How is that your job?"

He shakes his head as if he doesn't understand the question. His eyes settle on the poster on the opposite wall.

"Sam, look at me. This isn't like you, and you're doing things that could get you in trouble. I don't need to tell you that because you already know it. It's why you didn't tell Brenda."

"I want to help her. Why is that so hard to understand?"

"Because it's not your job."

She lets out a breath and he can see she's exasperated with him, but he doesn't care.

"Which job?" he asks. "Columnist or human being?"

"Sam, I know you're going through a lot. You miss Lisa and as much as you like your ethics column, you miss the adrenalin rush of a good story, but getting involved like this isn't a solution. If you're having a midlife crisis, buy a convertible or find some young hottie. Don't risk your job."

"I'm not risking my job. You're overreacting, and I really don't want to talk about it anymore."

She gets up again and shakes her head. "You *are* risking your job. You know how Brenda will react if she finds out you're doing this behind her back."

Molly waits for a response, but Sam doesn't offer one.

After she leaves, he thinks about what she said. He's not having a midlife crisis. He just wants to help a young woman in trouble. Yes, it's unorthodox, and yes, he'd probably tell someone else in his position not to get involved. But if there's one thing he's learned about ethics, it's that it's rarely black and white. The situation matters, and sometimes doing the right thing means recognizing that and acting accordingly.

Sam goes back to his emails and picks two questions for his column. One deals with an employer's right to read a worker's email, and the other asks whether movie theaters should be able to stop patrons from bringing in food. Both are easy to answer and will allow him to polish off the column quickly.

As he works on them, though, his mind keeps drifting back to what Molly said. He knows she has a point, but at this stage in his life, he wants to make a difference, and he thinks he can help this young woman get through a difficult time.

Still, it won't hurt to get another opinion, both on what he's doing and how he can help.

He decides to do what he wanted to do all along.

But he gets Lisa's voicemail.

"Hi, it's Sam," he says, purposely not saying "it's me." He swallows, then goes on. "I know I promised not to call, but I could use some help with a work problem and wondered if you might be able to meet for a drink. Or even dinner. I wouldn't bother you, but I've got a serious problem, and no one can help me think it through the way you can."

He hangs up without saying anything else. He hopes he hit the right tone, making it sound so important she can't ignore it while not sounding needy or threatening or scheming.

He doesn't have to wait long. She calls back in ten minutes, making him wonder if she was screening her calls and intentionally avoiding his. He answers with an upbeat hello, but she dashes his hopes quickly.

"I'm sorry, Sam. It's not a good idea."

A Daughter's Concern

Sam leaves the office earlier than normal and heads straight back to his apartment, not fighting his disappointment and figuring it will be easier to think if he's alone at home.

He pours half a glass of wine and turns on cable news before discarding both for the bourbon he prefers and the thinking he's been trying to avoid.

Is it truly over with Lisa? There will always be the kids to keep them in touch, but he wants more than that. Even if they can't be married, he wants some kind of friendship. He can understand how that would be awkward if there were someone else, but he doesn't think there is. Maybe she just needs some time.

Her refusal to see him rankles. Does he really need her advice or is it an excuse to see her? Both. He doesn't think he would turn her down if the shoe were on the other foot, though she often accused him of not being there when she needed him. In any event, she is making a statement.

His phone rings. He retrieves it from the desk and smiles when he sees it's Betsy.

"Hi, Dad, how are you?" she says.

He hesitates and then tells her the truth. "A little low, to be honest."

"Something going on?"

"A problem at work," he says.

"That usually gets your juices going. What is it?"

For a second he considers telling her, but something stops him. "Just a thorny ethics question. Trying to figure out how to stop someone from doing the wrong thing."

He asks about his grandson, and they chat a bit more before she returns to his initial answer.

"Is it work that's got you down or something else?" she asks.

"Mostly work."

There is a pause, as though she expects him to continue, but he doesn't.

"Maybe you're spending too much time alone," she says. "You should find something you're interested in and get out and meet some new people."

"Not now. I'm not ready for that."

"I know it's hard," she offers.

"I'll get there. Give me some time."

"I worry about you."

"You don't need to. It's just something I have to get through."

"But maybe not alone. Have you thought about seeing a counselor? It might help."

He has thought about it, but he doesn't want to say that. He decides to end the call, and as soon as he can, he does. "Thanks for calling. I love you."

"Love you too."

He sits down, aware that he feels worse after the phone call than before. He is alone and cut off. He wonders why he never made more friends of his own, but he knows he's never been that type. Never needed anyone beyond Lisa.

He can understand her reluctance to see him, but that doesn't make it hurt any less.

His mind drifts back to the meeting with his still-anonymous pen pal. He really wants to help. How can he not?

She's in trouble and that's his primary concern. But he can't help wonder if Molly is right that his loneliness—the lack of meaning and connection in his life since his separation from Lisa—isn't part of his need to get involved.

Theirs had been an improbable marriage. They met in high school, lean years for both of them, in Salisbury, a small town in eastern Maryland, and while they hung out with the same crowd, they were never more than casual friends. But Lisa wrote to Sam after he went off to the Marines, and one night while he was home on leave, they went out drinking and woke up in the same bed. Lisa avoided Sam on his next leave, and it wasn't until he came back for good that he discovered he was the father of eight-month-old Betsy. When he and Lisa married six months later, neither was sure they were doing the right thing.

But they grew to love each other. Sam was sure about that. It'd been tough at first, working part-time jobs while he earned a college degree, and then patching together childcare so Lisa could go to law school while Sam worked long days to build a career, first as a reporter covering Congress, then as an investigative reporter, later as an editor managing coverage of politics and the federal government, and now as a columnist. Throughout it all, they struggled to manage two stressful careers and a family, but those struggles—and the kids they were raising—brought them together in ways that a more idyllic courtship never could have. It was true that Lisa always seemed to want more from him, a level of support and intimacy that he could never quite deliver, much as he tried. Still, they had years of happy times to remember. Nothing could change that, at least not for Sam.

His glass is empty, but he knows better than to pour another. His thoughts drift to the woman he met, the one he knows as Truly Desperate. She masked her call to him, so he doesn't have her cell number, but he has an email address. He hopes she'll let him help her.

He gets up and heads for his computer, then stops to steady himself, surprised to find he's a little dizzy, unusual after two drinks. Or was it three? He's no longer sure. At his laptop, he retrieves the woman's email address and sends her a short note, saying he hopes she'll consider what he said, won't do anything rash, and will give him a chance to help.

He doesn't get an answer.

A Dead Body

Two weeks pass and Sam begins to assume the problem has been resolved—or at least that his pen pal has moved on and is no longer his worry. But then he walks into the newsroom and immediately feels a buzz. A few senior editors are in the bullpen area and the room is noisy, even with the cubicle walls separating and muffling the sound. Everyone is on the phone.

Rather than go to the bullpen, he pokes his head into Molly's corner. "What's up?"

"Senator Morgan is dead. There's a hint of foul play."

"What happened?"

"Don't know. The cops aren't talking, and I'm not having much luck on the Hill. It only broke about thirty minutes ago—on Twitter, of course." She picks up the phone and starts to dial, but Sam interrupts.

"I can help make calls. Tell me what you have," he says.

She looks at him for a second as though she's debating with herself and then plunges in. "You really miss reporting, don't you?"

He tries to ignore the comment, in part because the question rankles. He does miss it at times, but he'd followed the natural career progression from reporter to editor to manager and now columnist, each involving a promotion and a raise.

"You want help or not?" is all he says to Molly. "Tell me what you need."

"Okay. The Majority Leader's office made a brief announcement, only saying he was dead and they had no further details. They wouldn't even say where it happened. It doesn't sound like natural causes, though, and AP says his office has been sealed off."

"What about his house?" he asks. "He lives in Georgetown, right?"

"Yes, Margo sent Jimmy, but CNN already has a live shot. Looks too quiet, though. Only a few cop cars, so I'm betting it happened somewhere else, and that's where the main action must be. Everyone I've called says they have no idea."

"I know a few people in the South Carolina delegation who might know something. Morgan was close to Woods. And I know somebody in Charleston I can try. I'll feed you anything I get."

She nods, takes a sip from her water bottle, and turns back to her phone. Sam hurries into his office.

He fires up his computer and scrolls through his contacts and finds a number for Senator Peter Woods, the senior senator from South Carolina. He hasn't used it in several years and isn't sure it's still active, and when it rings through to voicemail, he gets a recording repeating the number he called and inviting him to leave a message.

"Senator, it's Sam Turner. I know it's been awhile, and I hate to bother you right now, but I need to talk to you about Senator Morgan's death. If you can spare a minute, please call me back on this number."

His next call is to Woods's office, but the line is overloaded and he can't get through. Sam takes a minute to check the latest news online. His own paper has put up a barebones story, but CNN is far ahead with lots of new details. They quote an unnamed police source saying he was found in Rock Creek Park with a bullet in his head and there's a hint of suicide—a gun was apparently found at the scene—but there's nothing conclusive. No one knows, or at least no one is talking. He considers checking the latest on Twitter, but he knows he can't rely on anything he sees there.

Instead, Sam calls a friend at the Capitol Police. Howard Stone and Sam served in the Marines together, somehow survived the bombing of the barracks in Lebanon, and formed the kind of bond that only combat veterans understand. Sam was overjoyed when they both ended up in the Washington area, and though they don't see each other that often, when they do, the connection is strong.

Sam hates to ask for favors from Howie and has never used him as a source, but he needs help and he knows there's a good chance Howie will have some idea of what's going on. He's worked for the Capitol Hill force, which has responsibility for the safety of members of Congress, since getting out of the service and now holds the rank of captain. Sam puts aside his reluctance and calls Howie's cell.

"I know why you're calling," Howie says right off. "But if I tell you anything, you'll have to invite me to that new golf club you joined."

"I haven't joined a golf club."

"Yeah, but imagine how much more cooperative I'd be if you did."

They chat a bit, asking about each other's families, Sam saying nothing about his separation from Lisa, carefully avoiding it without telling an outright lie. He'll tell Howie in time but not on the phone.

"Can you help?" Sam asks when they finish catching up.

"Off the record?"

"Background. A Capitol Police source?"

Howie pauses before responding. "No, make it a Hill source."

"How about a police source."

"No, just Hill. Or congressional."

Sam consents, smiling inwardly as he thinks of how this would play in his seminar. Using the word 'police' would give the information far more credibility, lifting it above the level of a Hill rumor that, for all anyone knows, could come from an intern, but it's early and whatever he hears from Howie is likely to be overtaken by events long before it gets into print. He's calling mainly for guidance.

"Okay, what do you have?"

"It's a complete clusterfuck at the moment. Everybody wants a piece of it, and it may set a record for conflicting jurisdictions."

"But you guys are involved."

"Definitely, though that may only mean we get blamed for not protecting him. Metropolitan has all murders in Washington, but we provided security for Morgan, and Rock Creek Park is under the Park Police, so we're all involved. But it's the FBI who'll be running this thing."

"The FBI doesn't do murders."

"They do when the president wants them to. He and Morgan were good friends, and he's already asked the FBI to put together a task force. They'll be in charge, but D.C. will do the heavy lifting and we'll all have some input. At least, that's my guess."

"Back up a minute. You're confirming he was found in Rock Creek Park?"

"Yeah, early this morning, in a parking area near one of the picnic sites. A bullet wound in the head."

"In his car?"

"Yeah."

"Is it murder or suicide?"

Howie pauses. "Where'd you hear suicide?"

"There's a hint of it in the early stories."

Another pause and Sam knows Howie is thinking carefully about how much he wants to reveal. "Too early to say for certain, but they don't believe it's suicide. More like someone hoped to make it look that way. Too many things don't add up."

"CNN said the gun was found at the scene. Does that mean in the car? Has it been traced?"

"In the car and in his hand. We're tracing it now, but it fits the description of his own gun, which he may have been carrying for protection. He'd gone off without his security detail."

"So, someone overpowered him and killed him with his own gun, then tried to make it look like suicide."

"You said it, not me."

"But it's possible."

"You're getting way ahead of what we know."

Sam asks more questions—exactly where he was found, when and by whom, how Morgan was dressed, whether police have any early theories.

"He wasn't a popular guy," Howie says. "Every time he went on TV, he made more enemies."

"He got threats? Can you be specific?"

"You know what he was. Anti-gay, anti-abortion, anti-immigrant, anti-Medicaid. He didn't even like food stamps. No shortage of enemies. It will take a long time to check everyone who had a bad word to say about him."

"But if a political extremist or someone like that set out to kill him, they'd probably bring their own gun. They'd have no way of knowing he was carrying one."

"Until we get ballistics back, there's no way to be sure it was his gun that killed him."

"What about his personal life?" Sam asks. "Was he a skirt chaser? Anything like that?"

Howie hesitates and Sam offers to go off the record, meaning he won't publicize what Howie tells him.

"It wasn't unusual for him to dismiss his security and go off on his own. His wife caught him at least once. His kid was in a car accident—nothing serious—but when she couldn't find him, she asked us for help."

"But nothing came of it?"

"They're still married. That's all I know."

"Will you be working the case? I mean personally."

Howie laughs. "I've been appointed liaison. They need someone with rank to be the scapegoat if something goes wrong."

"So, I can call you for updates."

"You can try. But think about that golf membership. Congressional would be nice."

Sam smiles. They both know the six-figure initiation fee is out of the question. He thanks Howie and writes up his notes for the team that will be updating the internet version of the story for the rest of the day. He sends a copy to Molly and calls her to tell her it's there.

No one from Woods's office or his sources in Charleston have returned his earlier calls, and he takes a moment to review what he's heard and to let himself consider the thought he's been avoiding: Morgan fits the description of Truly Desperate's ex-lover, and if she hears about Morgan's reputation as a skirt-chaser, Molly will make the connection. Say what you want about Molly, her instincts are good.

He does wonder about the woman he met. Her email threat was ominous, but he can't see her as a killer. Far too timid and weak to do something like that. If she killed anyone, it'd more likely be herself.

He finally admits this was his concern from the beginning—not that she'd do something drastic to the ex-lover—but to herself.

Still, how well does he know her? And don't they always say that anybody is capable of murder if the circumstances fit?

He sighs and decides he might be of more use on the Hill. He goes out to the bullpen, tells the assignment editor his column is done, and offers to pitch in. She tells him the stuff he sent from his source was great, and they can use all the help they can get. Can he make more calls? He tells her he'll have more luck going to the Hill and trying to buttonhole people in person. She warns him not to step on the toes of the beat reporters and tells him to keep Molly in the loop. As he starts to walk away, she suggests he take Molly with him, but he waves that off.

"We can cover more ground separately."

Sam Makes a Choice

Sam doesn't leave immediately. Instead he walks into his office and shuts the door. He considers going to Brenda and telling her about the email, but he knows then it will become part of the story, and he thinks that would be premature, as well as a violation of trust. He knows that won't apply if it means concealing a crime, but he doesn't know that's the case. He has to make sure.

He decides to email Truly Desperate but not from his computer and not from his cellphone. Until he knows more, he doesn't want to leave any unnecessary tracks. The secrecy is beginning to weigh on him and he wonders whether he should have listened to Molly and not gotten involved. But only briefly. He had to help. Sometimes journalism ethics and personal ethics don't lead to the same conclusion. In any event, it's too late now. He grabs a notebook and heads out the door.

Instead of hailing a cab for Capitol Hill, he walks down K Street, finds a place that rents computer time and buys an hour, paying with cash. He creates a new Yahoo account, using a fake name. He's not sure she'll answer a message from an unknown account, but he writes Mr. Ethics in the subject line and hopes for the best.

The message he composes is simple. "I need to know if Wade Morgan was your ex. Contact me ASAP or I'll have to go to the authorities."

Sam asks himself whether he's breaking any laws, risking his job, or, more important, doing the wrong thing. He's not sure, but he hits the send button anyway.

In the back of the cab, he mulls his situation, his mind jumping around. It could be a coincidence. He doubts that the frail, nervous young woman he met could have had an affair with someone like Wade Morgan. It's even less likely that she'd be a murderer. But she'd threatened to kill someone and the timing fits. So does the description of her ex-lover as someone too powerful to take on through normal channels.

It's okay to wait, he tells himself. Even if she did kill Morgan—and he still can't believe that—she's not a danger to anyone else. Reporting the email to the police would make her an instant suspect, assuming they find her, or at least cause her endless grief. He needs to talk to her again before deciding. Being ethical doesn't mean you always follow the scripted route. He's right to consider the consequences, but if she is the killer, it could blow up on him, even cost him his job, to say nothing of his reputation.

And there's still something that makes no sense. He can't believe that Morgan is the kind of stalker and harasser that his pen pal described. Why would he behave that way? Even if he cared that much for her, why would he risk everything he had?

He arrives at the Hart Senate Office Building before he's even considered what he'll do there. He goes through security and heads directly to Senator Woods's office.

When he opens the door, he finds a chaotic scene at the reception desk, mostly made up of reporters, judging by the rude jockeying he sees. He scans the staff for someone he knows, but he's been away too long and there's no one he recognizes, though he does recognize the type. Young men in pressed khakis, blue oxford shirts and ties, the most respectable clothes they can afford on entry-level salaries. The women show a little more variety, but they too are all in their twenties. At least that's the way they look to him.

When he finally reaches the receptionist, she acknowledges his press pass, making it clear the newspaper—and maybe his age—carries more weight with her than the credentials of some of the others competing for attention. She tells him the press secretary is tied up, so he asks for the chief of staff, and to his surprise, he gets ushered in.

But she has nothing for him. She says how shocked the senator is and how his heart goes out to the Morgan family, but when he makes it clear he's seeking real information, she says she has none. He hesitates, then shares some of what he learned earlier from Howie. She is surprised by some of the details, but she still can't help him. The best she can do is promise to tell the senator and get back to him if she picks up anything else.

He goes over to the press gallery, which is full and frenetic, but there's nothing there except news releases expressing shock and sympathy. He leaves and starts wandering the halls and spots the longtime senator from Georgia, who used to be a prime source.

"I'd help if I could," he tells Sam, "but I only know what I heard on the news."

Sam spends the next two hours in similarly fruitless pursuits and returns to 11th Street empty-handed.

Kelly

I call in sick. I don't have a choice. I didn't sleep and when I see the CNN report in the morning, I throw up. Not much, mind you. I've hardly eaten in weeks and I've been losing a lot of weight. Best diet known to man. Or woman. Get trolled and sexted by the creep you once thought you loved and watch the pounds slip away.

I don't know what to do about the email to Mr. Ethics. Why on earth did I do something so stupid? It's going to come back to screw me. I know it is. What was I thinking? Though thinking is not a real possibility when you don't eat or sleep. Even if it were, there was no way I could predict how it would play out. No way.

Why did I believe some stranger who writes a newspaper column might understand? What man could? I don't care how smart and sensitive he claims to be. I shouldn't have listened to Danny. Ariana had no right to even tell him what was happening. I only told her because I had to tell someone. I should have known she'd share it with him. She trusts him with everything. Someday that will come back to bite her. She says he's different. Maybe. Or maybe not.

The cable channels can't get enough of Wade's death, though they've had no new information in hours. Fox only says his body was found in Rock Creek Park and that police discovered the gun. One of their reporters mentions possible suicide before admitting he doesn't have a clue.

I turn to CNN and they are already in full speculation mode. There's a laughable panel talking about how controversial Wade is. Was. A frequent guest on Fox TV, they say, as if that is relevant. They even have statistics on how often he appeared. Of course he was on Fox. Who else would have him?

I make a cup of tea and consider eating something, but the thought makes me gag. Maybe a piece of toast. No, I can't eat anything. But Lassie reminds me that she wouldn't mind a little breakfast. She's been at my side constantly, sensing a crisis, I suppose. She's like that. I open a can, empty it into her plate, and place it on the floor along with fresh water.

I sit down, then move to the floor and lie flat, trying to do my breathing exercises. But I can't. Too tense to relax. The thought makes me laugh.

I go back to the TV, and Lassie joins me on the couch. I want to light a cigarette, but that will drive her away—sometimes I think she's read articles on second-hand smoke—and I'd rather have her than a cigarette.

The news anchors are still talking about how controversial Wade was, how he sometimes said things just to get the other side riled up. It's true. But I agreed with the ideas he supported. The need to put some sanity in our immigration and abortion policies. The Second Amendment. How we had to stop giving away handouts to those who haven't earned them. Wade believed the country was going to hell and wanted to stop it. How could I not admire him for that?

I turn the TV back to Fox. They're more specific in trying to tie Wade's murder to his politics, though no one goes quite so far as to blame a left-wing fanatic. The liberals would certainly blame us if a Democrat had been killed. So typical of their bias.

I wonder how Mr. Ethics is taking the news. I so wish I hadn't gone to him. Can he find out my name? Maybe he already has. If he tells the police about my email, they can probably track me down. Even if Mr. Ethics—how supercilious is that name?—doesn't tell them about me, they'll go through Wade's email and computer. Did he erase all trace of me? Obviously not. He kept those pictures. Oh God. I can see the cops gathered about a computer leering at them. But maybe Wade never wrote my name down. He was cautious. I can only hope, I guess.

I get up and walk away from the TV, go to the window, then the kitchen, then back to the bedroom, then the bathroom. Maybe I should take something to calm down. I still can't believe this is happening to me. What's worse is I know it was my own fault. I've acted like a criminal since the moment I first invited him to my apartment.

Mr. Ethics will probably try to contact me. No doubt about that. Only question is whether he tries before or after he goes to the police. I should be careful. They might bug his phone if he's told them. I have to find a way to get him to back off and leave me alone. It was such a mistake to involve him.

And of course, it's only a matter of time before Ariana shows up. As soon as she hears the news, she'll be here. Telling her about Wade was a big mistake, but I was so happy, and she knew I was seeing someone and kept asking. But why did I tell her who he was?

She was shocked that I was with someone twice my age. And married, no less. Not that it was a real marriage. They haven't had sex in twelve years. Imagine that. They stopped only weeks after the honeymoon. Nothing there, he said. Cold as ice. Talk about a marriage of convenience. Pure political convenience.

But sharing my good times with Ariana backfired big time when it went bad. I holed up in my apartment for three days, and she came to see what was wrong. She was a princess about it. Even cleaned up after he sent the pictures and I vomited. She wanted me to go to the police. Like they would have done something about a senator. I refused, of course, and I guess that's when she told Danny. He came up with the great idea of going to Mr. Ethics, their professor. Why did I agree to that? Desperate, I guess. Truly Desperate.

I don't answer the knock when it comes, but she keeps at it, won't go away, and finally I let her in.

"Are you okay?" A stupid question and she knows it, but what else can she say? She's dressed for work, a smart white blouse that looks good against her brown skin and slacks that look more expensive than they are. Seeing her makes me realize how I must look, still in a bathrobe I haven't washed in almost a month.

I don't answer her question, and she comes in and gives me a hug, then walks me to the couch. She sits in a chair close enough so she can watch my every reaction. I feel like I'm on trial already. Lassie comes over and jumps onto my lap, and I start stroking her back.

"I don't know what to do," I say. "They're going to blame me."

"No one will think it was you," she says, but what does she know?

"I threatened him in that email to the newspaper guy. What if he tells the police?"

"You threatened him?"

Another mistake. "Not exactly," I lie. "But I sounded desperate enough to do something drastic."

"Sam won't tell the police. Not without your consent. And even if you had a motive, they won't blame you without evidence. A motive doesn't prove anything. Anyway, do you know it was murder? I heard it might have been suicide."

I shake my head. "They've moved on from that idea. And I'm scared they'll find out about me. I could still be on his computer or phone."

I start to cry. I can't help it. But not many tears come. I'm dried out.

Ariana moves over and hugs me. "Have you eaten anything? Can I make you something?"

"I can't eat."

"What about a shower? Cleaning up might make you feel a little better."

"Nothing will make me feel better."

"I'll just sit with you for a while."

I'm not sure I want that, but she has no intention of "just sitting" anyway.

"If you're worried about the police finding out about you and Wade, maybe you should go to them first."

I stare at her in what must be a look of horror. "No. I'm not going to volunteer to be a suspect."

She relents, but only for a few seconds. "What if he left evidence of your affair on his phone?" she asks.

I get angry at the word 'affair.' Don't ask me why. I know that's all it was.

"He was careful. I have to take my chances. If they find out, they'll have all the reason they need to suspect me. I'll come off as a jilted and unhinged ex-lover."

"They won't want any of that made public. They won't do anything with it. It might even help protect you."

And I thought I wasn't thinking straight. Ariana is in dreamland, but I don't tell her that.

"I don't know. I'll think about it," I say, knowing I won't.

"Maybe Sam can help. He could be your go-between with the police."

Him again. Last thing I need is help from Mr. Ethics. I need to make him go away, not get more involved.

"No, I'm done with him."

"Danny could help. He's close to him and he could talk to him."

"Danny's done enough," I say, meaning it in ways Ariana won't pick up on.

We sit in silence for a while, until I feel like I'll go nuts if she doesn't leave. "I have to take a pill and try to get some sleep," I tell her, standing up and being obvious. "Thanks for coming over. I'll call you when I wake up."

She looks at me, a mix of doubt and concern and fear and resignation. "I'll call you later," she says.

After she goes, I check my various email accounts and sure enough, Mr. Ethics is trying to get in touch with me. I do another check of the news websites and Twitter but find nothing useful. I decide that a sleeping pill isn't such a bad idea, and lo and behold, it works.

More Pressure on Sam

Sam gets back from the Hill a little after one and after reporting in, he calls Lisa again. She's a lawyer, and though her specialty is now antitrust, she started as a public defender and is no stranger to murder. To his surprise, she answers his call on the first ring.

"I'm sorry," he says. "I know what you said, but I really need your help. It's about Morgan's murder. I might have some information and a legal obligation to share it. I wouldn't ask if I didn't really need to see you." He stresses the word *need* almost to the point of begging.

Lisa hesitates but then agrees to meet him for drinks.

He can't help being pleased with that and immediately starts to think about what he'll tell her. Then he sees he has voicemail and starts going through his messages. One is from Danny, which is a surprise. Sam dials the number.

"I need to see you about something urgent," Danny says, echoing Sam's plea to Lisa.

"I'm swamped here," Sam says. "I'm trying to help with the Morgan murder."

There's silence on the line before Danny speaks again. "That's what it's about. I need to tell you something."

Sam takes a moment to absorb that. "How soon can you get into the city?"

They set a meeting in Sam's office for late afternoon.

"I owe you an apology." Danny says. He's chosen the rarely used chair opposite Sam's desk and is leaning forward, eyes open wide and mouth pursed. Sam waits for him to continue.

"That email you got a couple weeks ago? I'm not sure exactly what it said. A woman looking for help in dealing with a vicious stalker. That was my doing. I told her to write to you. I thought you could help."

Sam leans back in his chair. "You didn't see the email?"

Danny shakes his head.

"She didn't ask for help exactly," Sam says. "Not directly. She said she was going to kill him. She tried to frame it as a question of ethics. Justifiable homicide and all that."

Anguish shows on Danny's face. "That bad?" he says. Then he brightens. "That's what you were getting at in class that week. Her email."

Sam ignores the comment. "So Morgan was the one harassing her? You know that for a fact?"

Danny hesitates. "That's what Ariana says."

"What's the emailer's name?"

"I can't tell you that."

"So why are you here?"

"I told you, to apologize. And to ask for your help."

Sam frowns, rises, and turns his back, but only for a second. "You're as bad as she is. You want help, but you won't tell me enough to be of any use."

Danny smiles tightly. A guilty smile.

"Do you think she killed him?" Sam asks.

"No. No way," he says, shaking his head vigorously. "She's the most timid person I know. She would never resort to violence."

"She threatened to."

"I can't believe she meant it."

"How well do you know her?" Sam asks. He's pacing around the room, making Danny turn in different directions to talk to him.

"Well enough," Danny says. "She's closer to Ariana. They're best friends, actually, but we hang around together sometimes, the three of us."

"If she didn't do it, her best move is to go to the police and tell them the whole story. That's my advice. That's what I'd tell her."

"Which is what Ariana did this morning. She won't listen, but maybe you can convince her."

Sam sits back down. Thinks for a minute. "Why would she listen to me? And why did you tell her to write to me in the first place? You're smart enough to know she needs real help. A shrink. A lawyer. The cops."

Danny leans back and shakes his head. "Ariana tried all that and she wouldn't listen. She does see a therapist, but she was so afraid of giving up the guy's name, she wouldn't go to anyone else. She figured he was too powerful, that he'd get it quashed or worse, turn everything on her. I wasn't involved in the discussions. I was hearing it secondhand from Ariana. I hit upon writing to you because I couldn't come up with anything else."

"But what did you think I could do?"

"What you did. Meet with her. Try to talk some sense into her."

"It didn't work."

"She didn't kill him."

"Sooner or later," Sam says, "the FBI will find some link between her and Morgan, and when they do, they'll suspect her. And maybe rightly so. Either way she's better off going to see them on her own. You need to make her see that."

"If I can set up a meeting, will you talk to her?"

Sam thinks about it, or pretends to. He'd made up his mind as soon as they'd started talking.

"On one condition," he says. "She has to give me her name."

Danny shakes his head. "She won't do that."

"That's the deal. Take it or leave it."

"Are you sure that's a good idea?" Danny asks. "If she won't go to the police, won't knowing her name make your situation even more awkward? Then you'll really be holding out information the police need."

Sam smiles. Danny has obviously been paying attention in the ethics seminar. Not knowing her name might protect him, but that's not his big concern right now. He sees it as a matter of trust. The woman may prefer to remain anonymous, but Sam figures she's less likely to lie to him if he can identify her. He's no longer operating on the basis of the journalism ethics he teaches, he's in a different world. He still needs to do what's right, but his concern is the people involved, not the job.

"Yes, I'm sure," Sam says. "That's the deal. Tell her to take it or leave it."

They stare at each other for several seconds before Danny speaks. "I'll do my best."

Sam skips the five o'clock editorial meeting. He knows they'll be discussing the Morgan story, reviewing what they know and how to frame their coverage. He has a clear conflict of interest now. He knows things he's not telling them, and he's becoming part of the story, playing both sides of the fence. Even if Truly Desperate didn't kill him, she still has valuable and relevant information that is part of the story, and she's let him into her confidence. He shudders to think what Brenda might do if she discovers what he's been up to.

As soon as the meeting ends, Molly is at his door.

"Tell me it's not true," she begins, taking the chair next to him, leaning forward in a no-nonsense pose. "That woman who sent you the email was talking about Morgan, wasn't she?"

"I don't know for sure," Sam says, telling himself that strictly speaking that is true. "But I can't take a chance. I'm going to recuse myself from the story."

"But I can use the email," she says.

"Absolutely not. It's confidential. I shouldn't have shown it to you."

"But you did. I can't exactly wipe it out of my mind. It's a huge clue. It shows he had issues with women."

"If you can't put it aside—truly put it aside—then you have to recuse yourself from the story too."

She looks at him with complete incredulity. "As in take myself off the biggest story to hit my beat in a million years?"

Sam shakes his head and shifts the subject by asking about the story she's planning for tomorrow's paper. Molly tells him that a source she has with the Park Police told her that the blood splatter suggests Morgan was shot by someone sitting in the passenger seat and then the gun was put in his hand in an amateur attempt to make it look like he committed suicide.

Sam sighs. "You can't use the email. You have to wall it off. If you can't, I'll have to tell Brenda that you're compromised."

"You wouldn't do that."

"You know I would, and you know she'd be furious with you."

"She'd be more furious with you. Look, it's not my fault you shared that email. If you'd listened to me and not gotten involved, neither of us would be in this position."

Sam knows she's right, but it doesn't matter now. "Molly, I may have made a mistake—I did make a mistake—but it's too late to take it back. Look, there's no proof that she was talking about Morgan so you couldn't write that anyway."

She looks at him for a few seconds before answering. "That's true. I can't write about it now. But if we get confirmation, there's no holding me back. You can't interfere."

He considers what she said. It's enough to buy some time, and without the name of Truly Desperate and confirmation that Morgan was her ex-lover, Molly can't do much damage.

"Don't you have a story to write?" he asks her.

"Yes, and I'll forget the email for now. But this isn't over."

He watches her walk out of his office, knowing she's right.

As soon as she leaves, he goes and finds Brenda, says he's sorry, but it turns out he's a little too well connected to people that may be involved in the investigation. He has to recuse himself from any further reporting on the story.

"Can you explain that? How are you involved and who do you know?"

"I'm sorry," Sam says. "I can't say anything more."

"And you just found this out?" She says, the anger spitting out.

Sam smiles tightly and walks back to his office.

A Grilling From Lisa

Lisa suggested they meet for drinks at the Tabard Inn, which is halfway between their offices. The choice surprised Sam. It had been one of their favorite spots, filled with way too much history. As he walks in, he can't help remembering one time in particular. They were in their thirties, newly established in secure jobs and more in love than ever. After one too many drinks, they were finding it hard to keep their hands to themselves. But they were attending a going-away party for Lisa's boss, unable to make an early exit, so they found a storage closet, barricaded the door, and made ample use of the tiny space.

There will be nothing like that today, he thinks, as he watches her approach his table, wearing a smart pant suit with a string of pearls he gave her for a long-ago birthday. He feels instantly shabby in his journalist uniform of wrinkled khakis and a blue blazer.

"You look good," he begins.

She smiles a thank you, and as she sits down, she looks carefully at his face.

"You doing okay?" she asks.

"Yeah, except for this stuff at work."

"Betsy is worried about you. She keeps calling, but she only wants to talk about you."

"I'm fine," he says. "Really."

The look she gives him tells him she doesn't believe him, and it occurs to him that she only agreed to this meeting because she's concerned about him. He tries to shake off the thought and asks about her work, and they talk a little without saying much. The conversation is difficult for him because it's so meaningless. Maybe for her too, he thinks.

"So tell me about the problem," she says.

He proceeds to tell her the first part of the story. He gives her a copy of the email and she reads it, shaking her head in what he takes for disbelief or sadness at the woman's plight.

"You know," she says, "the firm is representing two women who want to go public about a prominent news reporter who forced himself on them."

He asks which reporter, but he is smiling. He knows she won't tell him.

"It's like an epidemic," she says. "I always knew it happened, but I never knew it *always* happens."

A thought suddenly occurs to him. "Did it ever happen to you?"

She shakes her head. "I would have told you if it had."

He takes solace in that.

"Going to the police with this would be a waste," she says. "Even if they took it seriously, which is highly doubtful, there's not much they could do without names."

Sam takes a big breath. "That's the problem. I think I now have at least one name. I'm pretty certain she's talking about Wade Morgan."

Lisa's eyes open wider as she takes that in, and then she looks down at her empty wine glass. "I think I'm going to need a refill."

His mind turns suddenly to their intoxicated tryst in the storage room, but he shakes it off and signals for the waiter. Sam asks for the wine and another bourbon for himself. As soon as the waiter leaves, he tells her about his conversation with Danny, adding that he's taken himself off the story.

"That's a good start, but now that you know it was Morgan, you need to tell the police or the FBI or whoever is handling this."

"There's another complication," he says, ignoring her statement. "I showed the email to Molly when I first got it. I wanted another opinion."

"Molly," Lisa says, making it a sentence all by itself. Then she smiles. "You know, I always wondered about you and Molly. Something about the way you talked about her told me you were attracted to her. It made me a little nervous."

He frowns. Not that he hadn't guessed as much, but because there was never a reason for Lisa to worry. "I know things weren't always perfect between us, but there was never anyone else. And Molly thinks of me as an ancient species."

Lisa smiles. "The issue was how you felt about her."

He shakes his head again. "No lust in my heart," he says, and it's true. He likes and respects Molly, but he has always been aware of her shortcomings.

"Anyway, why was telling Molly a problem?" she asks.

"Because I transferred my conflict to her. I'm not sure how long I can keep her from writing about the email. It's the biggest story she's ever handled, and it doesn't seem fair to make her step aside."

Lisa sips her wine. Twice. "All the more reason why you need to go to the FBI. The sooner, the better."

"There's no evidence this woman was involved in his death."

"Determining that is their job, not yours. She had motive and she threatened him."

"I'm still not certain it was him."

"Yes, you are. You're asking for trouble if you keep silent. Even if you weren't Mr. Ethics, this could ruin your career. You're withholding evidence."

"Reporters withhold evidence all the time to protect confidential sources."

"She's not a source and you're no longer a reporter. And now you have reason to believe she may have committed murder."

"Lots of people had motive and lots of people threatened him. He was a right-wing nut. They say his mailbag makes for scary reading."

"Maybe so, but what you have in this email is far more specific."

"He was on TV all the time, stirring people up. Tweeting several times a day. He enjoyed waving red flags in front of bulls."

"True, but irrelevant."

He takes a sip of his bourbon. She's telling him what he already knows, giving him the same advice he'd give anyone who came to him with the same problem. What did he expect?

"Sam, can I be honest?"

That surprises him, mostly because it makes him feel distant. When did she begin needing to ask that kind of question?

"Of course. That's why I wanted to talk to you."

She looks at him, hesitates, but then she goes ahead. "This whole thing doesn't sound like you. You're always so careful to do the right thing. Your instinct always made you weigh the ethics involved. And this is a no-brainer. You know you're breaking the rules. You should go to the police. Now. What are you trying to prove by doing your own investigation?"

He shakes his head. "I'm not trying to prove anything. She came to me for help and I thought she needed it. I still do. And I'm close to finding out who she is and whether she's mixed up in Morgan's death. I need to know more before going to the police. And it'd be better for everyone if I can persuade her to go in on her own."

She doesn't respond, and he feels compelled to add a comment. "I want one more chance to persuade her that she should do what she should have done in the first place—go tell the police everything she knows."

"What if she won't? You'd go to them then? There's a real possibility she did it, and you can't believe this justifiable homicide stuff."

"No, but she was in an awful place. She felt she had no way out. I do feel for her. I do."

Lisa takes a sip of her wine and acts like she's considering what he said, but he knows she disagrees. They sit in silence for a minute until Lisa breaks it.

"Is that really it? You want to help her? Or is this the old investigative journalist in you? You want to get the story. You have a head start and you want to run with it."

He considers it. "I want to help her. I'm not going to be writing the story."

"But you want to get to the bottom of it."

"Of course, but that's neither here nor there."

"I think it is. It's what's going to get you in trouble."

"Just the opposite. Figuring out what happened may be the only way to save my job."

"You can't believe that."

Sam looks away and when he turns back, he takes a sip of his bourbon instead of responding.

"Look," Lisa says, leaning forward. "I know this is a difficult time for you. For both of us. But losing yourself in a story isn't the answer to either problem."

He looks at her and their eyes meet for several seconds before he looks down. "I don't think that's what's going on. I just need to go a little farther with it and then I'll either drop it or turn it over to the police."

She sighs. "Well, you asked for my advice. I can't make you take it."

The comment reminds him of what Molly said when he first showed her the email. It has some truth, he knows. He's looking for validation, in part because he knows he's breaking his own norms, but no one can or will absolve him. He has to settle for his own view that the ends justify the means, at least in this case. Of course that is only true if his emailer is innocent, which is exactly what he needs to find out.

"There's one other thing," he says, smiling sheepishly. "I wanted to ask a favor."

Lisa waits.

"Do I remember that you know his wife, Peg Morgan?"

"Yes, she's on the KidsPlace board," Lisa says, naming an organization she's long been involved with. "I've gotten to know her a little bit. She's completely different. Their politics are polar opposites, and she's on the board of several really good organizations. Her heart's in the right place, at least on the issues, though she has a bit of a mean streak. She can be brutal if someone tries to stand in her way when she really wants something."

"Could you get me in to see her?"

Lisa makes a face. "To what possible end?"

"I'm not sure, but meeting her might help me understand better."

"How exactly? You want to find out if she knew about the affair? Or if she's somehow involved in his murder? That's crazy."

"I need to get a sense of her," he says. "If you know her, you could pay a sympathy call and take me along. You can make sure I stay in line. She doesn't need to know we're separated. Unless she already does."

Lisa looks at him. He can't tell what the look means, another reminder of how they've grown apart.

"No, I won't help you get in deeper. You need to stop this. Go tell the police what you know and then take a vacation. Get out of town. It's only going to get you into trouble. You of all people should know that."

He doesn't agree. He's already in too deep to walk away. He tries to explain that to Lisa, but she counters with all the reasons he should stop what he's doing.

"Sam, there's something else going on here. A year ago, you'd have known exactly what was right. It's like you're trying to prove something, but I don't have any idea what it is or who you're trying to prove it to. Do you?"

He considers that. He can't exactly refute it, but he doesn't agree with it either. And he's not sure why.

Lisa interrupts his thinking to say she needs to go, and he signals for the check. Then she turns to him.

"I need a favor," she asks.

"Anything."

"I'm going to Houston the weekend after this one. My sister's throwing a baby shower for Susan. Would you housesit for Dodger?"

Sam would like nothing more, but he can't. "Normally, I'd love to," he says, "but with so much going on ..." He leaves the sentence unfinished.

She nods and he can tell she thinks there's more to it.

"I'm sorry," he says.

"I'm sure it'd be hard being back in the house, but I know you miss Dodger." Then, with a smile, she adds, "and she misses you too."

He considers it. Bethesda's not exactly far away, but Dodger needs regular walks and attention.

"It's not that," he says. "It's just that with this crisis, I'm not sure what time I'll have."

"Well, maybe by then, this will be over. Why don't you think about it?"

He agrees to do that much.

"But, in all honesty," she adds, "I think you're making a mistake. This is not something you should get in the middle of."

The waiter arrives with the check and Sam picks it up, takes out a credit card, and puts it at the edge of the table where the waiter can spot it.

"I have to talk to the email writer again," he says. "If she won't go in voluntarily and can't convince me she had nothing to do with Morgan's death, then I'll go in and tell them everything."

"She needs to convince the police, not you. It's not your job."

He knows that's true but won't say it.

They leave the table and walk outside. Sam thanks her and gives her a peck on the cheek.

As he walks back to his office to get his car, he realizes he still doesn't have a clue about how to deal with Molly. And he needs to come up with a plan fast.

The Bargain

Sam knows he's on shaky ground. He tells himself as much right after settling in on his couch with another bourbon—his third counting the two with Lisa. And he's still telling himself that after one more.

He often tackles the problems of people who write to Mr. Ethics by asking himself what's the safest ethical route to take and what's the riskiest, and then figuring out what point in between will do the most good with the least harm. It's his own variation of Aristotle's Golden Mean.

The safe route in his own case is to go right to the police and tell them everything he knows. But he has to consider what he's already done, however mistaken that may be, and whether dropping everything in the lap of law enforcement is likely to produce the best outcome.

He has no regrets about not going to the police when he first got the email. Even Lisa agreed with that. Contacting the woman, trying to help, was the right thing to do. But sharing the email with Molly was a mistake. Not ethically, but tactically, because it has put both of them in an awful bind.

He doesn't want to tell Molly he plans to investigate on his own, but he knows he must. Staying in touch with her is the only way to keep track of what she's doing and make sure she doesn't tell anyone about the email.

That's his fear. If Molly mentions the email in a story, all hell will break loose. All attention will turn to his pen pal, perhaps even prompting the FBI to drop other avenues of pursuit and take the easy way out. And even if she's not guilty, it will ruin Wade Morgan's reputation and hurt his wife, to say nothing of what it might mean for Truly Desperate. And to Mr. Ethics.

He also knows the risks of investigating on his own, though he can't see a choice, having messed up the situation as much as he has. The problem will be keeping his plans secret from everyone at the newspaper and holding Molly at bay.

He knows he has to give Molly something, offer some kind of deal to keep her in check for at least a few days. It takes him until early morning to come up with an idea.

"Here's the deal," he begins, trying to ignore Molly's skeptical and somewhat bratty look as they sit across from each other in Sam's office. "I'm going to take a leave of absence and stay away from the newspaper, but I'm going to keep looking into this. I may have another meeting in the works with my secret pen pal, and I'll try to revive some contacts that might prove useful. I'll feed you everything I have that can be confirmed, and you can use it as your own."

"You'll hold back."

"Not if it's solid and can't be easily traced to me."

"You'll give me her name when you find out what it is?"

He pauses. "No, not that. Not without her permission. But I'm hoping to persuade her to go talk to the police, and if she does, you'll be the first to know."

"You'll get me an interview?"

"I can ask if it comes to that, but I can't force her if she doesn't want to."

"How do you know I won't follow you and find out her name?"

"Because I'm smarter than you."

She smiles. "Is this ethical?"

"For you, it is. Might not be for me, but it is what it is."

"If this goes wrong, it could really hurt your career."

"No, if it goes wrong, it will end my career."

They shake on it, but after Molly leaves, he sits in his office and wonders whether he can trust her. In the end, he has no choice.

He goes out to find Brenda and tells her he needs to take a week of vacation time.

Enter the Wife

Before leaving the office, Sam goes out to the newsroom one last time and checks the bank of television monitors, but within seconds, he is shaking his head in disgust. The Morgan murder, which is what they're all calling it now, is still "Breaking News" on all the cable channels, though no one has new information to report. Instead he finds endless speculation on political motives and the possible repercussions, with everything from terrorism to leftwing extremism under consideration. One network is even showing a Twitter feed filled with far-fetched speculation and misinformation, with some critics wondering why the FBI is moving so slowly.

Sam is about to turn away when one of the stations switches to Morgan's home. A dozen reporters are waiting outside, for what he can't imagine. He doubts Peg Morgan is there, and even if she is, she's certainly not about to come out and face the press.

But like the reporters standing outside the Georgetown home, Sam wants to talk to Morgan's widow, and when he gets back to his office, he spends a few moments trying to figure out a way to reach her.

It doesn't take long for the obvious to occur to him. It's another move he wouldn't sanction under normal conditions, but he doesn't dwell on it, letting his reporting instincts take precedence over the ethical niceties. His need for reaching Morgan's widow seems more important. He calls Lisa's office rather than her cell and is glad when her secretary says she's in a meeting. He wonders for a second whether Lisa has told her receptionist about the separation, but it's too late to turn back.

"This is Sam, her husband," he says, not knowing how much longer that will be true. "Can you do me a favor? Could you check her contacts and give me a number for Peg Morgan? I want to call her and express my condolences."

She asks him to hold and he wonders briefly if she's checking with Lisa, but soon she is back and she gives him the number, and then for good measure, throws in the email address. He thanks her and hangs up, hoping it was too small a request for her to mention to Lisa.

Now that he has the number, Sam realizes he doesn't have a plan. He'd like to see her face-to-face, but she's unlikely to agree to see someone she doesn't know, especially a newspaper reporter. He can't play the Lisa card—pretending he's representing her somehow, though he doubts what he ends up doing is much better.

He sends her an email. He starts by offering his sympathy and apologizing about bothering her, adding that he's heard good things about her from his wife. Then he tells her who he works for and says he's sorry, but he's come across some allegations against her husband and before his newspaper gets too far in its investigation, she needs to know about them. He reads it over, decides it's true enough, swallows his guilt, and sends it.

He waits ten minutes, but there is no response. He sends a text asking her to check her email, saying it's important.

Still no response.

He closes up his office and heads back to his apartment, but just as he's parking, he gets the ping. Peg Morgan's text says she's staying with her sister, would love an excuse to escape, and suggests they meet in the bar of a boutique hotel in Foggy Bottom at four p.m.

He sees it's noon and goes up to his apartment to have lunch and plan for the meeting. He's entering the building when Danny calls him to tell him that Truly Desperate will see him. They set a meeting for that evening at Ariana's apartment, and he gives Sam the address. Ariana will be there, but only as a hostess. Danny, however, has been barred.

"And she'll give me her name? That's the deal," Sam says.

"Yes."

"Give it to me now."

Danny hesitates. "It's really for her to do." It's the answer Sam expects.

Sam hangs up and a wave of doubt grips him. He's not happy about the whole situation, but he needs to talk to her again. If she denies killing Morgan, he won't know for sure whether to believe her, but he'll have a gut feeling and that's better than nothing. If he thinks she's lying, he'll turn her in.

In his apartment, Sam makes short order of lunch, opting for a container of cottage cheese and an apple. He sits down at the computer to sketch out his thoughts ahead of the two big meetings and then decides to call Molly.

"Checking in as promised," he begins.

"With what?"

"Nothing yet, but I'm making progress." He tells her about his scheduled meeting with Peg Morgan.

"What do you expect to get from her?"

"I'm not sure exactly. Maybe she knew he was fooling around and has something that will help me sort through it."

"Most women know. How could they not?" she says.

Sam smiles to himself. He's learned from his own kids not to challenge the wisdom of twenty-somethings who are convinced they know what life has in store for them. "I'm not sure, what I'll get," he says. "I just thought it'd be good to talk to her."

"And you'll share, right?"

"That's the deal," he says.

"Nothing from the email sender?"

Sam hesitates. "I heard from our mutual friend—the one who sent her to me in the first place. He set up a meeting for tonight."

"That's terrific."

He hears the excitement and tries to tamp it down. "The ground rules are likely to be tight. I'll tell you what I can, but I have to get her permission to share."

"You promised."

"I'll do what I can," he says, choosing his words carefully. "What about you? Anything new?"

"Maybe. You know the feds are looking pretty hard at Morgan's mail, electronic and otherwise. I got a tip that there is one guy who wrote often and with increasing anger, enough to get Morgan nervous. The guy's an antifa type. He was apparently all over Twitter and sending emails. Morgan saved some rather specific threats that were sent anonymously and used some of the same language as was in the tweets. The FBI believes it's the same guy. They want to find him and talk to him."

"Do they have a name?"

"Not yet."

"Makes it hard to talk to him."

"They're working on it."

They chat about other details and the speculation that has emerged since the shooting, but nothing is particularly useful.

"Call me after you talk to them," Molly says, and then abruptly hangs up.

Peg Morgan is wearing sunglasses. It's the first thing he notices. Before the security detail sitting discreetly off to the side.

Before the black but suitably stylish outfit she's wearing. And before the drink—a neat serving of whiskey—sitting in front of her. It ought to be a more ladylike glass of wine, he thinks, before chastising himself for the burst of sexism.

He walks over to her table and introduces himself. The two security guards sit up a little taller, and he wonders why she needs them, then realizes her husband was just murdered. Of course she has protection.

"Thank you for seeing me," he says as she gestures for him to sit down, which he does.

"I'm not sure why I did," she offers.

"Me either," he admits. "Perhaps curiosity."

He tries to see through her sunglasses, which remind him of his meeting with Truly Desperate. The bar is dimly lit, dark in fact, and he wonders how she can even see the glass in front of her. As if to confirm his suspicion, she takes off the glasses, and the puffiness around her eyes signals her grief.

"Perhaps I agreed to see you because of your wife," she responds. "She's always been kind, treats me like a real person, not just a senator's wife looking for amusement or trying to make her husband look good. I wouldn't say Lisa and I are close, but we could be. But I gather she didn't send you."

"No. In fact, she'd be angry if she knew I used her name."

"Not that her anger would matter. I hear you moved out."

So word has spread.

"Every marriage has its ups and downs," he says. "I'm sure you know that." When she doesn't respond he adds, "Surely your marriage wasn't perfect."

She looks at him, meeting his eyes and holding them. He's not sure what it means, but it means something.

"Why are we here exactly?" she asks finally. "You said the newspaper had some information about Wade."

"Yes, I'll get to that. I also have a few questions. I thought maybe you could help me with them."

He's implied a bargain, but she plays hard to get. "And why would I be interested in helping you?" she asks.

"I'm going to guess the police aren't telling you much. They never do. First rule of homicide is to suspect the spouse and keep him or her in the dark. I might be able to tell you as much or more than you can tell me."

She looks around at her security team, as though wondering whether they can hear. She puts the glasses back on, but after a second removes them and puts them down on the table again. She takes the last gulp of her drink and signals the waiter. They both order and the waiter nods. Sam can tell he knows who she is.

"This has to be off the record," she begins. "Not even deep background."

"Of course." He's not surprised she knows the rules. Someone in her position would have to.

"I won't promise," she says, "but we can see how it goes. Tell me what you've heard."

The drinks arrive and he takes a sip. She takes a bigger one. He decides to give her what he can.

"They're going through his hate mail."

"No lack of that."

"No, it will take a long time, but I hear they've already found something. A guy who seemed to hate your husband's guts and didn't make much of an effort to hide it. He wasn't the only one, but his threats were the most ominous in tone and they put him at the top of the pile. They want to talk to him."

She looks around to see who else is in the lounge and then settles again on the security team. One is staring at his nails and the other has a cellphone to his ear, but he's not saying anything, either listening to a long monologue or pretending.

"So far, you're not telling me anything I don't already know," she says finally. "I told Wade he was going too far, but of course he wouldn't listen. He loved the attention he was getting. Are they close to finding this guy?"

"I don't know. And it's not the only avenue of inquiry."

She pauses as if waiting for him to go on, but he doesn't. He's staring at her shoes, which have six-inch heels.

"What other lines of inquiry?" she asks.

He looks into her face. "What was Wade doing at Rock Creek Park in the middle of the night?"

She shrugs. "I don't know."

"Why was he alone? Didn't he have a security detail?"

She shakes her head. "He used one when he thought it necessary, but not when he wanted to be alone. He did have a private life, you know. It wasn't all politics."

"Did the private life include other women?"

She looks away.

"How was your marriage?" he asks.

"That's a rather impertinent question."

"Why? You brought up my marriage."

She laughs at that and takes another gulp of her whiskey before answering. "How many politicians do you know who are true to their wives?"

"I don't keep score."

"But you're interested in Wade."

"Wade has been murdered. And you must know of the rumors."

"Is this the 'negative' information you used to lure me here?"

He doesn't respond.

"You're being foolish," she says. "There are rumors about every senator. Wade loved me. I never doubted that. He may have had a dalliance or two, but he loved me. I won't let you ruin his reputation with crazy rumors when he's not here to defend himself."

"It's more than crazy rumors—and you know that."

She shakes her head hard enough to bounce the dark brown hair that touches her collar. "I don't know what you think you know, but you're wrong. I won't pretend he never strayed, but our marriage was on solid ground."

"How can you be so sure? What if he got attached to someone else? Or she got attached to him?"

"Wouldn't happen."

"I think it did. In fact, I know it did. With unpleasant ramifications."

She pulls away, apparently surprised, then gathers her bearings and takes another sip of her drink. They let a moment of silence pass to ease the tension.

"What do you know? What is your paper going to report?"

Sam considers whether he's gone too far. "My paper won't report anything without proof. I can't speak for other media outlets."

"What are you suggesting?" she asks. "That one of his dalliances killed him because he jilted her?"

"Is it possible?"

"How do I know? I assume a woman has to really hate someone—or really love them—to go that far, and I can't believe anybody fits that description."

He thinks about that. It's a strange thing to say.

"Was there someone recently?" Sam asks. "Anybody I can talk to?"

She laughs at that. "I wouldn't tell you if I could." She looks around again. "And, in fact, I can't imagine why I'm even talking to you." She stands up. "Good day," she says loudly, then more softly, "Don't call me again."

Kelly

I wish I hadn't let them talk me into seeing Mr. Ethics again. I really do. No good can come of it. I kept saying no and they kept insisting. Asking what I had to lose.

"Everything" is the answer, but how could I say that without explaining what I've done.

After all the nights I spent with Ariana, crying my eyes out, curled up in a ball, screaming, choking, she still doesn't understand.

"You're innocent. You have nothing to hide," she says, showing me how naïve she is. "Innocent people don't go to jail."

What a fool! No one's innocent, not in today's world. I made so many mistakes that sometimes I think I deserve what happened to me and the guilt I'll carry around for the rest of my life.

Danny's even more naïve. Still believes in truth and justice. Makes me want to puke.

But I had to agree to this meeting. I could see my refusals confused them, made them suspicious, thinking there's more than I've told them. Of course, there is.

In the end, Danny made the only argument that scared me—that Mr. Ethics would tell the police about my email unless I can talk him out of it.

We meet at Ariana's apartment. I don't want her to be there. I don't need two people studying my every word and movement, but I can't say no without arousing suspicion. At least Danny's agreed to stay away, although I know she'll tell him everything. She's already proved she can't keep her mouth shut.

Mr. Ethics—or Sam as he insists I call him—arrives promptly at seven-thirty, wearing jeans and a pullover that make him look a lot less professional than the first time we met. Obviously, he didn't come from work.

Ariana greets him as Professor Turner and offers us cold drinks even before he's seated. I stick with water, but he asks if coffee would be a problem. Already he's making demands.

Ariana leaves to make it and I understand the ploy. Making coffee will keep her out of the room longer than grabbing a soda. Maybe that's for the best.

"How are you holding up?" he asks as soon as she leaves the room.

But I don't want to waste our time on stupid clichés. "I'm not sure why Danny and Ariana wanted us to meet again," I say, "but they said you insisted."

"That's a little strong. Danny came to me and I thought it was best if we talk. I know you probably didn't mean to, but you've put me in a difficult position, and I need to hear what you have to say before I figure out what to do."

"I don't understand."

He takes a breath and stares at me. "I gather Wade Morgan is the man you wrote to me about, but I need to hear it from you."

I knew it would be the key question and I'd rehearsed answers, but somehow I freeze when I actually hear it. Still, denying it isn't an option. He already knows.

"Yes," I say, "but I didn't kill him, if that's what you think."

"It doesn't matter what I think. That's not my role."

"I don't see that you have a role at all."

"I do," he says. "And frankly, that's your doing. It's why I'm here."

Ariana arrives with his coffee—too quickly—and takes a seat. She doesn't say anything and I do my best to ignore her.

"I don't understand," I say. "How is this your problem?"

He gives me a look that says I must be kidding, and when he answers, he raises his voice to show me he's getting annoyed. Let him. I don't care. I don't care about anything. It feels like my life will never be the same. There's nothing I or anyone else can do to get me out of this.

"You sent me an email threatening to kill a man who was harassing and abusing you, a man who then turned up dead. You've involved me in a murder. How can you not understand that?"

I'm not sure how to respond. I hadn't anticipated the anger.

"I didn't kill him. I understand if it's hard for you to believe that after what I wrote, and I'm sorry if I put you in a difficult position. Can't you just forget it?" It sounds weak even to me. I wish he'd go away and leave me alone. I wish they'd all leave me alone.

"No, it doesn't work that way," he says. "I promised we wouldn't print what you told me, but if there's evidence you committed a crime, it changes everything."

He leans back, and I guess he's giving me time to think about that.

"Look," he says after a few seconds. "The FBI will eventually find evidence that Morgan had an affair with you, and they'll get a search warrant for all your communications. They'll discover you wrote to me and called me, and they'll want to know why I didn't report it."

"I sent that email from a public library. There's no way they can trace it."

"Don't be silly. Once the FBI finds out you were involved with him, they'll turn your life upside down, and they'll find everything. You've put me at serious risk. And if you don't understand that, it leaves me no choice but to go to the authorities right now. A man's been murdered."

He sits forward and takes a sip of coffee, giving me a moment to think about what he said, though what I'm really thinking is how much I'd love a cigarette, something Ariana would never allow in her apartment. When I don't answer him, he stares at me and then stands up.

"You're leaving me no choice," he says. "I'd like to help you if I can—and that's a big if—but I'm not breaking any laws or taking any more chances if you won't cooperate. And you need to think about Ariana and Danny. You've involved them in this too."

He starts to walk toward the door and I watch him. Then suddenly a mix of guilt, anger, and hopelessness overtakes me. "Wait," I say.

He turns around and I lose it. My tough-girl façade, never too strong to begin with, is gone and the tears I don't want to shed form in my eyes. He sits back down, but instead of showing sympathy, he leans forward and presses harder.

"If you didn't kill him, and there's something I can do to help, I'd like to try, but you have to be honest with me. You have to tell me the whole truth."

Ariana has been sitting quietly, but this sets her off. "Sam, you can't possibly believe she killed him. Look at her. She's a total wreck. He had all the power and he ruined her life. Yes, she had motive, but she's no murderer. She's the victim here."

"Look," he says, staring at me and ignoring Ariana. "You need to trust me. And I need to trust you. It will help a lot if you tell me your name."

I shake my head. "I don't see why it's necessary."

"It's part of being honest. I told Danny that was a condition of seeing you, and I meant it."

"I could make up a name. Or are you going to ask for a driver's license."

"No, I'm trusting you to tell me the truth."

I pick up my water, but my throat is too tight to swallow. "Kelly," I say.

"Kelly what?"

I can't help sighing. "Lancaster."

He thanks me. "And just to get it out of the way, did you kill Wade Morgan?"

I shake my head, but he waits until I say "No" out loud.

"Where were you the night he was killed? Do you have an alibi that will satisfy the police?"

"I was in bed, trying to sleep. Unsuccessfully of course. But I was alone. Except for my cat."

"When was the last time you were in touch with him?"

This is beginning to feel like an interrogation, but it occurs to me that it might be good practice for what now feels inevitable.

"Shortly after you and I met. I tried one more time to get him to stop. I begged him to leave me alone."

"And he refused?"

"He not only refused, he continued to deny everything. Said it was someone else. It was ridiculous."

"And after that?"

"He sent another photo. It wasn't explicit, but it was his way of telling me there was more to come."

Turner considers that, drinks more of his coffee, and then asks me what I plan to do. I consider saying suicide, but that might be overly dramatic. And no one needs to know how often I think of that.

"Nothing. What can I do?"

"You need to go to the police and tell them the whole story. You should get a lawyer to go with you."

"Telling the police my story will only make me their biggest suspect. I have no alibi. Why would they believe I didn't kill him?"

"If you didn't kill him, there can't be any evidence that you did. If you tell them the whole story up front, it shows you're being honest, and you're giving them important information about what kind of person he was. That'll send them looking for other victims."

"Other victims?"

"Kelly," he says, a little loudly and with a hint of impatience. Then he takes a breath and when he resumes, he's calmed down. "You probably weren't the first woman he's treated this way. There could be a slew of women out there with the same motive, and one of them could be guilty."

I think about that. Wade never denied there were other women before me, but he insisted they meant nothing, that he'd never been in love until he met me. I never believed it, not for a second, but it was nice to hear.

"Did he have a reputation for that?" I ask.

Turner nods. "I spoke to his wife this afternoon. She admitted that she knew he had other women. Said she accepted it as long as he didn't rub her nose in it."

"You spoke to his wife?" I try to keep the surprise and shock out of my voice but can't be sure I'm succeeding. "What did she say? Did she say anything about me?"

He shakes his head. "I didn't get into specifics with her, and I certainly didn't mention anything related to you. She said she never cared or tried to find out any details of his affairs, but you never know what she knew or how she really felt."

I get angry. "She's a cow. She never loved him."

"Kelly, you don't know what went on between them or what other women Wade had. That's why it's best to come forward now."

"I don't know," I say. "It would be awful to go to the police and tell them the whole story. I'm so ashamed that even you know."

"But they will find out whether you tell them or not," he says firmly.

Until this point, Ariana has said little, but she can't keep quiet any longer. She tells me that he's right and reminds me that Danny said the same thing. It would look better for me to go voluntarily rather than wait until they discover me on his phone. And then she hits me where I'm most vulnerable.

"They'll probably find those pictures," she says. "If you explain the circumstances, they'll understand the pressure you were under."

What she really means is they're less likely to think I'm a total whore. What she doesn't seem to realize is that the pictures gave me a strong motive to kill him.

"I need to think about it," I say, more to get this over with than anything else. A part of me believes they're right, but I can't imagine going through with it. I'm not that strong. I honestly don't know if I can.

Turner seems to realize he's pushed me as far as he can. "Okay, that's fair," he says. "But I'm afraid you don't have much time. Once they find evidence linking him to you, it will be too late. And that could happen at any time. They may be focused on his hate mail right now, but they're looking at all of his personal accounts and they'll recover anything he deleted."

Again, I realize he knows things that are useful, but I don't want him to get too close. I'm still shocked that he talked to Wade's wife. He's as big a threat as the police. I need more time to figure out how to handle him, so I just promise to get back to him tomorrow and he leaves.

Afterwards, Ariana wants to talk, but I go in the bathroom and throw up instead. When I return, I tell her I have to go home, and she lets me. Reluctantly.

Molly's Scoop

As soon as he gets to his car, Sam pulls out his phone and sees a series of text messages from Molly. The first is a link to a story posted on the paper's website. The others ask for his reaction, each with increasing urgency.

He scans the story quickly to make sure there is nothing about Kelly's email, then waits until he gets home to parse it more carefully.

The story bears the bylines of three reporters, with Molly mentioned first, telling Sam she did the heavy lifting. The report, based almost entirely on anonymous "law enforcement" sources, says the FBI has identified the man who threatened Morgan in tweets and letters, and they want to find and interview him. Sam is surprised and mystified by that. Not that authorities have his name, which isn't in the story, but that they are admitting it. If the suspect sees the story, he'll know who they're talking about and go to ground.

It's too late to give Molly advice on the story, but he still owes her a call. When he tries, her phone tells him she is on another line, so he leaves a message. It's almost midnight and he is exhausted, so he pours himself a drink and sits down to consider the day's events. A lot has happened in twenty-four hours.

He begins his mental review by going over his conversation with Kelly. Does he believe her?

He doesn't know her well enough to be sure, but Danny and Ariana seem pretty convinced she can't possibly have killed Morgan, that she doesn't have it in her. He knows that's not true. There's no telling what someone will do when pushed into a corner—and Kelly certainly was pushed into one. She admitted as much, saying she saw no other options.

What surprised him was her temperament, different in many ways from their first meeting. Less frail and lost. Stronger, though still with a sense of defeat and indecision. She certainly wasn't rejoicing at Morgan's death, and she seemed genuinely afraid of being accused of it. He didn't get the sense that she was prepared for the predicament she's in. He's inclined to believe her because he too can't see her as a killer, but he knows part of that is that he *wants* to believe her. And he is more than aware that his own role in the affair—his failure to go to the police right away—is less of a problem if she's innocent. He hopes she will go to the police now. That would release him from the burden. Let them figure it out.

His phone buzzes and he picks it up. "Good story," he tells Molly, trying to muster at least a little enthusiasm.

"Thanks."

"You're going to get pushback. The feds will be furious you gave away their progress. It gives the guy a warning and he may now disappear. Or do they already have him?"

"No, they don't. And I'm already getting the pushback. I just got off the phone with the head of the FBI task force. He's livid. Threatened to call Brenda and insist I get taken off the story."

"So he wasn't your source?"

"No," she says, not offering more. But when he waits out her silence, she gives in. "Actually, I got it from my Park Police guy, but another source confirmed it."

Sam knows better than to ask for the names of her sources. She'll have told Brenda, and Brenda obviously thought they were good enough, but he does question their motives.

"Whoever first tipped you off must have known you'd print it," he says. "Why would anyone want it out?"

"Not my job to figure that out, as I kept telling Brenda."

"But in the end, she approved the story," he says, choosing his words with care.

"Not easily. She had her doubts. Knew it could prompt the guy to run and swore at you a few times while we debated it."

"Swore at *me*?"

"Wanted your ethical take on it."

He nods to himself but doesn't say anything.

"What would you have told her?" Molly asks.

"It's a difficult situation."

"So you would have said not to run it?"

"It doesn't matter now. Frankly, I'm surprised anyone told you they had a name. Let's hope they find him quickly."

"Yeah, and that my source tells me first."

This time when she mentions her source, Sam can't help probing a little. "How sure are you that he knows what he's talking about?"

There is silence, which he takes for disapproval. Correctly.

"I wouldn't have written the story if I wasn't sure."

"Sorry," he says without adding what he's actually thinking. That someone might be using Molly, though he's not yet sure how.

"What about you?" she adds. "Did you meet with Morgan's wife?"

"Yes, but I didn't get much from her. She knew he played around and didn't care as long as it never got serious. Insists it never did."

"You believe her?"

"Up to a point." He realizes that's the most he can say about anyone involved in the case. Even Molly.

She asks more questions about the conversation and he tells her what he can, but when she moves on to ask about his conversation with Kelly, he tells her he's sorry, but he has to keep that to himself for a while longer.

"She denies killing him?" Molly asks.

"I'll tell you what I can as soon as I can."

Sam has a restless night and gets up early, but he waits until nine to call Howie.

"You've seen the paper? The story about the guy who threatened Morgan?" he asks.

"Oh, yeah. Heard about it last night," Howie says.

"I'm sorry if we screwed things up for you."

"I have to assume whoever leaked it had a reason. Above my pay grade."

"Your FBI friends don't seem too happy about it."

"They'd complain even if they were the source. Have to keep up appearances."

Sam is surprised by that. Howie doesn't seem at all upset. He asks if there is any other news, but Howie won't add to the story already in print. After he hangs up, Sam wonders what it all means.

Since he talked to Molly he's been wondering about her source—not who he is so much as why he gave her such valuable information. Now he begins to wonder if it was all planned. He knows, as any experienced reporter knows, that sources who leak usually have less than pure motives. Genuine whistleblowers are pretty rare. Most want to get their side of a story in print in order to influence the debate or prompt someone else to take some action.

His thoughts are abruptly interrupted when Molly calls. "I got a message from the guy," she says without the usual preliminaries.

"The suspect?"

"Sounds like it. He called the tip line and asked to speak with me. Insisted he won't talk to anyone else. Made me buy a burner phone and told me to hide the number inside a tweet he dictated."

"Did he call?"

"He texted. Said he wants to meet. Told me where and when and to be sure I'm alone."

"You can't do that."

"How can I not?"

"Molly, it's too dangerous. You have to tell the police."

"I can't. He said I have to come alone."

"Molly, you're dealing with a murder suspect."

"He says he's innocent."

"At least give me his phone number."

"I'm sure it's a burner. Won't do you any good."

Sam has seen Molly in moments of insane naïvety before, but never when it was so dangerous. He tries another tack. "You have to tell Brenda."

"She'll react the same way you did."

"With good reason."

He hears her sigh.

"When is this supposed to happen?" he asks.

"If I tell you, you'll tell someone or have the police follow me. You can't say a word."

"Then why did you call me?"

"What do you mean?"

"If it's so secret, why tell me? I could hang up now and call Brenda and tell her everything."

"You wouldn't do that."

"I will if you put yourself at risk."

"The meeting will be in broad daylight in public. What could he possibly do to me?"

"Why can't he talk to you on the phone?"

"He wants to do it in person. I understand that. He wants to know he can trust me. What's that silly phrase you always use? Something about knowing the cut of the jib? Well, you ought to understand then."

"And you want to see what he's like. Get color for the story."

"It won't hurt."

"I'm calling Brenda."

"I told you in confidence."

"I never agreed to that."

"Sam," she says, drawing it out, then pausing. "I've got another call, let me take it. I'll think about what you said and call you back."

Sam sees right through the trick and as soon as he hangs up, he calls Brenda. But she's not in. He tells the receptionist it's an emergency and to please find her, and in the meantime, he calls her deputy and asks that they keep Molly in the office.

But the deputy calls back two minutes later to say that Molly is nowhere to be found. She must have left the building without saying where she was going.

Call Me Peg

My sister is really getting to me. She was nice to take me in, not that she had much of a choice, but now I want to be alone. So much to process, and she won't leave my side. The three boards I'm on have let me sit in on meetings through Zoom, but they've become so solicitous and condescending that I tend to bow out early. They don't seem to be taking me as seriously as when Wade was alive. I've worked so hard for them, and there's so much I can contribute. I thought they realized that, but now I get the feeling it was only my money and Wade's influence that made me important to them. So much for all the work I've put in.

The security guys don't want me leaving the house. They even follow me on walks, though no one is supposed to even know where I am. They say I can't go home yet—there are still reporters hanging around there—but I want them to at least take away the minders.

Except for Larry, of course. It's a good thing I made a "special friend" of him. Having a source in Wade's security detail has been valuable all along, and now it's essential, well worth the occasional indignity of spreading my legs and thinking of the queen. Of course, with Wade dead, Larry is already talking about seeing me more often, although even he knows he has to wait until the noise dies down. It's a problem I'll have to face at some point. Just not now. That's the only good thing about sheltering here.

Larry tells me everything the FBI won't. If Wade were still alive, he'd be getting regular briefings from the Director and maybe even the Attorney General. Being chairman of the Judiciary Committee had its perks. Being the wife of the dead chairman has none. Less than none. Which is too bad. I've got to find a way to keep Wade's affairs out of the news. I put up with them when I had no choice, but I'm not putting up with the press turning me into another Hillary Clinton.

"We're working several leads," the FBI keeps saying. They probably got that line off some TV show. Problem is, they won't tell me what those leads are.

So I rely on Larry and the newspaper. Today's article was helpful. I'm glad they're onto the antifa guy. Lord knows Wade got threats, and he thought it impressed me to hear about them, but this guy was by far the most vicious, and he certainly sounds like someone who could commit murder. He practically threatened it. I know they're taking a hard look at him, which should take the focus off of Wade's extracurricular behavior.

There were always threats. Why do people get so worked up over politics? It's not like it matters. Swings back and forth, and each side is worse than the other. It was a game to Wade. All he cared about was getting re-elected. Taking extreme positions was a way to get in good with the people who mattered. The guys with money and the stupid voters who blindly follow whatever they hear on Fox. It was a ticket to easy re-election, which is all that ever mattered. And being on TV all the time didn't hurt. He didn't care if half the world hated him, as long as the other half cheered him on.

Marrying him was the biggest mistake I ever made, but I was young and foolish. Weren't we all at that age? I did love Wade once, and in my own way I even loved him at the end.

It just wasn't enough. I did my best, but it's hard being married to a senator who loves all the attention that goes with it. The change in our relationship was gradual and by the time I noticed, it was too late. I had too much to lose.

How much does Turner know? He's undoubtedly heard the rumors, but he implied he knew some specifics. I've got to find a way to get him under control. I can live with the nasty inuendoes, but I don't want any details to come out. That would be humiliating.

A Devious Plan

Molly's not answering her phone, and Sam begins to feel desperate. He debates telling Brenda everything but figures there's nothing she can do that he can't. He wonders whether to call the police, tell them everything, and hope they can track Molly's cellphone, but he knows there isn't enough time.

He glances at the clock. Eleven a.m.

He pushes himself to think of everything he might say or do to get through to Molly but knows he probably can't even get her on the phone again.

Then an idea hits. He calls Danny, who thankfully answers. "It's Sam. I need to talk to Kelly."

"She still hasn't made up her mind about going to the police. I think she will, but more pressure from you won't help."

"That's not what I'm calling about. I need her and it's urgent."

"Can I tell her what it is?"

"No. Just find her and have her call me as soon as possible. Tell her it may be a matter of life and death."

Danny doesn't try to hide his confusion but agrees to do his best.

Ten minutes later, Sam's phone rings. It's a blocked number, but he knows who it is.

"Kelly, I need a favor," he says. "Someone who means a lot to me is about to make a horrible mistake, and you're the only one who can stop her."

He quickly explains what Molly is up to and then makes his request. "She's seen your email. I showed it to her the first day when I wasn't sure it was for real. She doesn't know your name or anything and she's not going to write about the email, but you're one person she'll take a call from. Text her that you're the one who wrote the email and you want to talk to her to give your side of the story, but that you have to do it now because you plan to go to the police this afternoon."

"But I don't want to give her my story."

"You don't have to. Just set up a meeting. Once you've done that, call me with the time, and I'll go in your place. I have to stop her somehow and only you can help me."

"I don't know," Kelly says. "You want me to lie? It sounds kinda weird."

Sam sighs. She's reminding him what shaky ground he seems to be walking on with increasing frequency.

"I don't like asking you to lie," he says, "but it's necessary and I really need this favor. Tell her you'll meet her at the JW Marriott next to the Press Club. Say you'll be at a table on the lower level outside the bar. Insist on that exact location, but let her pick a time."

"But when I don't show up, she'll know I tricked her and that may come back to haunt me. She's more likely to write about the email if she finds out."

"I'll make sure that doesn't happen," he says, then wonders if he can really make such a promise. But he can't take time to think about it.

"Please, Kelly. I wouldn't ask you if I had any other option."

Kelly doesn't sound convinced, but she takes Molly's phone number and hangs up. She calls back a few minute later.

"It's set for one p.m.," is all she says before hanging up.

Sam arrives early, finds a seat on the main floor where he can watch the two tables outside the bar without being seen from below, and for the third time reviews his options for handling Molly. He's already rejected the two safer moves—getting either Brenda or the police involved. Instead he's decided to follow Molly to the meeting. He knows that's problematic. He's hardly trained in surveillance, and he could easily lose her. Then an idea occurs to him, and he calls Danny again. He gets his voicemail and leaves a message asking him to call back as soon as he can. Sam checks that his phone is on vibrate and sits down to wait.

Molly shows up a moment later and goes down the front stairs to a table outside the bar. Sam has a clear view.

While she waits, Molly reaches into a tote bag and takes out her water, then pulls her phone out of a pocket and starts scrolling. Sam's too far away to see what she's doing, but he watches her push her hair off her face and wet her lower lip. She waits for twenty minutes and then gives up. Sam gives her time to leave and then follows her out. He's already wearing what he thinks is a good disguise: a Washington Nationals hoodie, jeans, and a baseball cap pulled low over his forehead.

He follows Molly up 14th Street, assuming she's headed back to the office, but then she turns into a fast-food restaurant with a big salad bar. While he waits outside, Sam's phone vibrates. It's Danny and when Sam asks if he's available to help, he agrees to hurry into the city and stand by for more detailed instructions.

When Molly comes out, Sam follows her to the Metro Center station. When she takes a red line train north, Sam panics briefly, then hops on an adjacent car. He tries to remember how they do it in the movies and stays by the door and carefully sticks his head out at each stop. Then an idea occurs to him and he uses his senior editor privileges to tap into the newspaper's private staff list, where he finds Molly's home address. His hunch looks right, and he guesses that Molly is headed back to her apartment to hide out until her meeting with the suspect.

He expects her to get off at the Van Ness stop and he's ready when she does. More confident of where she's headed, he stays back and follows at a distance. When she stops to wait for a traffic light to change, he sends the address of Molly's apartment building to Danny and tells him to text him when he's a block away. Danny confirms the plan.

Molly's building has a doorman, and Sam makes no attempt to enter. He does prowl around a bit, as discreetly as he can, to check for side or back entrances. He can't tell, but he sees no reason why she would use anything but the front door. He spots a small deli across the street, and he goes in and finds a seat to keep watch. He updates Danny on his location and settles in to wait and worry.

The deli is light on amenities, but it has what he needs: a table by the front window and coffee. He takes a seat and uses the time to rethink his plan. He can still call Brenda or the police. He wonders whether his friend Howie at the Capitol Police could have helped and gets annoyed at himself for not thinking of it earlier. He's worked himself into a jumpy high, only partly fueled by the caffeine, by the time Danny slides into a seat next to him.

"Why are we here?" he asks.

Sam explains the dilemma and his decision to follow Molly as briefly as he can.

"Is this ethical?" Danny asks with a mischievous grin.

Sam takes the question seriously, pauses, and says, "We're trying to keep her from doing something really stupid and dangerous."

"Why not call the police?"

"And say what? Think about how that conversation might go. And anyway, for all I know, the cops set this whole thing up. They may be watching her door the same as we are."

Danny gets up and goes outside, and Sam watches him walk the block, cross the street, and return.

"Nope. Nobody's watching but us," Danny says.

Sam can't help but smile. Danny gets himself some coffee and a refill for Sam, plus a muffin that they share, Sam eating with a fork, Danny using his fingers.

"So how long have you and Ariana been an item?" Sam says, still staring out the window at the front of the apartment building.

"Almost a year now. We were teamed up in investigative journalism and did our project together. We hit it off."

"Serious? You live together?"

"We've started to talk about it, but I'm not sure. Our hours don't mesh—I start work very early and she waitresses most nights, and neither of us has a big enough apartment for that to work."

Sam turns from the window to look at Danny, tries to read whether that's a real problem or an excuse, decides he can't tell.

"And Kelly? How well do you know her?"

"Only through Ariana. They've been friends since high school. Went to Montgomery College together and then both transferred to Maryland. Roomed together off campus for two years. They're still very close."

"But they don't live together now?"

Danny smiles. "I promised I wouldn't tell you where Kelly lives, but no, they don't live together."

"But they both live in College Park. Or near it. Is Kelly still in school?"

Danny shakes his head. "She works in one of those big physician practices with eight doctors, mostly handling insurance paperwork."

"So, what is Kelly like?" Sam asks.

Danny takes a moment and Sam wonders why.

"She's not making any of this up, if that's what you're asking," Danny says.

"I'm only asking you to tell me what she's like."

"Well," Danny says, drawing the word out and making Sam wonder why he's stalling. "I don't know her that well. I met her at a party that Ariana dragged me to. And I've seen her on a few other social occasions. She and Ariana were both bridesmaids at a wedding last year. She seemed happy. Normal. Outgoing. Friendly. Nothing that would make you think badly of her or worry about her."

"When did you hear about her relationship with Morgan?"

"Not until after it ended. Ariana knew for a while but kept it a secret."

Sam notices a change in tone. "Sounds like you were surprised they kept it from you."

"At first, but it was none of my business. Ariana promised not to tell, and I understand that."

"So what made her finally bring you into it?"

"After the breakup, Kelly went downhill fast, and it was hard to hide it. Her whole personality changed. One night Ariana asked if she could go out to dinner with us. She was trying to cheer her up. But that night, I couldn't help but notice something was very wrong, and when I asked Ariana, she finally told me what was going on."

"Was Kelly unhappy about the breakup or the harassment?"

"Oh, definitely the harassment. It was driving her to the edge. Ariana was afraid she was having a nervous breakdown. That's why she told me. She wanted advice on what to do."

"But your information is all from Ariana. You never actually talked to Kelly about it or saw it firsthand?"

"Except for that night at dinner when she could barely say a word. And it was obvious she'd lost weight and wasn't sleeping."

Sam had kept his eyes on the apartment building throughout the conversation, with only brief turns of his head toward Danny, but now he took a harder look at him. "You don't have any doubt that she's telling the truth?"

Danny shook his head. "No. I don't know about every detail, and I don't know what led to the breakup, but I know he's been doing the porn revenge thing. Ariana and I looked at the pictures on the internet together. That was a pretty awful thing he did."

"And it was definitely Morgan? No other unhappy boyfriends in Kelly's life?"

"She's had other boyfriends, but I never heard any suggestion it could be someone else."

"She was popular?"

Danny acts surprised by the question. "I'm not sure what you mean. She dated. Nothing out of the ordinary. I don't know the details."

"I'm just wondering why she would get involved with a married man twice her age."

Danny shrugs. "It happens. Isn't power supposed to be the ultimate aphrodisiac?"

Sam nods. "That's what they say."

The afternoon passes slowly. Sam continues dividing his attention between the apartment building across the street and Danny. They talk about Danny's job and how he juggles it with school, and Sam hears out his complaints about some of the classes in the journalism program.

"The younger students, the ones who don't have jobs yet, are so into the web and they think the rules of journalism don't apply to them. If ethics weren't required, you wouldn't have anyone in your class. They just want to know the flashy stuff. My investigative reporting class only had six of us, and we're all interested in jobs at the big, serious papers."

"Both of them," Sam says, then feels bad when he sees Danny's grimace. "It's not that bad," he adds. "Just keep at it."

"How'd you get into teaching ethics?" Danny asks, obviously eager to change the subject.

"A fluke, like so much in life. I'd been in Washington a lot of years as a reporter and editor, and I'd spoken a few times at the university, so I knew the head of the program. One day she called out of the blue. The instructor they'd lined up had suddenly dropped out and they were desperate."

"Were you writing the column then?"

"No, that came much later. I had no preparation for the class—my master's is in political science and I never took a journalism class of any kind, ever. So I took a week off and read everything I could about ethics—from Kant and Aristotle to Peter Singer and Kelly McBride. I ate it up and soon I was preaching in the newspaper office to anyone who would listen. When they suggested I put my passion into a column, I jumped at the chance, and we came up with Mr. Ethics. Stole the basic idea from the *New York Times*, of course, but we take different approaches."

"So it wasn't something you were shooting for."

Sam shakes his head. "I never would have expected it."

It's nearly five when Molly emerges from the apartment building, and Danny leaves immediately to get his car in case she takes a taxi or calls a service. Sam watches Molly take a moment to look around, walk to one end of the block, and turn back the other way. He's glad he's shielded by the deli and wonders why

Molly is being so careful. He doesn't think he tipped her off, but she obviously wants to be sure no one is following her. He notices that she's wearing a red scarf on her head. He's not much into style, but it doesn't look like the kind of thing she normally wears. He guesses it's a marker that the suspect will use to recognize her.

Molly fiddles with her phone and Sam assumes she's checking on an Uber or Lyft that she's summoned. Danny pulls up and Sam texts him to wait. When Molly's car arrives, Sam hurries out and slips into Danny's back seat. "Follow that car," he says, but Danny is tense, in no mood for joking.

They keep two cars back as the Uber heads north on Connecticut Avenue. The rush-hour traffic makes it hard to keep up but easy to remain undetected. Molly's car crosses into Maryland and turns right on East-West Highway, then left on Grubb Road and into an area that Sam doesn't recognize, but soon they are on Georgia Avenue, a busy thoroughfare this time of night, and then the car turns into a big shopping mall in Wheaton.

Sam grows more confident with every mile—he can't imagine that Molly came all this way to do her shopping—but when the car drops her off at the big Costco store, he senses a problem. He tells Danny to pull over and go after her while he parks the car, fearful that if he goes himself, she'll spot him. He parks quickly and enters the mall, then hides at a snack bar, hoping to hear from Danny. When he does, it's to say that Molly has disappeared.

"She went into the Costco, but I didn't have a membership card and they made me go to customer service. I never got in."

"Why didn't you wait outside?"

"I don't know this place," Danny says with a defensive tone. "I thought there might be another way out and I'd miss her."

They hang around another half hour in hopes she'll show up, but she never does.

Twitter Calls Me Antifa Man

I recognize her as soon as she arrives, thanks to the red scarf I made her wear. I watch her flash her Costco membership card and enter the store. She walks around quickly to the checkout line and slips through empty-handed and exits the other door. As far as I can tell, no one is with her or following her.

She's younger than I expected, close to my age. And prettier. Neither of which is a problem. Maybe she'll understand where I'm coming from. Plus, she works for that liberal rag, though it's hardly progressive enough for my taste.

I take my time walking through the mall to the Target a couple hundred yards away, being careful to look for and avoid any security cameras, though I have a hat pulled down over my forehead so my face is hidden. There's a little-used Starbucks inside the Target, and I find her waiting there, as instructed. She's seated at a table with what looks like iced coffee. I see only two other patrons, and she's picked a table as far away from them as possible. I take one last look around and join her.

"I knew you'd come," I say.

"I thought you deserved to have your say." She opens her purse and takes out her phone. "Mind if I record this?"

"No recordings. No pictures. Give me your phone. I'll give it back when we're done."

She's reluctant but has no choice. She hands me the phone and reaches into her purse for a notebook and it occurs to me that she may have another phone in her purse already recording, so I insist on looking inside. She frowns but hands her bag over. I go through it quickly and find nothing worrisome, so I give it back. I look around to see if anyone has noticed the odd search, and then I begin.

"That was a load of crap you wrote today."

"Which part wasn't true?"

"I didn't kill the asshole. I'm not shedding tears over him, but it wasn't me."

"I didn't say you did, only that you threatened him and the police are looking for you."

"He's an asshole. I tried to shock some sense into him."

"By scaring him? You only egged him on."

"Do you have any idea how much damage his kind are doing to this country? Every day there's some new asshole policy that sets us back a decade or two. Think about the world we'll be leaving our children. Dirty air, dirty water, people living in the streets, not having enough food, no health care anyone can afford, businesses doing anything they want no matter how much it hurts people. To say nothing of discrimination against anyone who's not a White male. Do you know a woman can't even get an abortion in Alabama anymore? And we still lock immigrant children in cages. We're going back to the Middle Ages."

She's writing as fast as she can, filling notebook pages as if she's never heard any of this before.

"Why are you writing this down? Your newspaper reports on it every day on every page. I'm not telling you something you don't know."

"It tells me how you feel. It will help readers understand your motive."

"What?" I say, a little more loudly than I should. I look around, but no one has taken note. "There's no motive because I didn't kill him."

"You sound angry enough to have done it," she says.

I grab her wrist roughly to try to get through to her. "I didn't do it. And you better not write another story that makes it sound like I did."

She pulls her arm free and stands up. "Touch me again and I'm leaving."

I decide to apologize. I don't believe she'll leave, but I want to keep her off guard.

"I'm sorry," I say. "Look, his politics were awful. I don't know if he actually believed in what he was saying, but that doesn't matter. He was one of the bad guys, the guys who are destroying this country and putting us on the road to a dictatorship. He needed to be stopped, and I'm glad someone did it, but I'm not stupid enough to think killing one person will make a difference, and I certainly wouldn't sacrifice myself. I've got too many other ways to fight, too many other things I need to be doing."

"Like what?" she asks, pretending she cares.

I tell her no and stand up. "This was a mistake. I thought you'd understand."

"I do understand your politics. I'm not even saying I disagree with them. But the police are looking at you for this. They know your name, and it won't take them long to find you."

I sit back down so I can speak more softly. "They don't know my name. That's bullshit."

"How do you know?"

"Did they give it to you?"

"Of course not."

"Because they don't know it."

She looks around, like she's trying to figure out what to ask next. "If you're really innocent," she says, "you should go to the FBI. The more you hide, the more guilty you look."

"Yeah, that'll work out real well. They just want to pin it on somebody to take the pressure off, and once they have me, I won't have a chance."

She leans forward, her elbows on the table. "Do you have an alibi for the night he was killed?"

I don't answer right away. "I do, but it's not one I can tell anyone about."

"Why not?"

"Because I was with some friends, people who understand what we're facing, what needs to be done. I'm not giving them up. If I go to the feds, they'll make up some bullshit and lock me up."

"So, you were with friends planning something illegal?" she asks.

"I didn't say that."

"Then why won't they stand up for you and give you an alibi?"

I look at her. It's hard to believe she's so naïve. "The police probably won't believe them. They'll end up in trouble too."

"Are you all in this together? Did one of them kill him?"

"No way," I say with more conviction than I feel. Truth is, I had the same thought, but they assured me they had nothing to do with it, and we don't lie to each other.

"Okay," she says. "Let's try another approach. Tell me about your background. Where did you grow up? Did you go to college?"

This is beginning to feel pointless. She thinks I'm a fool. "You just want information that will help identify me. I'm not going to give it to you. I'm leaving."

I stand up again and start to walk out of Starbucks and into the main store, but she hurries after me, even taking my arm. "Give me back my phone."

"First, tell me what you're going to write."

She rolls her eyes, the first sign that she's no longer afraid of me. "I have no idea," she says. "I doubt my editor will let me write anything. I don't know your name or if you're actually the suspect the police have in mind. You haven't given me anything but a political diatribe. How do I know this isn't a hoax?"

I'd expected her to demand proof earlier, so I brought it with me. I hand her a copy of one of the threats I mailed. I doubt she's seen the original, but maybe she can check it. Even if she can't, it seems to have an effect on her.

"So, what will you write now?" I ask.

"I'm honestly not sure. You haven't given me much. I'll have to talk it over with my editors."

"At least tell them I didn't do it."

"I'll tell them you denied it," she says.

I can tell this has been a waste, maybe a dangerous one. "You go back to the Starbucks and stay a few more minutes. Don't leave until I'm well out of sight. Promise me that."

She nods. "But I need my phone back."

I reach out with it but then stop. It would be too easy for her to follow me and take a picture that could come back to haunt me. "Not now. I'll send it over to the newspaper in the morning."

"Shit," she says as I walk away.

Molly's Debriefing

Sam gets no reply on Molly's cellphone and wonders for a moment whether he should call the police. Danny tells him to relax. "He's probably leading her to a second location to make sure she's not being followed. That's what they do in the movies."

Sam's far from convinced. "Maybe we should call the police."

"And tell them what?"

Sam sees how ridiculous and futile it would be, so he asks Danny to drop him back at his apartment. He still can't get Molly on her cellphone or her office line. He calls again an hour later, and this time when she doesn't pick up, he rings the desk. Molly is in the building, an editor tells him, but she's in a meeting with Brenda and two other editors.

Relieved that she's safe, Sam bides his time. It's after eight when she finally calls him.

"Where were you?" he says more harshly than he planned.

"It's a long story and I'd rather tell it in person. Do you mind if I come by?"

"You met with him, didn't you?"

He hears a chuckle. "And Brenda told me not to say a word. Who told you?"

"Never mind. I'm here. Come on by. I'll try not to wring your neck." He gives her the address, and she promises to bring a bottle of wine as a peace offering.

She arrives in less than half an hour and hands him a bottle of merlot. He sees how tired she is, understandable considering the tension she's been under. She's wearing slacks and a cotton sweater, and there's no sign of the red scarf. On impulse he gives her a quick hug and then walks her into his tiny kitchen.

"Tough day," he says, leaving off the question mark, as he pulls out two glasses and a corkscrew. Soon they are sitting in the living room.

"I left you a dozen messages," he says. "You could have at least called me to tell me you were okay."

"He took my phone. I never got your messages."

Sam considers that. "He didn't hurt you? Try to scare you?"

She shakes her head. "No. We were out in the open. I was never scared. Not in the physical sense. Just afraid I'd blow it."

"Start from the beginning, and don't leave anything out."

She runs through her day. Most of it he can confirm, but she leaves out the diversion through Costco and only recounts the meeting, not saying where it was. It makes him wonder if she's leaving anything else out, though he doesn't let on that he'd been trying to follow her.

When she's finished, he asks her what kind of story she's written.

"None. What would I write? I went through the whole thing with Brenda and she said there was nothing I could confirm. I knew that's what she'd say."

"And she's right," Sam says.

"I know. I didn't argue. Well, I argued a little. I wanted to follow up on my scoop and say the guy the feds were looking for had reached out to me to insist he's innocent."

Sam looks at her to see if she's joking. "And then the FBI would be on your doorstep demanding you tell them everything," he says.

"I'd tell them it was all in the story."

"They'd get a subpoena for your notes, and you'd end up in a legal tangle that would take you off the story until it's resolved. Even if you win, you lose."

"Which is exactly what Brenda said. If I didn't know better, I'd think you two were in it together." She leans back and brushes the hair off her face.

"Besides, you're not even sure it's the right guy," Sam adds.

"He gave me a copy of one of his threats. I have someone who can confirm it."

"Which reminds me, you have one hell of a source. How did you get him?"

"The same way any reporter gets a source. He was using me and I was using him."

"But you have more than one source, right?"

"I have one guy who gives me great stuff and a couple others who'll confirm it indirectly."

"Indirectly? What does that mean?"

"They'll tell me if it's wrong. So far, they haven't had to."

"So why is this source so helpful?"

Molly looks at him, then turns her head away. "He flirts a lot. I let him."

"Molly," Sam says sternly. "Flirts how? What are you doing?"

"Calm down. I have it under control."

But the way she says it is unconvincing. Sam opens his mouth and then closes it, deciding this is no time for a lecture. It will only push her away.

"Be careful," he says. "You took a big risk today. How is your Antifa Man going to react when he finds out you didn't write a story."

"I already warned him that was likely."

"So, what are you hoping will happen?"

"I think I got through to him when I told him to go to the FBI. He refused, but he'll come around. He doesn't have any other option except to go on the run for the rest of his life."

"You're assuming he's innocent?"

"No. But even if he's guilty, it's his only chance to get away with it. Hiding makes him look guilty."

He sees her wine glass is empty and asks if she wants more, but she shakes her head. "I better get home. I'm totally exhausted and I have another big day tomorrow."

At the door, she stops and gives Sam an off-centered smile. "One other thing. I got a text today from your email friend."

Sam tries to look blank.

"She said she wanted to talk to me and set up a meeting, but she didn't show."

"Maybe she got cold feet."

Molly stares at him intently. "Maybe."

It's two hours later when Sam's phone wakes him. He glances at the caller ID and answers.

"Molly, you okay?" he asks, shaking himself into consciousness.

"Do I sound like Molly?" the voice says.

Sam is sure the call came from Molly, but then he remembers that she gave up her phone.

"Who is this?" he asks, trying to sound confused rather than hostile or suspicious.

"Let's just say I'm a friend of Molly's."

Sam pauses, trying to figure out where this might go but comes up blank. He's still not fully awake.

"Why are you calling me?" he asks.

"Because you called her nine times today and I kinda wondered why Mr. Ethics was so concerned." The caller's voice is louder than it should be, and Sam recognizes something between anger and fear.

"We work together," he tells him, aware of the reference to his column.

"You didn't sound like someone who just works with her. You sounded like someone worried about her."

Sam tries to remember the messages he left. He doesn't think he gave anything away, but it doesn't matter.

"Look, what's this about? What do you want and why are you calling from Molly's phone?"

"She lent it to me today. I'm helping her with a story. You'll see it in tomorrow's paper."

Sam decides on a more aggressive tack. "No, I won't," he says. "And neither will you. You didn't give her enough to work with, and her editors won't print anything."

There's a brief pause and then the caller hangs up.

Sam spends the next few minutes pacing his apartment, trying to decide what to do. It's almost one a.m. and he doesn't see any point in calling anyone right now. It occurs to him that if the FBI knew what was happening, they might be able to zero in on the location of Molly's phone and catch this guy, but he's not sure that really happens other than on TV.

As he often does when he's not sure what to do, he considers the ethics. He knows that Molly promised the suspect confidentiality and that she wouldn't alert the police to their meeting, but technically that doesn't apply to him. It would if he were her editor, but he's not, and anyway, the suspect brought him into it by calling without setting any boundaries. Still, Sam feels some obligation to act as a journalist, rather than a cop.

But he also can't do nothing. He picks up his phone and calls Molly's number, well aware that he's doing exactly what he told Molly not to do.

But he gets no answer.

Sam waits ten minutes, plans what he will say and calls again. There's still no answer, but the guy hasn't turned off the phone either. That gives him enough hope to call again a few minutes after that.

"What do you want?"

"I want to finish the conversation you started," Sam says.

"Your friend was pulling my chain. I was counting on her to write a good story. The feds have already convicted me. I don't stand a chance."

"Of course, you do," Sam says. "If you're innocent."

"I didn't do it. I told her that. Why doesn't she believe me?"

"Actually, I think she might, but it doesn't matter what we believe. If you didn't do it, they can't prove you did. It's as simple as that." He says it with more conviction than he feels, and quickly he regrets it.

"I know that's not always the case," Sam adds. "The newspaper can help if you can show us you didn't do it, but you need to go to the FBI. Voluntarily. Hiding out only makes you look guilty."

They talk for a while, and Sam senses the suspect's resistance fading, helped by his disappointment that Molly is not writing a story about him. It's not lost on Sam that he's using the same argument with this guy that he used with Kelly, but it feels appropriate.

"Do you have a lawyer?" Sam asks.

"I can't afford a lawyer, and I trust them about as far as I trust the cops."

"You need a lawyer. If you want, I can put you in touch with someone who might help."

"You only want to know my name and where to find me."

"No, you don't have to give me a name, and lawyers are bound to confidentiality far more than journalists. They'd lose their license to practice if they gave you up. And a lawyer can explain why you're better off going to the police than running away."

"I don't know," he says, but Sam gets the feeling he's thinking about it.

"Who's this lawyer you'd get?"

"I'd have to ask her," Sam says, "and she might not be willing, but I think I can talk her into it."

"And who's going to pay?"

"She might do it pro bono. For free."

"I know what pro bono means. Don't treat me like an idiot. I went to college."

"Sorry," Sam says, aware that he's got a new clue, though not a very helpful one.

"Why would she do it for free?"

"I'm not sure she will, but she might. Or know someone who will."

The suspect doesn't say anything, and Sam senses more skepticism. He considers his next comment carefully. "Look, I think I can persuade her because she's my ex-wife. We're still friends and she's a good person."

"Your ex-wife?"

"Yes," Sam says, having decided that he needs to put a little distance between himself and Lisa so his caller doesn't believe they'll work together. But, in a superstitious kind of way, he feels bad about saying 'ex.'

"To be honest, we're still technically married, but we're separated. It's complicated."

"What's her name?"

"Let me first see if she's willing."

"I can Google your wife in twenty seconds. Save me the trouble."

Sam knows he's right. He shouldn't have mentioned the relationship without asking her, but now it might earn a bit more trust. "Lisa Turner. She's with Fisk, Akhtar and Wainright. I'll call her first thing tomorrow. She can be hard to get to, but I'll call you on this number as soon as I know."

"And I'm supposed to believe she won't give you my name?"

"She's a lawyer. She can't do that"

"If this is a trick, someone will pay."

"It's not a trick. I'll let you know tomorrow. Just think about it."

Antifa Man grudgingly agrees. "But I'll call you if I want to see her. I promised to return this phone first thing tomorrow."

After they hang up, Sam thinks that is a good sign. He could have decided to keep the phone, but instead he's keeping a promise.

KELLY

I've never been so scared. I don't even think about breakfast; holding down coffee is hard enough. I've had my one cigarette for the day, and now I'm considering a Xanax or a Valium. No, better not. I'm going to need my wits about me. I have another cigarette, then I reconsider and take half a Xanax, figuring my anxiety is more than anyone should have to handle.

I know I don't have much choice about this. I've come around to that view. It's best if I'm the one to tell the cops about Wade and me. It's the one thing everyone keeps telling me. Knowing the FBI is looking at some guy who threatened Wade makes it easier. That might get me off the hook. I can say something about all the threats—how Wade laughed them off when I told him to take them seriously. I might even embellish that point a bit. My hope is they're looking at lots of threats and lots of potential killers, so they won't want to spend time on me.

My biggest fear—besides the obvious—is that what I tell them will end up in the newspapers. Everything in Washington does. I spent enough time with Wade to know how it works. Someone wants the story out to gain some advantage, and reporters are all too willing to go along. A mutual arrangement that usually ends up deceiving the public.

I keep thinking about Wade's wife. How could I not? Wade always said she knew and didn't care if he was with other women as long as he was discreet. Could that ever have been true? Even in the beginning? What kind of woman lends her husband out like that?

I smile slightly at the thought. What kind of woman borrows another woman's husband?

Danny and Ariana have agreed to drive me for moral support. They again suggested a lawyer, which doesn't make sense. A lawyer will make me look guilty. I need to convince them I'm not hiding anything, that I'm scared and didn't know what to do.

Most important, Ariana keeps telling me, is to remember I'm the victim. And that's true. No one should have to go through what I went through. It made me crazy, and they shouldn't blame me for the mistakes I made. I did what I thought I had to do to get free.

Danny suggested that I take Turner with me, but he's the last one I want by my side. Not after that email. I would never have written that if I had any idea how this would turn out.

Danny and Ariana arrive at ten. Danny is driving and after some polite and awkward debate about who sits where, Ariana and I take the back seat. She tries to hold my hand, but it is clammy and I prefer to clasp my own hands together. We don't say much on the drive.

"Do you want me to go in with you?" Danny asks.

I hesitate. "Just Ariana. No offense."

"I understand."

I'd read about the task force they formed to handle the investigation, and I asked Danny if we could approach the D.C. police rather than the FBI, which would be infinitely more intimidating. Danny says it wasn't hard to arrange. He called D.C. headquarters and asked for the detectives working on the case, and they were eager to talk to me. I know they're all working together, but going to the cops rather than the FBI will make it at least a little less dramatic.

When we arrive, it's clear the front desk is expecting us. This is an important case. The cable networks talk about it all the time, and even the *New York Times* has put it on the front page several days running. I know it's a big story. How many senators manage to get themselves murdered? I also know it's a black mark against those who were supposed to protect him, and they probably think solving the case will get them off the hook.

A uniformed officer escorts us up to what I presume is the homicide division, and we're greeted by a detective who isn't at all like what I expect. Latisha Thompson is heavy and not trying to hide it, wearing a blouse, slacks, and beat-up black shoes that look both comfortable and tough, the kind you'd want to wear if your plan for the day included kicking somebody. She's Black and has something resembling a mini afro. The only thing stylish about her is her glasses, which are some kind of designer knock-off.

"There's a room we can talk in," she says and then takes closer notice of Ariana. "Are you her lawyer?" she asks.

"Just a friend," Ariana says. "Is it okay if I come with you?"

Latisha takes a moment before answering. "Sure, if it will make you feel more comfortable," she tells me.

I nod. So far, Ariana has done all the talking and I haven't said a word. My throat is tight, and I wonder what will happen if nothing comes out when I try to tell my story.

The room Latisha takes us to is nicer than I expect. It's not like the cold interview rooms on TV, and when I look around, I don't see any cameras or two-way mirrors. It helps me relax a bit. It's not exactly comfortable—it's chilly and I can smell disinfectant—but it's surprisingly roomy.

"You said you had some information for us," Latisha begins. "Do you mind if I record this?"

I look around for the microphone, but she's pulled out her phone and placed it on the table. I nod my consent—what choice do I have?—and she senses my discomfort.

"It's easier than taking notes," she explains and then looks at me expectantly.

"I'm not sure where to begin," I say.

She smiles, trying to be friendly. "Did you know Senator Morgan?"

This is the moment. I know there's no going back, and I want to get this over as quickly as possible, so I don't mince words. "I was his lover," I say, watching her carefully. I get no reaction.

"When was this?"

"We met in September and we slept together a month later. It went on for four months and then it got to be too much for me, so I ended it." I take a big breath. "He took it badly."

"What do you mean it got to be too much?"

"I was stupid. I let him seduce me, and I fooled myself into thinking that he really cared about me. I even thought he loved me. But hiding everything became a huge burden. It took all the pleasure out of it. I wanted it to stop."

"And he took that badly? How exactly?"

I shake my head and I try to talk, but nothing comes out. I start crying. The detective slides a tissue box over to me. Until then, I hadn't even seen it on the table.

"Do you want me to tell her?" Ariana asks as she reaches for my hand.

Latisha objects. "It's better if I hear it from her."

I regain control and tell her how he got angry and threatened to ruin me. How I didn't take it seriously until I realized he'd broken into my computer and stolen my identity, run up charges, not to steal but to make trouble for me.

"I begged him to stop, but he ignored me. When he finally answered, he said it must be somebody else. I did everything

I could to make him leave me alone, even threatened to tell his wife and make it public, but he knew I wouldn't do that. It would be as bad for me as for him if word got out."

Latisha sits and listens, nodding as though she understands but not saying anything. She knows there's more.

"And then it got worse," I say. "There were pictures. I let him take intimate pictures of me, and he used them on the internet. Not so I could be identified but with an implicit threat of what might come next."

I tell her about the dating profile and the threat to post my picture and contact information on a site where men look for prostitutes.

"Did he do that?" Latisha asks.

"No, but he might have. I wouldn't put it past him."

"But now he's dead."

"She had nothing to do with that," Ariana blurts out.

"I wasn't saying she did. But the fact is, your problem got solved when he got killed."

"She came here to help you," Ariana says.

"I know, and it's good she did. Can I ask why, though? This can't be easy—telling me all this. Why do you think it's relevant to the case? To solving his murder?"

I pretend to think for a minute. "I figured I wasn't the only one. There may be lots of women who hated him."

"Did you hate him that much? So much that you thought of killing him? I'm not saying you did. I'm only wondering if you ever thought about it."

I shake my head, but I tell her yes. "Of course. He was driving me insane. I couldn't eat or sleep or work or do anything. Of course, I thought about killing him, but I didn't."

"Would she be here if she had?" Ariana says foolishly.

Latisha ignores her. "I'm sorry you had to go through this. No one should have to go through this. If what you say is true, he was an incredibly cruel man."

I note the "if" clause in her sentence. "It is true. And I wouldn't be at all surprised if he did it to other women."

Ariana takes my hand again and asks Latisha if we are through.

"A few more questions," she says.

"You mentioned other women? Did you know that there were others or are you only assuming it?"

"I could tell he'd done it before. It was obvious. I'm not that naïve."

"Do you know of anyone in particular?"

I shake my head.

"Any reason to think he was seeing someone else during the period he was seeing you?"

"He came over to my apartment frequently. And he was busy with work. I doubt he had time for simultaneous affairs." There, I've used that word.

"Did he talk about his wife? How they got along? Did she suspect he was seeing you?"

"It was a marriage of convenience. Obviously, he didn't love her if he behaved this way. She knew there were other women, but he said she didn't care enough to find out who they were."

"So you talked about her?"

"He complained a lot about his wife. Mostly how she wouldn't have sex with him."

"How did you communicate with him when you were apart? His cellphone?"

"One of them. He said it was too risky to use his primary phone, so he carried an extra. It was one of those prepaid deals."

"Do you have the number?"

I know it by heart of course, but I go through the motions of checking my own phone before I give her the number.

"This is the number I used, but he may have gotten a new one since then."

"What makes you say that?"

"When I sent him a text asking him to leave me alone, I didn't get an answer."

"But you said he denied being the one who harassed you. Was that in person?"

"That was earlier. We did talk once on the phone and he denied it."

"He was using the number you gave me?"

I shake my head. "It's all a blur. I don't remember."

Next, she wants the email addresses we used to communicate. I give them to her, and then she reads them aloud to check that she has them right. I decide I better be more forthcoming.

"I did send several emails pleading with him to stop bothering me. He ignored them. Just as he did with the texts."

Though she's recording everything, she writes that down, and when she finally looks up from her pad, she changes the subject.

"Did he ever talk to you about receiving threats because of his political views?"

At last, she's asked what I most want to talk about. I've rehearsed my speech and it comes out just the way I want it to. It's the first time I can string sentences together without gulping for air or struggling for control. I watch her for a reaction as I tell about all the threats and how Wade refused to take them seriously, often dismissing his security detail so he could do what he wanted.

"In a strange way, he saw the threats as a badge of honor," I conclude.

"Did he give you specifics? Did you ever see any of the threats or hear them on his phone?"

I shake my head.

She stares at her notes for a second, then goes back to when he posted the pictures of me. She asks me to tell her as many details as I can about where and when the revenge porn appeared.

"We'll need to trace everything," she says.

I run through the details, but she keeps pressing for more, including dates and descriptions of the pictures so they can be identified.

When she's finished her questions, I ask one of my own. "Does this mean you don't already have the pictures? They weren't on his phone?"

Latisha frowns. "I can't discuss the case with you."

"But if the pictures are there, there's no reason why anyone else has to know, right?"

She looks at me and our eyes meet. "Not unless they prove relevant to the case."

I don't have to ask what that means.

"Is there anything else we should know?" she asks.

Ariana looks at me. Danny had advised me to tell her about my email to Mr. Ethics, but I know how damning that would be. I have to trust he'll keep it confidential.

"No," I say.

"One last question," Latisha says. "And this is just routine. Can you tell me where you were on the night he was killed? Between ten p.m. and four the next morning?"

I'm not surprised, but I don't have a good answer. "I was home. Alone. With my cat."

A Tangled Web

Sam wakes up with a massive headache, aware he's brought it on himself. He had one bourbon too many, to say nothing of getting involved with one too many murder suspects. He owes Molly an update and has to call Lisa to see if she'll talk to the antifa guy, but before he can do either his phone rings. It's Danny.

"Kelly went to the police yesterday," he says. "I should have called you last night, but we were in crisis mode."

"It went badly?"

"I wasn't there, Ariana was, and she thought it went better than expected. The detective asked a zillion questions but without getting hostile or giving Kelly a hard time. But Kelly didn't see it that way. She thinks the detective was cruel."

"Didn't he believe her?"

"She. And who knows? Ariana says the detective could win a contest for keeping a straight face. She gave nothing away, including whether she knew about Kelly even before she came in."

"So, what was the crisis?"

"Kelly's a wreck. Having to tell the whole story again was hard. The detective asked a lot of questions about Morgan's harassment and the pictures. They're obviously going to track everything down, and Kelly is hung up on the idea that a lot more people will end up seeing the photos."

"She knew that going in."

"She's truly embarrassed by it, but the bigger problem—at least in my mind—is that the pictures are a pretty strong motive for murder."

"We knew that going in too," Sam says. "You have to have faith that if she's innocent, the truth will come out in the end."

"I suppose."

Sam doesn't like the way that sounds. "You are still confident she's innocent, aren't you?"

"Yes, that's not what I meant, but it wouldn't be the first time the police got it wrong."

"Going in to see them was the right thing to do. They would have discovered her eventually."

"I know. It's just hard."

Sam is about to end the call when Danny asks about Molly. "Have you heard from her?"

Sam hesitates. He made no promise to keep Danny in the loop, though he owes him some courtesy for his help in following Molly to her meeting with Antifa Man.

"She met with the guy," he says. "He insists he's innocent."

"Does she believe him?"

"How can she know? I ended up talking to him by phone—long story—and I told him he had to go the FBI. I promised to try to find a lawyer to help him."

Danny is silent for a few seconds. "You sure are getting in the middle of this."

"Yeah, but not by choice. I'm actually doing my best to dump it all in the lap of the FBI."

They end the call after agreeing to keep each other up to date.

Sam knows Danny is right, but he's willing to live with it. Kelly came to him for help and he felt some obligation to give her advice. And in an odd way, the antifa guy also came to him for help, at least through Molly. Plus, he does feel an obligation to try to keep Molly out of trouble.

But he knows he is doing more than giving advice when asked. He's met twice with Kelly and went to a lot of trouble trying to follow Molly, and he gave advice to Antifa Man. In each case, he could have washed his hands of it more quickly by going to the police. Yet he convinced himself that the more ethical choice was to persuade the people involved to go to the police on their own. It worked with Kelly, and he hopes it will work with Antifa Man.

Satisfied with his conclusion, at least for now, Sam calls Lisa, but he has to leave a message. He then calls Molly.

"Nothing new," she says by way of an answer.

"Well, that's not exactly right," he says. "Your man called me last night."

Molly is apparently too stunned to respond, so Sam explains. "He has your phone, remember? He got all the voicemails I left you, so he had my number."

"I can't believe this," she says with real anger. "That's not possible."

"It's not only possible, it's true."

"No, I'm sure I turned it off before I gave it to him. He would have needed my password."

"Is your password hard to figure out?"

Sam hears the hesitation. "Reasonably hard," she says, but he can tell she's not so sure. "He must have known how to break into it."

"Whatever," Sam says. "The fact is he called me. Wanted to know why I was so concerned."

"This is crazy."

Sam gives her a second to absorb it all, but then a question occurs to him. He assumes his name shows up on Molly's contacts, but how did the guy know he was Mr. Ethics? He obviously did his research.

"Well, what did he say?" Molly asks finally.

"He wanted to know what my interest in you was. I told him we worked together and asked him who he was. He said I'd read about him in the paper tomorrow, but then I dropped the pretenses. I told him I knew about your meeting, that there'd be no story, and that if he's innocent, he ought to turn himself in."

"That's what I told him."

"I know, but I went a bit further. I told him I'd try to get a lawyer to go with him, no charge. I'm going to ask Lisa."

"She'd never agree. Would she?"

"Not sure. Maybe. I'll let you know, and if I can, I'll give you a heads up."

Molly doesn't seem to know what to say to that, but she grumbles a sound that he takes for assent.

"I guess he hasn't returned the phone yet," Sam adds.

"Not yet."

"There's something else," Sam says, suddenly remembering. "My email writer went to the police. Told them her whole story."

"She told me she would. Then she set up that meeting she never turned up for. But who told you she went to the police?"

"Our mutual friend," he says, "the one who told her to write to me in the first place."

"What did the feds tell her?"

"Not much, according to him. She went to the D.C. police, not the feds. She thought that'd be less intimidating. Anyway, they just listened and didn't give away anything."

"Do you still think she's innocent?"

"I still lean in that direction, but who can be sure at this point?"

He hears her sigh and guesses what's coming next. "You know her name, don't you?"

"Yes, but I can't tell you."

"I need to talk to her. Did you ask her why she stood me up?"

"How about this?" he says. "I'll ask her if she'll call you. I can't make her and, in fact, I can't think of any reason why she would, but I'll ask."

"I'll give you a reason," Molly says. "Tell her I'm going to ask the police about her and print her email if she doesn't talk to me. I'll make it public without her help and then she'll have no control over what gets written."

Sam considers confessing his role in Kelly's fake appointment but decides against it. He's relatively sure that Molly's threat of writing a story about Kelly is an empty one. She doesn't have a copy of the email and doesn't know enough details, and he doubts the police will fill her in. He's tempted to tell her that, but then he remembers Molly's Park Police source, whose willingness to talk is still a mystery to him.

"I'll do my best, but no promises," he says.

Lisa tells Sam he's crazy, but after they discuss it for a while, she agrees on three conditions.

"Which are?"

"One, I'll arrange for him to go talk to the task force and go with him if he wants, but that doesn't mean I'll represent him on a murder charge. We'll see what happens."

"Understood. What else?"

"You back off and stay out of this. I can't figure out why you keep getting in deeper, and I don't want to see you hurt."

"And number three?" he asks, without agreeing to number two.

"Remember I asked you to dog sit? Well, Betsy has decided to come in and do it, and she'll stay a few extra days to visit. Ben has to work, but she's bringing Logan. She wants you to stay at the house too. You don't have to spend the whole weekend—you can come and go as you please—but it's a chance to spend time with them. And with Dodger."

This is obviously a condition he can accept and he readily agrees. Only after he hangs up does he realize there's more to it. They've concocted the arrangement so Betsy can see for herself how he's doing, and maybe keep an eye on him to make sure he stays out of the case. He wonders how much Lisa has told her.

Sam isn't sure what his next move is, but before he decides, Molly calls. "He returned the phone, but guess what?"

"What?" Sam doesn't try to keep the concern out of his voice.

"He deleted your voicemails and erased any record of talking to you. The history is completely wiped out."

"Why would he do that?" he asks.

"I don't have a clue. Do you?"

"I can't think of why he'd bother, unless he doesn't want you to know he talked to me, which doesn't make a whole lot of sense."

They bat around other possibilities, but neither has any convincing ideas.

"You need to take it to IT and have them check that he didn't load it with some kind of malware," Sam tells her. "Better yet, toss it and buy a new one. The paper will reimburse you."

Sam ends up staying home, and it's not until four that Antifa Man calls him. Sam tells him that Lisa has agreed to talk to him. He gives him her number and leaves it to them to work out the details.

Talking Ethics

Sam starts his seminar with an unreasonable question. "Are you a journalist first or a good citizen first?" He lets it settle over the seminar group and watches in silence. He knows it's a question they've heard before and he can see they have little desire to tackle it again, but he doesn't care.

"Let's start with an extreme instance. You're a war photographer and the soldier who's been escorting you is hit with shrapnel. There's no medic nearby and he's bleeding badly. Do you put your camera down and help him or do you keep filming because that's what you're paid to do? Josh?"

"You have to help him. Do what you can and as soon as a medic or someone else arrives to help, you go back to work."

They all agree and Sam shifts to another possibility. "You're covering a political campaign and you notice that the candidate who's about to take the podium has his fly open. Really open. Do you tell him or let him embarrass himself?"

No one raises a hand and Sam surveys the room, a little surprised that Danny and Ariana are both absent.

"I'd take a picture first and then tell him," Eliza says to laughter around the room.

"Fine, but would you then use the picture?"

Eliza actually gives it some thought. "Not unless it was relevant to a story. Like if the candidate was really old and people were wondering if he was losing it."

Sam smiles and asks if anyone else has a thought.

"I think you keep your mouth shut," one student says. "You're there to observe and report. The open fly is not newsworthy, so you pay no attention to it, but you can't tell him about it. That's the job of a campaign aide, not a reporter."

"I agree with you," Sam says. "He's not bleeding to death or anything like that. You have no reason to cross the line.

"Here's another one: What if you're talking to an aide and she has her hands full and she drops her pen. Do you pick it up for her?"

"Of course," two people say in unison.

"And how is that different from telling the politician about his fly."

"The aide's not running for office. It's no more than common courtesy."

"Let's try a more complicated example," Sam says before anyone else can comment. "You're doing an investigative story on how schools handle children with behavioral or cognitive issues, and you find that a certain school isn't always providing the specialized care it claims to provide. You become aware of one kid in particular who's being left out, not getting what she needs. You witness a few specific examples that would give the parents grounds to file a complaint, maybe against a negligent teacher or administrator. You're allowed to write about it in general terms, but you can't name names. That was the school's condition for letting you in. But you're upset. Do you go to her parents with the details so they can take action?"

No one is smiling now. Sam sees a lot of wrinkled brows, several in the class are staring at their notebooks, and a few have pursed their lips in thought.

"It's wrong to do nothing," says Cynthia Bergman. "I'd tell the parents." Cynthia is the oldest student in the seminar, probably close to fifty and Sam figures she's the only mother, not that this matters.

"Is that breaking the ground rules?" he asks. "You promised confidentiality. What right do you have to approach the parents, let alone share the names of any school officials involved?"

"As long as you don't print it, you're not breaking the rules," Cynthia says. "But you can't do nothing."

Sam thinks about that. "But what can the parents do with that information? If they tell the school they got it from you, you're going to be in trouble."

Cynthia shakes her head. "It's up to them to decide what to do. They can raise a stink. They can complain without citing a source. Or maybe they can switch to another school. They need to know."

"But isn't it a parent's job to know how their kid is doing in school, to take an interest, to care?" Josh says.

Cynthia disagrees. "Tell that to a couple holding down two jobs and caring for three kids, one of them with special needs. It's not that easy to know what's happening at school."

Sam lets them go on. They're making good points, and he sees no reason to intervene until the conversation starts to wane.

"One more," he says, "and this relates at least a little bit to the dilemma we discussed here, back before spring break.

"What if you're covering health care and you're investigating whether a state-run program to get more people on an insurance plan is working. In the course of your discussions, you see someone struggling to fill out an application. He's been helpful and it's a simple chore, so you step out of the reporter role to help him. You're doing a good deed that doesn't seem in any way related to your story. But then his application gets rejected, and you figure it might be your fault—maybe you made a mistake—and you want to correct it, so you help with an appeal.

And then you discover it wasn't a mistake, and it begins to look to you like the system might be prejudiced against Muslim applicants. That's a bigger story if it's true, but now you're in the middle of it. You're no longer an objective reporter looking at a problem. You've become an advocate for the person, so what do you do? Does this mean you can't investigate and report the discrimination?"

No one raises a hand and Sam nods to the clock. "That's your assignment for next week. A thousand words on where your obligations lie and what the ethical implications are of personally intervening to help, using the power of the press, or stepping away. Note the slippery slope. You start with a simple gesture, almost like picking up that pen in the earlier example, but before you know it, it's turned into something far more serious, more like the school not providing necessary services or even the soldier who's bleeding to death."

Peg

Why do they always show up in pairs? Is it so there's a witness? To make sure no one misbehaves? Or to play good cop/bad cop?

This is the third pair to question me, and I know instantly this is different. The first two, from the Capitol Police, only came to inform me of Wade's death. Then came two FBI agents who asked pretty routine questions, and they called ahead to make an appointment. The new pair have D.C. badges and show up unannounced. Not a good sign. More threatening.

The cops make an odd couple. Sven Bergström is tall, thin, and blond, just as his name suggests, but when he opens his mouth, a southern accent comes out. The other one, a Black woman named Latisha Thompson, is a foot shorter and heavy and all business. Not even a smile.

"Sorry to show up without calling ahead," she says, making it clear she's not sorry at all. "Some new questions came up, and we thought it best to get them sorted sooner rather than later." I resist pointing out that a phone call wouldn't have delayed this encounter.

"Of course," I say. "Come in."

Once seated in my sister's living room, there are no preliminaries. "Were you aware that your husband was having an affair?"

I make a point of raising my eyebrows, but I can't exactly feign shock. "The senator wasn't perfect," I say, subtly reminding them who they're dealing with. "I've yet to meet a man who is."

"So you *were* aware," she says. No doubt who's the lead detective on this one.

"Why does this matter?"

"It could suggest a motive and possible suspects in your husband's murder."

"I see," I say, trying to think two moves ahead of her. Is it me or the other woman who has the motive? "Are you referring to anyone in particular?"

"Ma'am, do you know the names of any women he might have been involved with?" It's Sven who asks. The "ma'am" strikes me as cute until it occurs to me that it may be a trick. He knows I'm from the South, though I long ago rid myself of the accent and telltale mannerisms.

"No," I say, and leave it at that.

"Ever had suspicions about anyone in particular?"

I shake my head.

"Did you know he was seeing someone else recently? Like several weeks ago?" The Black woman is back in the conversation.

"Are you married?" I ask her.

"I was," she says, "but he cheated on me, so I dumped him real quick." The defiance is in her voice as well as on her face.

"Well, good for you," I say with as much sarcasm as I can muster. "I chose differently."

"Meaning what exactly, if you don't mind my asking," Sven says.

I suddenly feel tired. "Look. My husband was a very powerful man, and that attracts women, and he was hardly the kind to resist that. I knew he had some affairs, but as long as they never got serious, I wasn't about to throw myself out the window. I put up with it. It didn't mean we didn't love each other, and in many other ways, we had a good marriage. Not that this is any of your business."

Neither of them says anything to that. They both appear to be writing in their notebooks, but I suspect they're stalling while they think of what to ask next.

"Tell me," I say. "This woman you say he was seeing. Do you know who she is? Do you think she's involved?"

"We're not saying that," the Black woman says. "But recently your husband broke up with her and it allegedly got ugly. The woman says he stole her identity and did various other things to make her life miserable. We need to look into that."

"You've talked to her? Who is she?"

"At this time we'd rather not say."

"This sounds like something from a cheap novel. A bad cheap novel. At any rate, I don't know of anyone or anything about what might or might not have happened. I don't see how I can help you."

My knee is shaking and I cross my legs to steady it. Unfortunately, she notices. But maybe I can make it work for me.

"Are you okay?" she asks. "Can I get you some water?"

I look at her, hoping my disdain shows. After all, I'm the hostess here, even if it is my sister's house. I shake my head. "I'm fine," I say. "This is all very upsetting. I'd like to be alone right now."

"I'm sorry if we upset you, ma'am," Sven says.

"I'll be fine," I say. Then I stand up, an obvious sign, I hope, that we are done.

They rise with me, and I stifle a sigh of relief. But at the door, the Black woman turns to me. "Do you know if your husband used more than one cellphone?"

I shake my head.

"And as far as you know, we have all his computers and tablets?" she asks. "There's nothing in a second home or anywhere else like that?"

"No," I say, trying to sound firm. "Nothing."

House Sitting

Sam is set to pick up Betsy and Logan at BWI at ten-thirty. He packs an overnight bag, though he's not sure he'll feel comfortable sleeping in his old house—it's his first time back and he's bracing for all the emotions that may stir. He's glad Betsy and Logan will be there to keep him occupied and, to some extent, make the weekend seem like old times.

Before he goes, he calls Danny and tells him of Molly's request for an interview. They discuss all the reasons why Kelly is sure to refuse, but Sam says he promised to try. He asks Danny to make the case but then realizes that's unfair and instead suggests he ask Kelly to call him. He's on his way to the airport when she does, so he's forced to talk to her through the car speakers, which he hates. She's no fan of it either.

"Is there anyone with you?"

"No, I'm alone." He tells her about Molly's request for an interview, trying to walk a fine line between doing Molly's bidding and understanding that he's making an impossible request.

"I know you don't want to meet with her," he says, "but on the off chance she ever does write about you, this gives you a chance to tell your side of the story. You can set ground rules that prevent her from publishing anything unless your name becomes public."

"But you said she doesn't know my name."

"Correct. And you don't have to give it to her. Just be sure you set the rules before you begin talking."

"And if I refuse?"

"Worst case is that she hears it from the police and writes about you, though even then she'd want to contact you for comment."

"You're talking me out of it. Why risk calling her now if I'll get a chance later?"

"Because a million other reporters are chasing this story. If someone else gets it and takes it public, you might not have time."

Kelly is silent for a few seconds, and when she speaks again, she sounds choked up. "So what should I do?" she says.

Now he's caught. He would like to be helpful to both Kelly and Molly, but he has to choose.

"Tell her no," he says.

"You tell her for me," Kelly says and hangs up.

He immediately asks his all-knowing car to call Molly, and he tells her that Kelly isn't ready. He doesn't say that she will never be ready.

Sam gets to the airport, parks in the hourly lot, and walks over. He's early and the plane is a half hour late, which gives him a chance to check his phone for any news. There's nothing new in his own paper, so he looks at the South Carolina media to see what they're saying. He finds articles on Morgan's legacy, plans for a memorial service, and the inevitable speculation about who will be chosen to succeed him. He reads it all but learns nothing of importance.

The airport display sign blinks and then shows Betsy's plane arriving, and he ambles down to the baggage area where they planned to meet. It takes another twenty minutes before she and Logan come into view and Sam smiles broadly. They haven't spotted him yet, and that gives him a chance to admire his daughter and grandson. They're both dressed too warmly for what is a nice spring day, but they've come from Minneapolis, where it's much colder. Betsy wears a parka, but Logan has already taken off his jacket and carries it with one hand, not caring that he's dragging it on the floor. He's at that cute six-year-old stage, and Sam goes over to greet them. They talk somewhat awkwardly about the flight and the weather until the baggage conveyer belt rumbles into motion. Soon they have their bags and are loading them into his car.

Logan is quiet at the airport, but once in the car, he chatters nonstop. He's an outgoing kid who makes friends easily, both with other children and adults. Logan hasn't spent nearly enough time with Sam to know him well, but that doesn't stop him from recounting his own views of the trip and his hopes for the weekend.

"We're taking care of Grandma's dog," he says. "I'm going to be in charge of feeding her and Mommy's going to walk her."

"What will that leave for me?" Sam asks.

Logan considers that. "You can help us, and if she runs away, you can go after her because you have a car."

Sam agrees and says he hopes they can do some fun things together in addition to caring for Dodger while Grandma's away.

"He's your dog too," Logan suddenly remembers. This is their first visit since the separation, and Sam doesn't know what Logan's been told. He looks at Betsy, but she offers no clue. Just the opposite, in fact.

"You remember when we all stayed together at Christmas, don't you?"

Logan looks out the window instead of answering, and Sam figures that's okay. He doesn't want to press the point or prompt questions about living arrangements.

Soon, they reach the house, which sits back on a residential street in a well-off neighborhood, a stately colonial with a large, well-landscaped yard, the kind of home a successful lawyer and a somewhat-successful journalist can afford.

After pulling into the driveway and getting out of the car, Sam takes a few seconds to look around. He takes a big breath. Bethesda isn't exactly country, but the air smells fresher than in the city. Maybe his imagination is working overtime, but he feels invigorated by it.

When they open the door, Dodger is waiting, her tail wagging so hard her whole back end is moving. She greets Sam like the old friend he is, and soon remembers, or at least accepts, Betsy and Logan. Logan is careful, but not afraid, and Dodger seems to appreciate that. Sam figures Dodger needs to go out, so he opens the backdoor and gives her a few minutes in the fenced yard.

Betsy and Logan unpack and settle in their rooms. Sam slips his bag into another guest room and realizes it's lunchtime and he hasn't talked to Lisa about food. But he needn't have worried. The pantry and refrigerator are well stocked, and Sam gets to work making tuna fish sandwiches, with help from Betsy and kibitzing from Logan, who only likes mayonnaise on one side of his sandwich. He asks for a pickle, and Sam finds a jar in the refrigerator.

Sam cleans up after lunch and sits down with Betsy and Logan to plan an active weekend. It's already after two, and Betsy and Logan say they want to spend the afternoon hanging around.

"Fine, but Dodger needs a walk," Sam says. "Who wants to come?"

Betsy says she'd rather lie down, but Logan agrees to tag along. He acts tentative, though, reminding Sam that they don't have a close relationship. He tells himself that's what this weekend is for.

But the walk provides little opportunity for talk, mostly because Logan keeps leaving the path to explore the park. He's avoiding Sam, or so it seems, and Sam doesn't push it. They have all weekend. He asks a few questions about school and Logan's friends, but the loquaciousness that Logan had in the car and at lunch is gone. Without his mother in attendance, he's more reserved, or maybe he's just getting tired.

When they return, Betsy is napping and Sam tries to engage Logan in a game of checkers, but Logan doesn't know how and doesn't want to learn. He asks instead for Betsy's iPad, and soon he's lost in some video game. It gives Sam a chance to think about his problem.

He starts by checking his phone for news, finds none, and calls both Lisa, who doesn't answer, and Molly, who's focused on Antifa Man. When she finally asks again for Kelly's name, Sam asks what her source is telling her, and she gets defensive.

"It's more than one. I always get two sources."

Sam lets that go without comment and offers to call his friend Howie, and she doesn't object.

"They've got several leads they're chasing, but it's taking a long time," Howie says when Sam asks for an update. "Everyone from the president to the mayor is on their back, and everyone's frustrated. The pressure from the media doesn't help."

Howie then goes off the record to tell Sam about a conspiracy story gaining traction on the web—that operatives for the Democratic National Committee put out a contract. Sam laughs, but Howie doesn't see the humor in it.

"They still looking for the antifa guy?" Sam asks.

Howie hesitates. "I never said antifa."

"That's what the media is implying. The speculation on cable news is nonstop, and Fox is sure he's a fanatical lefty working with a group."

"As far as I know, he's a loner. No known ties."

"You know his name?"

"No comment."

Sam wonders if Howie would have been told, then figures that if they are looking for a specific person, they must have spread the word. Sam thinks about telling Howie that he talked to the guy and he may soon turn himself in, then realizes he can't be sure of that, so he says nothing. He tries another tack.

"Is the widow a suspect?" Sam asks.

"You know the drill," Howie continues. "Everybody's a suspect until they're not, and the spouse is always first in line. There's enough reason to look seriously at her."

Sam is tempted to ask about ex-girlfriends to see if Howie has heard about Kelly but decides he better not. It's bad enough he's milking his friend for details while getting cute about it and withholding his own information. He doesn't want to cross the line into outright deception.

"What about Morgan's phone and computers?" he asks instead. "Forensics on the car? Anything come back yet?"

"He left his official cell at home, but the officers on his security detail said he had more than one. There wasn't one in the car, so if he had one with him, the killer must have taken it. We're trying to track it down, but so far, no luck. We've got his computers and they've put all manner of rush on going through them, but it's always slower than you want."

Howie hesitates and then adds. "There's one thing I can tell you. The ballistics confirm that the gun that killed him was his own, the one in the car with the body. We pretty much knew that. He had a permit to carry and often did when he wasn't with his security detail or in the Capitol. The thing is, I can't see that many people would know he carried, which makes it unlikely his killer was a stranger or someone pissed off about his politics. They would have brought their own gun."

"You sure about that? He didn't mention his permit at some gun rally or on TV?"

Howie hesitates and Sam guesses he hadn't thought of that. "That's worth checking," Howie says. "But I can't believe he'd be that stupid. I still think an outsider would bring his own gun."

"Maybe he did, but Morgan pulled his, they wrestled, and it became the murder weapon. The killer left it in the car to confuse you guys."

"Possible, but that requires a lot of luck and coincidence."

"Then why do you think it was the wife?" Sam asks.

"I never said that. Might be her, but it could also be a jilted lover."

Sam hesitates at that. "Only if she knew he'd have his gun with him."

"Or if she knew he always kept it in the glove compartment or something like that. Maybe got to it when he had his guard–or his pants—down. Can't rule it out."

Sam is surprised Howie is so forthcoming, but by the time the call concludes, they are back where they started. Lots of suspects to look at.

Sam feels obligated to give Molly something, so he calls her back and tells her about the gun, but she tells him it's all old news. She already had that.

"Anything else?" she asks.

"Not really," he admits, "but my source says they're still looking at a lot of people, not just your antifa friend."

"He's still number one on the list. They had a lead on him, but he's gone underground. That's pretty suspicious."

"Not so underground that he didn't contact you," he reminds her. "And I think he's serious about turning himself in."

"Has he called Lisa?"

"Not that I know of."

"Then not so serious, I'd say."

Sam lets it go. She may be right, but he doesn't think so. "Have you heard anything to suggest they're looking seriously at the wife?"

"No more than usual. You know the drill, the spouse is—"

He cuts her off before she can repeat it. "It might be more than routine. Maybe she was fed up with his affairs."

"Is that the feeling you got when you talked to her?"

Sam thinks about it and admits to himself that Peg Morgan had seemed at peace with it. He thinks for a moment how he would feel if Lisa had ever had an affair. He knows how much it would have hurt and finds it hard to believe that anyone could live with that without constant anxiety. But he doesn't tell Molly that.

"Who knows how anybody really feels?" he says instead.

Antifa Man

Andy and Stevie can never agree on anything, at least not without a lot of arguing, so it surprises me when they respond in unison.

"Are you crazy? It's gotta be a trap!"

I've just finished telling them about the offer of a free lawyer and the suggestion that I go to the FBI.

"I can't believe you're even thinking about it," Stevie says.

He's the smart one. At least the smarter one, while Andy is what we sometimes think of as our goon. Big and strong and willing to do things—or push us to do things—when we might otherwise err on the side of caution. We usually stay away from the rough stuff, preferring to make life difficult for our enemies by exposing their lies, hacking computers, and spreading embarrassing stuff on the internet. That's our usual MO. Though not always.

I'm not as good with the techie stuff as Stevie, but I'm no slouch either. I had no trouble with the Galaxy that reporter was using. Waste of money, those things. Airtight security, my ass.

Not that I found much. I did download all her contacts and text messages, some of which clearly related to her reporting about Morgan. But her sources were careful. Nothing from them. Be a lot better if I could get at her computer. I've got her home address, and we might see how hard it would be to break in, but I bet the good stuff is all at the office, and that would be far too risky.

It was Stevie's skills that allowed us to go after Morgan and get into his computer. Found some good stuff, including amateur porn, that we had some fun with. We found some memos that let us leak some good stories to the press, and we even got into his bank account. The harassment can be fun, but I have to admit it's more satisfying to know there's now one less asshole to worry about.

Anyway, Stevie says we ought to lay low and maybe even get out of town. He doesn't trust the newspaper, was against my contacting them, and thinks they'll turn me in.

I don't see it that way. I still think I can manipulate the girl. She's so desperate for a story. I just have to handle her better than I did the first time.

Stevie says I'm being foolish, and he has Andy on his side. It was Stevie who came up with the plan to run the reporter through Costco to lose any tail, and it's a good thing. He's sure some guy was following her, but we shook him. At first, I thought it was Ethics man, but Andy says the guy was young and Hispanic, which isn't true of Ethics man. I know, I checked.

I do worry a little about Ethics man. It was weird for him to suggest a lawyer. That could be a trap, but how ethical would that be? Not very.

I checked out his wife on the internet and she's legit. Stevie says that doesn't matter. He doesn't believe the feds know my name—how could they?—and he keeps saying the minute I walk in there, I'll be arrested for something. Maybe not murder, but no telling which of our other good deeds they're chasing as crimes. They'd arrest Robin Hood if they could.

The big problem is my alibi. Stevie and Andy would back me up if I asked them to, and Stevie says if I tell the feds I was home alone, they'll never give me a minute's peace. But it would be too risky to bring them into this. Andy has a few burglaries he's wanted for, though that was before he hooked up with us, and Stevie is on probation for hacking into the EPA computer. Never mind that we found all that shit they were trying to hide about the pollution in Lake Ondingo. It turned into the biggest scandal in EPA history.

Stevie wants to use the money we stole from Morgan to get out of town and stay quiet. But running will only make me look guilty, and I'd never be able to relax. No way. And we really should move on to the next target, that asshole Marie van Hart. Be good to go after a Democrat for a change and if we work it right, we can get her defeated in the primary. Every day that passes is a day closer to planet extinction. We can't afford to waste any time. Anyway, I think it's worth talking to this lawyer, at least see what she says. If Stevie's right that it's a setup, I'm smart enough to recognize it. Andy and Stevie don't need to know.

But I'll call the reporter first. She's desperate for a story and if I can give her a little more to explain what we're trying to do, I might get through to her.

Oh man, it's too confusing. Hard to know what's the right thing to do.

Family Ties

Sam and Betsy take turns looking through the refrigerator and suggesting possible dinner menus, all of which Logan rejects.

"Pizza," he says. "I haven't had pizza in days."

"You had it Thursday," Betsy points out. "That was two days ago."

"You said I could choose."

Betsy and Sam exchange glances, silently asking each other who made such a promise. But after a day at the zoo, neither is in the mood to cook, so they order a pizza and salads from the menu that Lisa has conveniently left out on the counter.

Sam makes gin and tonics for Betsy and himself, and they pry Logan away from the iPad so they can all talk while they're waiting. Logan gets a little wild, racing around the circle made up by the kitchen, dining room, and living room until he flops down somewhat exhausted. He's talking nonstop, and Sam has trouble understanding him, so Betsy has to translate.

"He's the airline pilot from our flight and he's warning us about the static. I think he means turbulence."

"The shaking. It almost made me throw up."

The pizza arrives, and they settle around the small table in the kitchen. Logan eats half a piece and then starts stacking all the pepperoni he can get his hands on. Sam takes one from the middle, toppling the stack, and sticks it in his mouth, which doesn't please Logan. "Mom said you want to be friends with me. That's not the way to do it."

Sam looks at Betsy, who gives him a sheepish grin but doesn't say anything. Sam looks back to Logan. "We are friends, aren't we?"

Logan won't commit. "Don't take any more pepperoni."

Sam promises to behave.

When Betsy starts clearing the dishes, Sam pulls out his phone again to check for any news on the Morgan killing, but he finds little. The early stories for the Sunday papers are about the planned memorial service and speculation about who will take over the Judiciary Committee. There's competition between another outspoken senator and one who is more moderate and productive. One of the papers even calls him more judicious.

Sam reads *Curious George at the Baseball Game* to Logan before he goes to sleep, and then Sam and Betsy settle in the great room, Sam with bourbon and Betsy with herbal tea. The room is Sam's favorite, with built-in bookshelves and a leather couch and chairs that still smell new. Betsy puts her feet up on an ottoman, and Sam senses they are about to have a serious talk. He's soon proven right.

"So," Betsy begins, and lets the word hang. Sam waits with a Cheshire cat smile on his face.

"Mom says you've got yourself mixed up in a big story that could get you in trouble."

He cocks his head but doesn't comment.

"Want to tell me about it?"

He's tempted to ask what Lisa has said but decides it's better to give his own version. He begins with the email and takes her through the chain of events.

When he finishes, Betsy reaches for the teapot, stirs it, and refills her cup. He knows she's formulating her response, which isn't like her.

"So does this have anything to do with your split with Mom?" she says. "It's not just a way to keep busy so it doesn't hurt so much, is it?"

"Is that what she thinks?"

Betsy raises an eyebrow but doesn't say anything.

"She's wrong," he says. "That's got nothing to do with it."

"Are you sure? You don't usually get so involved. You always told us your job was to observe and report, not try to fix the world."

"This is different. The email made me a participant."

"That was your choice, though. You could have ignored it or reported it to the police."

Sam sighs. "The separation does play into it, but not in the way you suggest. I can't deny that at another time when I was in a different place, I might have kept my distance from this woman and not tried to help her the way I have, but separating from your mom has changed my outlook. It's made me think a lot about what really matters in life. I don't want to feel sorry for myself. On the contrary, I want to be less selfish. I want to make a contribution to people, and this is a way."

"But doesn't your column do that? You do a lot of good through the advice you give. You do help people."

He considers that. "In a way, I do," he says. "But it's all at arm's length, and it's pretty superficial. The format means the questions and the answers need to be short, which often makes it hard to examine the circumstances. It leads to a lot of over-simplification, a lot of relying on black and white rules applied to very gray situations. This is different anyway. It's a woman who's really hurting and if I can help somehow, I want to do that. You can understand that, can't you? If someone in trouble came to you for help or advice, would you ignore it?"

"She came to you talking about committing a crime. If I did anything, I would urge her to go to the police, and if she didn't, I'd be tempted to go myself."

He reminds her that's pretty much what he did. "I didn't feel doing nothing was an option. She seemed genuine and she was a mess. Still is. I had to help. Once Morgan was killed, and it became clear he was the ex-lover she was talking about, she did go to the police. Now it's up to them."

"But you waited until after the murder. For all you know, you might have been able to prevent it."

"That's harsh. I didn't know her name. I didn't have enough to go to the police."

Betsy takes a breath, looks away, and waits several seconds before responding. "Anyway," she says after turning back to him. "You're still involved. There's this other guy the police suspect, and you hooked him up with the newspaper."

He corrects her about Molly's scoop and explains that he only got drawn into that to help. "I have an obligation to help the newspaper. They pay my salary."

"They pay you to write an ethics column, not to solve murders."

Now it is his turn to get up and refresh his drink, adding what he guesses is just an ounce of bourbon. He tells himself not to get annoyed, but it's hard.

"Is that your mother talking again?" he asks when he sits down. "I get the impression she doesn't think what I'm doing is ethical."

"How is it ethical to help the girl when she's one of the suspects?"

"Your mother's willing to help the other suspect, isn't she? Is that different?"

Betsy sighs. "You know it is. She's a lawyer. She's paid to take sides."

"No pay in this case."

"Dad, don't be silly. Besides, that was your idea. She's doing you a favor."

He looks at her and is reminded that his little girl has gotten older. Her hair is a mousy brown and a curl is out of place. He sees faint lines around her eyes, and she looks tired from the day's sightseeing. But none of that is relevant.

"I haven't done anything unethical. Nothing serious."

"What's the unserious part?"

He thinks a second, though he doesn't really need to. "I've kept some information from the newspaper, and I haven't been completely honest with Molly. Even tricked her into going to a meeting that wasn't real, but I only did it because I was worried about her safety. That's not truly unethical unless you take the extreme view that there's never a good reason to lie, which I don't. And, in fact, I've done a lot of good here. I was the one who persuaded Kelly to go to the police, and I'm trying to do the same with this other guy. What's wrong with that?"

"Maybe nothing, other than it's not your job to do that. But you know that better than I do. What bothers Mom is that you're withholding evidence and doing your own investigation, which is a little weird and maybe dangerous. You could lose your job or worse. And to be honest, what you've said to me tonight isn't reassuring. You're being inconsistent and giving a lot of explanations that seem more like rationalizations. It's not like you at all."

He makes a face. He knows there's some truth in what she's saying, and he knows he's cut some corners, but he really believes he's done more good than harm. "I'll be careful," is all he says, and the way he says it makes it clear he is done talking about it.

Betsy lets it go, moves over to the couch, and snuggles into him. Sam knows she doesn't want this to turn into an argument, and neither does he. He changes the subject and says how much he enjoys spending time with Logan. "He's a wonderful kid."

Betsy smiles. "He has his moments. I wish I could give him a sibling."

"I was an only child, and believe me, it has its advantages." When Betsy was pregnant with Logan, there had been complications, some of them scary, and ultimately the doctors told her she shouldn't have any more children. She and Ben considered adoption but decided against it.

"So how are you doing otherwise?" Betsy asks Sam. "You always say fine, but you never give me any details, and I'm never sure whether to believe you."

"I'm fine. Honest."

"You need something else in your life besides work. It doesn't have to be a woman—maybe it's too soon for that—but something. Maybe a new hobby."

He smiles. "I'm a little too old for new hobbies. I'm fine, really."

"Maybe you should write a book. About ethics. Or about Congress. You have the credentials."

"Is this your mother's idea too? Does this mean there's no chance of our getting back together?"

Betsy looks at him and their eyes meet. "I don't know about that. It's not my business, but she is worried about you."

Sam lets out a sigh that comes from deep within. "I know she thinks I'm lonely and that's why I'm doing this."

"Isn't it? You said you feel isolated and need to be connected and helpful."

"No. Really, no. I'm doing it because I have no other choice. And because I think I can help."

Molly calls early Sunday morning. "I got a text from him."

"From Antifa Man?"

"He wants to meet again. He says he can explain more and will give me what I need to write a story. He's desperate to tell his side."

"Molly, it's too dangerous."

"No, it's not. We're meeting in a public place—what could he do to me? Besides, you'll be there."

"Me?"

Her sigh is audible. "He's insisting on it. He's gotten it into his head that you're the boss and he needs to convince both of us."

The idea intrigues Sam—he wants to go. He hates the idea of missing out on time with Betsy and Logan, but it'll help him figure out what to make of the guy.

"Did he say anything about calling Lisa?" he asks.

"No, and I didn't ask. I'd rather he talks to me first. Did he call her?"

"Not as far as I know. When does he want to see you?"

"Today. At noon. We agreed to meet at the café in the National Gallery."

Sam thinks about it, but only for a few seconds. "Where exactly are you meeting him?"

"I told him I'd be at a corner table at the Cascade Café in the East Gallery."

"Okay, but go instead to the West Gallery, to that Garden café they have."

"What difference does it make?"

"For safety. Make him text you from whatever phone he's using and make him promise to keep it on. Wait until a few minutes before noon and text him the change in restaurants. I'll follow him as he goes across and make sure he's alone."

"But how will you recognize him?"

"By your description."

Molly hesitates. "This is silly. What could possibly happen? What are you afraid of?"

Sam admits to himself that he's not sure, but his gut tells him to take some precaution, so he insists. He asks her for a description of Antifa Man and keeps pressing for more details until he has enough.

He tells Betsy he has to go out and she'll have to take Logan sightseeing—they're headed to the Lincoln Memorial—by herself without offering an explanation. She looks at him as if she's about to ask where he's going and why, but then she holds her tongue.

Kelly

I wake feeling somewhat better. At least, there's no lead ball in my stomach, and it's easier to get out of bed. Showering helps, and I have a real breakfast of cereal and yogurt. No small thing for me.

The police interview was bad, though I suppose it could have been worse. I think the detective believed me, and maybe the cops won't feel a need to look too deeply. I hope so.

I tell myself I really am better, though my mood keeps shifting as I wonder what will happen next. At first, I felt nothing but fear, but that's changed. I'm able to think straight, at least some of the time. And that's the only way I'll get out of this.

I'm not sorry—he had it coming. What I really want to feel is relief. Wade is dead. Wade is dead. Wade is dead. I say it several times. I don't have to worry any more about what he can do to me. But there's no relief.

Even in my good moments, it's not like anything is back to normal. The fear is strong. I worry they'll arrest me or that our affair will get into the papers. I'm glad to see the newspaper stories focus on that nut who threatened Wade. Still, they've begun to hint about Wade's womanizing—God, I hate that word—but it's all pretty vague.

That's one thing I can be thankful for. Wade went out of his way to keep me a secret. Never went out in public after the first meeting. He always came alone, usually by Zipcar. No security. No aides involved in setting up our nights together.

I know he loved me, at least in the early months. And I don't believe I was one of many, but I guess there's no denying he was a serial cheater. I was a fool. I'll plead guilty to that. I was an ass, but he was an asshole.

As long as they don't think I'm guilty, the police won't make our affair public—and his wife certainly won't—so no one will ever know my name. And there'll be no more pictures circulating on the internet.

Now if I can persuade them I wasn't involved so they leave me alone. All of them. The police. Mr. Ethics. The reporters. And of course Ariana and Danny. Especially Ariana and Danny.

They are coming over this morning, so I pull on jeans and a cotton sweater. I've lost weight, and not in a good way. I look terrible. At least I washed my hair.

I make another pot of coffee and before it can drip through, the doorbell rings. I greet them, giving Danny a light hug and getting a kiss on the cheek. Ariana insists on a closer hug and doesn't seem to want to let go.

"How are you?" she says.

I've come to hate the question, especially from her. There's no right answer. "Better," I say. "Going to the police was a good idea."

"I knew you'd feel better. I'm glad you took the advice."

Typical. Rather than make me feel good about going, she takes credit for pushing the idea.

"I hope they believe you," Ariana adds.

Any sense of relief quickly vanishes, and I have a sudden desire to be alone. I don't know why they've come.

When we're seated, I get my answer. Danny says that the self-declared Ethics man told him I refused to talk to that newspaper reporter. "Maybe you should," he says.

"Why on earth would I want to talk to her?" I ask. "The last thing I want is publicity. Let the newspapers write about the guy who made the threats."

"Someone in law enforcement is obviously leaking parts of their investigation," Ariana says. "Who's to say they won't leak something about you? That's why it makes sense to take the initiative and get out ahead of it."

"Think of it as insurance," Danny says, speaking more calmly. "The press is beginning to talk about Morgan's affairs and they might find out about you. You can preempt that by talking about what a rat he was."

I can't believe they mean this. Danny is so hung up on journalism, he thinks it has all the answers. But I know better. Journalists never consider the consequences of their actions. Danny doesn't realize that anything I say will draw attention to the fact that I had a good motive for killing Wade. How can this possibly help?

"You want reporters on your side," Ariana adds, trying another tack. "It shows you have nothing to hide, right?"

I don't miss the implication in that or the fact that they are ganging up on me. "If you had the slightest understanding of what I've been through, you'd never ask me to talk about it with another stranger," I tell her, my voice rising. "Going to the police was pure hell. I'm not telling the same story to a reporter. What can I possibly say that wouldn't make me suspect number one?"

"You tell the whole story," Ariana says, "and she'll be sympathetic. And write a sympathetic story."

Were these people born yesterday?

"It's way too risky," I say. "If the newspaper runs a story, the cable networks won't rest until they get hold of my name. I'm not doing it."

"Waiting for it to leak could be more risky," Ariana says, but Danny softens her comment.

"No one's trying to force you," he says. "It's just an idea. It's obviously your call, and if the police don't consider you a suspect, you may not need to put yourself through it."

I thank him and we try to talk about other things, though not with much success. The conversation is awkward, and they finally get up to leave. It's then that my phone rings. I glance at it and let it go to voicemail.

"Anything important?" Ariana asks. "You look concerned."

"Just my mom," I lie.

After they leave, I listen to the message from Detective Latisha Thompson. She wants me to come back for another interview.

Confrontation Over Brunch

Sam picks up Molly outside her apartment building and drives down to the National Mall. Getting there by Metro would be easier on this April Sunday, but he wants the car for added flexibility.

They go early, which is good, because they have to circle several times before finding a place to park. It's twenty minutes before noon, and Sam sends Molly to the West Gallery and tells her to wait for his text. He finds a bench and checks to make sure his phone is on.

He has Molly's description of Antifa Man and his own powers of observation. He sees four people that might fit, but he can't be sure, and he knows it's possible that the guy has already been there an hour. At eleven-fifty, he texts Molly to send the message changing the location.

Sam gets luckier than he has any right to expect. A minute later he sees a possible match, a man walking toward the museum who suddenly stops, checks his phone, makes a face, and then heads to the West Gallery. Sam waits a bit before following. As far as he can tell, the guy is alone. So far, so good.

Molly and Antifa Man are already seated when Sam enters, joins them, introduces himself, and extends a hand to shake. A waiter appears and they hurry through their orders. As soon as they're alone, Molly opens her notebook and gets right to the point. She's already told Sam this is her story and warned him against taking over.

"You said you had more information for me?"

"Can we trade? I'll give you some information if you tell me what the police told you about me. Do they actually think I killed the guy? Because I didn't."

"Then go tell them that," Sam says, drawing a cold look from Molly.

"I need to know what to expect," Antifa Man says. "Do they think I'd be stupid enough to send him threats if I planned to kill him?"

"I don't know what they think," Molly says. "I thought you were ready to talk to me. If you give me information that I can verify, I can write your side of the story. Get it out there before you're named and assumed guilty."

"Do they really know my name?"

Molly consults her notes. "They do if it's Carl Wasserman."

He almost spits out the water he's drinking, his surprise leaving no doubt that it's his real name. Sam looks at Molly, equally surprised, and she gives him a look of satisfaction at having gotten the name and kept it from him.

"I didn't do it," he says, keeping his voice low. The other tables are closer than any of them would like.

"You ought to go to the FBI before they find you," Sam says, but Molly interrupts before Wasserman can respond.

"Leave the FBI for later," she says. "You got me here saying you wanted to give me more information. What information?"

He starts telling her his life story, where he was born and how his parents split and his mother often left him to fend for himself. How he survived because he was smarter than his parents and had an uncle who helped him and teachers who recognized his potential. How he did so well in school that he earned a full ride at Johns Hopkins. How he thought about public service, but gradually realized how intractable the problems were and how no one was interested in real solutions.

"I'm not crazy," he says when he finishes. "I can't sit back and do nothing when they're destroying the world. We need a revolution."

Molly writes it all down, while Sam sits quietly taking it in, trying to decide whether Wasserman is sincere, naïve, or a little off his head. All three, he decides.

"So you sent threats to senators?" Molly asks. "How was that going to help?"

"I thought shutting them up would allow a more reasoned public debate."

"And did the threats shut them up or did you need stronger medicine?"

Wasserman stares her down. "I'm sure it made them think twice."

They talk more about the threats, Molly wanting more details and Wasserman refusing to give them. After a while she gives up and says she has what she needs. She gives Sam a look to see if he agrees.

When Sam hesitates, she says she can write a story that gives a human element to what she's already written about the man the police are after. "Almost like a feature."

"Exactly," Wasserman says, "but you can't use my name."

"It's not your decision," Molly says. "I got it from a cop, not from you."

Panic spreads across Wasserman's face. "No, please. If you do that, I'll have to leave the country and never come back."

Sam knows Brenda would never allow the name into the story unless he's arrested, but he takes advantage of the fact that Wasserman doesn't know that. "There's another option," Sam says. "You call the lawyer I gave you and go to the police. We won't run the story until you've done that, and then we'll run it without your name unless you're arrested and the FBI gives it out."

"But you have to decide quickly," Molly says. "I won't give you more than thirty-six hours."

The waiter comes to clear their plates, giving them all a moment to think.

Sam knows that thirty-six hours is more than enough time for Wasserman to get out of the country, but he doesn't say anything.

When the waiter leaves, Wasserman gives in. "This is blackmail. You're not giving me any choice."

"One other question," Molly says, ignoring his last comment. "What about your alibi for the night he was killed? You said you were with friends, but you won't give the names of the others who were there. You're going to have to. The FBI will want to talk to them and so do I."

"I can't give up the other guys I was with. They've done some things and they'd get in trouble, to say nothing of how they'd feel about me."

"Did they threaten Morgan too?" Sam asks.

Wasserman shakes his head. "No, that was me. And none of us had anything to do with Morgan's murder, if that's what you're thinking. We were all together that night."

"You have to tell all that to Lisa when you talk to her," Sam says. "She needs to know the whole story. And being together doesn't cut it if your buddies do bad things. You need to prove you weren't together killing Morgan."

Wasserman shakes his head vigorously. "No. It wasn't us. I wouldn't be sitting here telling you all this if it were. I'd be in Mexico or Costa Rica already."

"Or maybe, that's what you want us to believe," Molly says.

Wasserman shakes his head again. "I didn't do it, but I can't use my friends for an alibi. The cops would never believe them anyway. I might as well say I was home alone. Same thing in the end."

They all sit silently thinking about that, but neither Sam nor Molly offers a direct response.

"Thirty-six hours," Molly says to end the conversation. "That's the deal."

Wasserman nods, stands, and walks away.

Sam signals for the check and hands it to Molly. "You can expense it. I'm still on vacation."

She takes it and then drains the last of her water. "You believe him?"

"It doesn't matter what I believe."

Molly bites down on her lip. "It's in everyone's interest for him to turn himself in. He'll come around to see that, and that will give my story a lot more punch."

Sam doesn't bother reminding her that there's another way it could work out—with Wasserman running as far and as fast as he can in the other direction.

Peg

How did she find me? That's what I want to know. No one knew I was at my sister's house but the task force, the security team, and Turner, and they all promised they wouldn't tell. But here she is.

"I'm sorry to bother you," she says, not meaning a word of it. "I just have a few questions."

"How did you find me?"

She doesn't answer, but I let her in. Why did I do that? Why didn't I send her away as soon as she identified herself as that reporter? I guess curiosity, especially when she said she was writing another story about Wade and wanted to "give me a chance to comment." I know what that means. I haven't been a senator's wife for twenty-two years without learning a thing or two.

Once I ask her in, I put on my polite façade (force of habit) and even offer her refreshments, which she declines. I take her into my brother-in-law's study where we can have some privacy from my sister and the housekeeper. She's dressed inappropriately in black faux-denim slacks and a tight sweater. What I notice most, though, is the dark roots of her hair and the fact that she needs a manicure. And why is she wearing sneakers?

"So how can I help you, Molly?" It's not quite as blunt a question as 'what do you want?' but I'm not sure yet where this is going, and I decide that as long as I let her in, I might as well play along.

"I've been covering the investigation, as you probably know."

I don't normally pay attention to bylines—not like Wade did, anyway—but I've been devouring every story about the murder I can get my hands on.

"Yes, I've read your stories," I say. "Are the police any closer to catching this antifa terrorist?" Nothing like starting with offense, Wade taught me. Or at least getting what you want before giving anything up.

"Well, that's not entirely clear. I suspect it won't be long before they find him, but he's only a person of interest. The FBI isn't saying he's a suspect. Of course, they're pursuing other avenues as well."

"But he threatened Wade. That's what you wrote in your story."

She nods. "That's why they want to talk to him, but your husband got other threats, as well."

"You said he was the most persistent and . . . specific."

She smiles at that. "That's what they tell me. Did your husband ever talk about the threats? Did he take them seriously? Anyone in particular he worried about?"

"He told me about them only in general terms. He never mentioned any names, if that's what you're asking. Not sure he ever knew them and in any event, he wanted to protect me, or at least keep me from being alarmed."

"Did it work? Did you worry?"

"I learned to live with it. What choice did I have?"

"So he never showed you any threatening letters or emails? You never heard any phone calls?"

"No, I'm afraid I can't help at all with specifics," I say, and when she stops writing in her notebook—I've no idea why she is because I haven't said anything worth writing down—I try to turn the tables.

"You said the police were pursuing other avenues. I haven't seen that in the papers. What does it mean?"

She looks at me and our eyes lock. I know what's coming and she knows I know what's coming.

"Mrs. Morgan, there's no easy way to ask this, but were you aware of your husband having relationships with other women?"

I give her my coldest stare, but she doesn't blink. "I assume this discussion is off the record."

"You didn't mention that before," she says.

I resist pointing out there was no need because I haven't said anything yet. "Well, I'm saying it now. If you can't grant that, I'll have to ask you to leave."

She closes her notebook. "Okay, off the record."

I call out to Rosa. My guest may not want anything, but I ask for coffee. "Are you sure you don't want some?"

She accepts and I realize it was a mistake because it will prolong the meeting.

"Well," she continues, "off the record, can you tell me whether there were other women in his life?"

"Are you married?"

She smiles. "I will be in May." But then she bites her lip and I pick up on the anxiety.

"Good luck," I say, hoping to keep it neutral. "Do you know what percentage of men cheat on their wives?"

"Is that a yes? You knew he saw other women?" She's losing patience with me, as if I care.

"Let's cut to the chase," I tell her. "What do you know that's relevant to Wade's murder?"

She considers that and decides on a more direct approach. "I've heard that he'd recently been dumped by another woman, and he didn't take it well. That he was harassing and threatening her."

"Hmm. Doesn't sound like something Wade would do. I doubt that very much."

"There's some evidence of it."

When I ask what, she won't say.

"If you want information," I tell her, "you have to give information, my dear."

She shakes her head. "You want me to respect the fact that this is off the record. I have to do the same with other sources as well."

"I'm not your source. In fact, I think you should finish your coffee and leave."

"Can you at least tell me, off the record, that you were aware of his affairs?"

"Of course, I was. Now you tell me whether the police suspect this woman you say he was seeing."

"They're keeping an open mind. Right now, they're more interested in the guy who threatened the senator, but if they find he's not the one, they're going to look more closely at this other woman."

I don't respond to that other than to stand. "Nice to meet you," I say, taking her arm and walking her to the door.

"Same here," she says, but she's not quite through. "I assume the other woman is a suspect, but if you knew about his affairs, that might make you a suspect too."

I shut the door, but not before giving her my best smile.

Cable News Histrionics

MSNBC leads with the story three hours later. Law enforcement has a new angle, a breathless reporter tells viewers, the usual "Breaking News" banner parked at the bottom of the screen. Police are now looking hard at Morgan's private life, which includes a series of affairs, including at least one that may have ended with recriminations and revenge porn.

The reporters in the newsroom have circled the TV, all listening carefully. Molly mutters under her breath, and Sam, who's standing next to her, shakes his head, before touching her arm and leading her back to her cubicle.

She tells him how angry she is at him for keeping her from using the email. "That scoop should have been mine," she says. "You should have let me push harder on it instead of wasting so much time on Antifa Man, who's probably a dead end."

"I didn't send you after him. Your sources did that. And anyway, it wasn't wasted time. You got a good interview out of it. Have you written it up yet?"

Molly reaches for her water bottle and takes a sip before answering. "I turned it in, and Brenda is doing her usual agonizing over whether I have enough. But I'm pretty sure she'll say yes once the lawyers give their okay."

"Does she know I was there?"

"Yeah. That surprised her, but I think she was glad. Not sure she totally trusts me."

"Of course she does."

"What are you doing here anyway?" she asks. "I thought you were on a stay-out-of-the-fray vacation."

"I don't see a conflict anymore. You and your law enforcement friends have everything I had, so what's the point?"

"Maybe keeping your job? You're still keeping that email secret, to say nothing about your conversations with the woman who wrote it. If you start working the story and Brenda finds out, she'll kill you."

"My email friend told everything to the police, which makes the email irrelevant."

"Hardly. I bet she didn't tell them about her threat to kill him."

Sam takes a breath, knowing she has a point. Does he have an obligation to tell the police about the email? He thinks about that. The email doesn't prove anything. He's delivered Kelly to the task force. Let them take it from here.

"Anyway," he says to Molly, who's busy rubbing moisturizer on her hands. "Brenda asked me to come in and help."

"She wouldn't have if she knew the whole story."

He doesn't argue. "What kind of story did you write about Wasserman?"

"I made it a kind of feature, and Brenda is talking about running it in Arts & Style, though I really don't think it fits there. Anyway, I just laid out the facts. That he contacted me, admitted the threats but denied having anything to do with Morgan's murder. Hopefully, I'll be able to add that he turned himself in, but I wrote it to run either way. I let him tell his side of the story."

"You didn't use his name?"

"No. I told him I wouldn't, and I know Brenda would have been against it. If they arrest him, that will change, obviously. In the meantime, I need to focus on your pen pal. I need to use her email. It's the way to get ahead of the networks on this."

"You've got the Wasserman story. How many scoops do you need in one day?"

"It wouldn't be the first time I had two bylines in the paper."

"But you don't know her name and you can't use the threat she put in the email."

"Why not?" she asks, brushing the hair off her face.

"Because that was our deal."

"Which you've broken repeatedly. Maybe now that the networks have the story, she'll talk to me."

"She won't. She knows she has nothing to gain."

"Maybe she'll feel different after the TV reports."

"They didn't name her," Sam points out. "In fact, they said Morgan had been involved with several women, which is true and which the feds know. And she didn't threaten him directly, only in that email to me."

"Maybe she did and maybe the FBI knows that. I'm sure they've been going through his computers and phones. I'll ask. If I get the story on my own, you can't stop me."

Sam sighs. He can see he isn't going to be able to talk her out of it, but if he's forced to, he'll tell Brenda the whole story, regardless of the consequences. She'll be angry, but she'll conclude that under the circumstances, it would be a mistake to write about the email even indirectly. This is one time when the lawyers might be on his side.

Molly reads his thoughts. "Don't you go interfering in this. You still have a conflict of interest. You talked to the woman and your wife may be representing Wasserman."

Sam knows she has a point, but he won't concede. "We'll see."

Molly sighs again and reaches for her water bottle. Sam sits down on the edge of her desk, waiting for her to calm down.

"I'll contact the email sender again," he offers, "and I'll check with Lisa to see if she's heard anything from Wasserman."

Molly looks at him. "Be my guest, but I'm not sitting on that email forever. I'll get it from another source."

That stops Sam. "If the cops don't have her email, I'll go to jail before I show it to them. You can't use it unless you get it from her. I guarantee you Brenda will refuse."

"No matter how mad she gets at you for keeping it a secret?"

"Even if she fires me, she'll defend our right to keep it secret. Besides, I told you that in confidence. You have no right to use it."

"You never said it was off the record."

Sam feels his muscles tense. "Try thinking of all the confidential things you've told me without going off the record."

"This is different."

"Why? Because it gets in the way of your ambition?"

"It's not that."

"Of course, it is. It's exactly that."

He leaves her cubicle, as disappointed in her as he has ever been, but he still doesn't think she'd do anything to get him fired.

Sam goes directly to Brenda's office. "You said you could use some help."

She smiles and invites him in. She has three television monitors in her office, and he can see that CNN has now confirmed the MSNBC report, not that there were many details to confirm. Fox is still focusing on the theory that left-wing extremists are behind the murder.

"Molly wants to go after this story about his woman troubles," Brenda says. "I told her to go ahead but to be sure she gets some new details and doesn't rely on rumors. I want a well-sourced story, not like that vague crap everyone else is putting out."

"I told her I'd help."

"Thanks. I know I can trust you do to what's right."

A moment of shame passes over him, but he tries not to show it.

Sam's phone rings as he enters his office. "You owe me," Lisa says.

"He called?"

"Woke me up at some ungodly hour. I cut my trip short and came back to town to see him."

Sam's first thought is personal. He's planned a last dinner with Betsy and Logan.

"Is he going to go talk to the feds?"

"You know better than to ask that," she says. "I've got to go, but I'll see you later on. Betsy said you're all having dinner at the house."

"If that's okay."

"Of course. Don't wait on me, though. Not sure how long I'll be."

Relieved that his dinner is still on, Sam sits back in his chair. He has the distinct impression that Lisa and Wasserman are going to the FBI tonight, and a part of him wants to alert Molly, but he knows he can't.

Sam is hoping to grill hot dogs and hamburgers for Logan and Betsy, but he gets home too late. Betsy has made spaghetti and meatballs.

"Sorry, but I was afraid you were going to be late, and Logan couldn't wait."

Logan is already eating and ignores them, so Sam hides his disappointment and opens a bottle of Chianti.

"Mmm. That's perfect," Betsy says after the first sip. Sam makes himself a plate and joins them at the small table in the kitchen.

"What'd you guys do today?"

"Museum of Natural History," Betsy says.

"I touched a rock from Mars," Logan adds before Betsy interrupts to tell him to swallow before he talks. "And we saw the Hope diamond. It's really big." He rattles on about other exhibits before he runs out of steam, pauses, and then pops a whole meatball into his mouth. Dodger is seated by his feet, having easily identified the one most likely to drop something edible.

"It was nice," Betsy says. "And Logan clearly enjoyed it. How was your day? You catch the killer?"

Sam knows she's joking, but the question bothers him. There's nothing funny about the killing or the role he's assumed for himself in the investigation. But he hides that feeling.

"The FBI is making some progress. And your mother's return probably means the guy the cops have been looking for is going in to talk to them."

Logan interrupts, apparently unhappy at being left out of the adult talk. He wants to know when Grandma is arriving and whether they are still staying until Wednesday.

"She may not get here until you're asleep," Sam tells him. "But you'll see her tomorrow. You're spending the day together, right?"

Betsy says they're going to the National Aquarium in Baltimore.

"They have sharks and jelly fish," Logan says with a grin. "Are you coming too?" he asks Sam.

"I think your Grandma wants a little time alone with you guys. But we had a good visit, didn't we?"

"So far," Logan answers, never one to jump ahead of himself.

Sam starts to clear the dishes, but Betsy says she'll handle the cleanup and suggests Sam and Logan play a game in the living room. They debate the possibilities and then start working on a puzzle. Dodger joins them, but soon falls asleep nearby. The first puzzle Sam picks is too easy, and Logan finishes it in minutes. He quickly does two more with similar ease. "I'm a puzzle-making machine," he announces.

Sam pulls out one with a hundred pieces and that slows him down. They work on it together and talk about school and Logan's friends. At one point, Sam looks up and sees Betsy is sitting in the corner listening, a smile on her face.

At eight-thirty, Betsy says it's time for bed. Logan wants to wait for Grandma, but his request is denied. Grudgingly he lets Betsy take him up to his room.

Lisa arrives just before midnight, after Betsy has gone to bed. Dodger greets her as if she's been gone a year, and she kneels down to play with her, but Sam can see how tired she is, and when she settles into a chair and takes her shoes off, Sam gets her a glass of wine.

"Thanks," she says. "I needed this."

"Tough night?"

"Let's just say you owe me one."

"More than one," he says. "Can you tell me anything?"

"Not much more than I told Molly."

"You called her?"

"I wanted to get it on the record that he went in voluntarily. I gave her a quote saying he's cooperating with the investigation."

"Have you read her interview story? Does it square with what he told you?"

Lisa smiles. "You know I'm not going to answer that."

Sam nods and when he looks at her, she is staring intently at him.

"Sam, you need to tell them about the email. It's only a matter of time before they find it, and it's better coming from you. Isn't that the advice you've been giving everyone else lately?"

He shakes his head.

"She met with me on the understanding that it was confidential. I can't tell the authorities."

Lisa gives him a look that he recognizes from the old days. *That's wishful thinking. Be careful where you tread.*

"I'm exhausted," she says, giving in. "You're welcome to spend another night here."

He starts to decline but then realizes how tired he is. Besides, it will give him another chance to see Betsy and Logan, however briefly, in the morning. "Thanks, I'd like that. And thanks for arranging this weekend. I really appreciate it."

She shakes it off. "It worked out conveniently for everyone."

He leans over and kisses her cheek, and she squeezes his arm before he goes up to the guest room.

Antifa Man

I can't sleep and I want to get high so bad, but I'm afraid to. I need to keep my wits about me. The feds were bastards, which I expected, though I had no idea they could ask the same thing so many times.

That lawyer was good. She let me answer most of the questions, and the only real hiccup was when they asked where I was the night he was killed. Andy and Stevie would have lied for me, but I couldn't get them involved, so I said I was home alone.

As it is, the guys are furious with me for going in to talk to the feds. Stevie is insisting we leave town. He's sure the lawyer and Ethics man are playing me for a sucker. I think Andy is worried I'll give them up, but I would never do that. It would be nice if they could vouch for me without getting into trouble themselves, but with their history, I can't see that happening. They were stupid, doing that shit, going too far too many times.

Andy won't even listen to me. He's really upset. I hope he hasn't done anything dumb that we don't know about. I asked Stevie if he knew where Andy was the night Morgan was killed and he doesn't. Still, I don't think Andy has the smarts to go after Morgan without our help. I'm sure he had nothing to do with it. I wish we really had been together—usually we are—but that night we were all zonked and never met up.

The lawyer said I did okay, didn't put myself in jeopardy. And she said they have nothing to hold me on. Fortunately, they don't seem to know we got into his computer and bank account.

And the gun thing was pretty clever of me. Once the newspaper said it was his gun, I had a big advantage. No way they could accuse me of killing him. "How would I ever get his gun?" I asked them.

The look on their faces was worth remembering. Like they hadn't thought of that, though they must have. One of them told me not to believe everything I read in the newspaper, but I wasn't buying that. Then he said Morgan might have carried it for protection and maybe I took it away from him. "Some protection," I said. "How would I manage that when he was bigger and stronger and armed?"

That was maybe a mistake. I shouldn't have even commented, and the lawyer told me to shut up at that point. Like I'd given them something to think about. But think is all they can do.

I'm not too worried, but Andy and Stevie—especially Andy—think I'm a jerk for letting Ethics man talk me into going to the feds. They're worried they'll find some link between me and them. I suppose they can if they look hard enough, but so what? That doesn't prove anything.

And what choice did I have once they had my name? If I hadn't made the gesture, I'd be on the run forever and what would that be like?

But I need to control Andy. He can be a little crazy, and he keeps insisting we have to fight back, whatever that means.

Stevie thinks we should throw them off the idea that anyone is targeting the right-wing nuts, and he still believes the best way is to threaten one of our allies. He even suggested a phony assassination attempt. He doesn't realize what kind of shit that would bring down.

Right now, I'm fine. The police have nothing. I just need to keep Andy and Stevie calm and make sure they don't do anything stupid. That gets harder and harder, though I've been doing it for a long time. Not always successfully. I admit that. But mostly.

Maybe I will get high after all.

No, better not. I still have to figure out our next move. Someone has to be the brains behind our cause. We're rid of one asshole, but there are plenty more like him, and we're running out of time.

The world is running out of time.

Maybe I can figure out a way to get the newspaper on our side. They are, sort of, but they're not nearly forceful enough. The girl is sympathetic, but I know the older guy has more influence. Isn't that the way it always works?

I wonder if he has something going with her. Maybe I can get to him through her. But how?

That's worth considering, but not now. Much too tired. I better try to sleep. I'll have to deal with Andy and Stevie in the morning. I better have some energy for that.

Although I'd much rather get high.

A Bittersweet Goodbye

Sam declines Lisa's offer of breakfast and tries not to get emotional when he says goodbye to Betsy and Logan and, of course, Dodger too. But he feels emotional. He knows Lisa deserves her time with them, but he hates being left out. He feels so isolated.

He stops at the Tastee Diner for breakfast, which proves to be another mistake because it reminds him of happier times, spending leisurely Sunday mornings here with Lisa lingering over the newspapers and bottomless cups of coffee. The weekday crowd at this hour is different, hurried white- and blue-collar workers chowing down and leaving.

He only reads one story in the paper, Molly's account of the interview with Wasserman. He'd read it online before going to bed, but he wants to see the update. The story is now on the front page and it leads with Wasserman's meeting with the task force. There are no details on what he said, but Lisa is quoted saying her client is cooperating with authorities. Molly has done a nice job of summing up the interview, giving Wasserman enough of a chance to speak his mind and make his points, but not enough to make the story one-sided. She's included the threats he sent—he hasn't denied those—and his passion is obvious, which helps explain why the police are interested in him.

As Sam hoped, the story on Morgan's extramarital affairs is short and on an inside page next to the jump from the Wasserman story. It mentions that police have talked to at least one woman, but it doesn't name Kelly, and quotes the task force saying they are still pursuing multiple avenues in their investigation.

When Sam calls Howie to ask if he can come by and pick his brain, Howie says he doesn't want to be seen with a reporter in his office, but he wants to talk, "providing this can be a two-way street." Sam agrees and soon finds himself at another restaurant tempted to have a second breakfast. He settles for a bagel while Howie orders eggs, bacon, and hash browns.

"Don't you eat at home?" Sam teases.

"With three teenagers? Let's just say I'm often needed in the office extra early. Plus, there's less traffic this way."

When the coffee is served, Sam asks if he's read Molly's story.

"Of course. That was another nice coup. You didn't happen to find out who told her about the guy in the first place?"

Sam scrunches up his face. "Even if I did, I couldn't tell you, as you well know. But the truth is, I don't know her source. If it's any help, I can tell you it's not from your crew."

"Oh, that's a big help. Leaves only five or six other possibilities."

Sam can't help but smile.

Howie hasn't gotten a report yet on Wasserman's visit to the FBI and when he finds out Sam was present for Molly's interview, he asks a million questions about Wasserman. He wants Sam's impressions of his demeanor, how crazy he is, how scared he is. Sam does his best to answer, knowing Howie trusts his impression more than what he'll get from the agents who interviewed him.

"You sound like you don't think he's guilty," Howie says when he finishes grilling Sam.

"I'll leave that to you guys. I can only tell you what I saw."

When Howie doesn't respond to that, Sam asks again about the reports of Morgan's extramarital affairs, feeling only a little guilty about asking. He probably knows more than Howie, but he wants to find out how much the feds know and how seriously they're taking it.

Howie answers with a shrug. "No doubt that he screwed around. I already told you that. But as you well know, he's not the only one, and as far as I know, no one ever got killed over it."

That's not quite true, Sam thinks, but he doesn't bother saying it. "Are they looking at any woman in particular?" he asks instead.

Howie dips his last scrap of toast in the last drops of egg yolk. "Apparently he had a problem—one of his own making—with the last one he broke up with. But I doubt she's the only one who thinks he was a bastard."

Sam waits for him to take another bite, knowing there's more to come. "This one girlfriend came in and talked to the D.C. police. Morgan supposedly took their breakup very badly and did some things he shouldn't have done. She figured we'd find out about her sooner or later so she came in to declare her innocence."

"They believe her?"

"Hard to say. It doesn't sound like him at all, but who knows? Could be true and could be a motive. Sometimes the ones who step up and say, 'not me,' are really saying the opposite."

Sam's not sure how to respond to that, feeling both awkward and guilty for holding back so much from Howie. "Well, the same could be said of the guy who went to the FBI yesterday," he finally says.

"Except they already knew about him, and he knew they knew, so he didn't have much choice."

"So they don't believe the woman who came in?"

"They don't believe her and they don't disbelieve her. Some things she said haven't checked out. At least not yet. And then there's wifey."

Sam raises his eyebrows. "So the wife's still a suspect?"

"The way he treated her would make a strong motive," Howie suggests.

"So could lots of other things. Being a bad boss, playing dirty politics, stepping on an ant."

Howie agrees. "I'm told his email and phone records leave no shortage of plausible villains. It's not just Wasserman."

"They found his phone?"

"Not his private burner, but there were plenty of threatening messages on the office phones. They only saved a few, but it's enough to give a sense of what was going on."

Howie puts his fork down and signals for a check. Sam knows he'll end up paying it, but Howie must need to get back to work.

"Wives are always suspects," Howie says, "but it's hard to see a real motive. She'd learned to live with his screwing around, so it wasn't that."

Sam is so lost in his thoughts that he's in his car with the motor running before he sees the paper under the windshield wiper. He gets out, thinking it's an advertisement, only to find an envelope with his name written on it. Inside, there's a note.

"You're making the wrong people unhappy and that's not something you want to do. Back off."

He reads it twice. It's pretty vague, and as threats go, it's pretty weak. It has to be related to Morgan's murder—he can't think of anything else he's doing that might upset someone—and whoever killed Morgan is obviously capable of violence. For a second, he considers calling the police, but that will only lead to questions he doesn't want to answer.

Sam gets out of the car and looks for Howie, but he's already out of sight. He gets back behind the wheel and starts to drive off, only to realize he has a flat. When he gets out to check, there's an icepick blade in his left rear tire. He has no doubt it's an exclamation point on the warning note.

Sam has changed his share of tires and he does it quickly, making a point of not looking around. If someone's watching, he doesn't want to show any emotion, though all of his senses are on alert.

When he's finished, he drives slowly to the office, watching his mirrors to see if anyone is following. He goes through the list of who might be rattled enough by his investigation to do this and who might have known where he was and be daring enough to pull it off in broad daylight. Someone must have followed him into town, which means they knew he was at Lisa's house. Could she be in danger? What about Betsy and Logan?

The list of suspects is short. Kelly is on it, but he's been helping her and she's already told the police everything he knows. Or has she?

Antifa Man is clearly capable, but Sam has been helping him too. Still, it could be one of his buddies in the antifa movement.

The most logical choice is Peg or someone working for her. He's asked her the toughest questions, and she seems most suspicious of his involvement. But Peg still has a security detail, and it would have been hard for her to get away and pull this off. Plus Peg seems way too sophisticated to resort to such heavy handedness. If she wanted to threaten him, she'd have far better ways to do it. And how would she have known where to find him?

But who does that leave?

At the office Sam huddles with Brenda and Molly, filling them in on what he'd learned from Howie. Molly dismisses it as useless. Sam gets annoyed but lets it go.

"Did you get a readout on Wasserman's meeting last night?" he asks her.

"A vague one," Molly says. "He admitted sending the threats but denied doing anything more. They kept him talking for three hours and then let him go."

"He didn't offer an alibi?" Brenda asks.

Sam waits while Molly says he told them he was alone at home. "He's protecting his buddies," she adds. "I'd still like to know why. He wasn't convincing when we talked to him. Something's not right with them."

"Any way of us talking to them?" Brenda asks.

Molly gives that some thought. "Not sure how, unless he trusts me enough to introduce me."

"Not likely," Sam says.

"Could they have killed Morgan?" Brenda asks.

Sam and Molly both shrug. They have no idea.

"I wish I could tell the police about them," Molly says. "They'd be able to track them down."

"But you promised you wouldn't."

Molly gives Sam a look that says she's not in the mood for one of his ethical lectures. Still, he keeps his eyes on her until he's sure she understands.

"Anyway," she says. "I have no idea who they are or how to get in touch with them."

Brenda changes the subject, asking how they'll pursue the other angle to the story, the reports of Morgan's affairs, especially with the woman who went to the police. Sam doesn't say anything. He still hasn't told Brenda about the email from Kelly and hopes he'll never have to, but Molly could force his hand. Even her special Park Police source has been less than forthcoming about Kelly, and Molly's been growing impatient.

They end their talk with Molly planning to try her sources again and to see if Peg Morgan has anything more to say.

Back in his office, Sam settles into his visitor's chair and stews for a while. He has to decide what to do about the warning. He's ruled out going to the police, but he could ask Howie for advice.

No, the warning was too amateurish to get upset about. Someone wants him to go away, but if it were the murderer, Sam figures he'd have gotten more than a warning.

Kelly

Maybe it was a mistake to come alone, but Ariana makes me nervous, even more nervous than I already am. I took a Xanax to relax, but now that I'm in the police station I wonder if that was a mistake.

The Black detective is here. Latisha Thompson, she reminds me, in case I forgot. I didn't. But she has an older woman with her, another detective who she introduces as Detective Flynn. No more first names.

What are the odds of them picking two female detectives to interview me? I'm guessing the force is overwhelmingly male. I know the police use women detectives to handle rape cases, but that's not what this is, though I certainly understand the feeling. Violated. I was violated. First by Wade's tricks and now by these prying busybodies.

Latisha asks me if I want water or coffee or a soda. "I'm fine," I say, my first lie of the day.

When we're seated in a formal interview room, Latisha starts a tape machine and goes into that routine you always see on TV, giving the time and naming everyone present. Then Detective Flynn asks me to go over everything again, like she hasn't heard the story from Latisha. "Just start at the beginning—when you met the senator—and take me though everything until today."

I swallow and begin to tell the story. It's not like I have a choice. I find myself telling it the same way I told it to Latisha. It's as if I remember that interview more than I remember the events. The thought gives me pause, and I hesitate just as I reach the point when he first came to my apartment.

"And that's when you became intimate?" Flynn asks. She's mistaken my pause for embarrassment.

I nod and then say yes out loud for the recording.

"Who initiated it? The intimacy?" Flynn asks. Why is she so hung up on this part?

"It was mutual. We both knew it was going to happen when we agreed to meet at my place."

We get to the part about the breakup, and Flynn, who is now asking all the questions, presses me on why I ended it. I hear skepticism in her voice, like she doesn't believe I'm telling the whole story.

Then we get to the harassment, and her skepticism turns into something more. "Whose idea was it to take pictures?"

"It was his. His all the way. I didn't want to, but I got tired of telling him no."

"So he asked on multiple occasions."

"Yes."

"And you finally agreed to it so he'd stop pressuring you?"

"Yes."

"But there were pictures on more than one occasion. If you regretted it the first time, why did you allow it again?"

So they have the pictures. And obviously they can tell the dates. "Same reason," I say. "It was easier than resisting."

"And you took pictures of him too. And selfies of you together?"

"He took the selfies."

"But in some of the pictures, you're holding the phone."

"I suppose. Why does it matter? It wasn't against the law to take the pictures. I know we were consenting adults, and I know I agreed. What was wrong was what he did with them after we broke up."

"You broke up or you ended it?"

"We broke up because I ended it. It's not an either/or question."

She sits back, looking a bit smug, and after a second, Latisha picks up the questioning. She goes easier on me, not challenging or probing any more deeply than the first time. I guess she's the "good" cop, though I suspect she can play either role if she wants to.

"Did you break up with Morgan in person or on the phone?" Latisha asks.

"In person."

"And that's when he reacted badly."

"Not at first. I don't think he believed me, and he proved that by calling me two days later and asking to see me. That's when he got angry. Said that was no way to treat him after all he'd done for me."

"Meaning what? What had he done?"

"Nothing really. Got me some job interviews that never panned out."

"And after you said no to his appeal, the harassment started?"

"Not right away. It took a couple of weeks."

"How did you confront him about that? By phone? In person?"

I admit the embarrassing truth. "I couldn't face him. I emailed and texted him. But he didn't respond, and the vicious games didn't stop. I eventually called him, but he denied knowing what I was talking about. When the pictures came out, which proved it was him, I sent him another email pointing that out."

"Why do you think he did that—deny it was him and then send proof that it was him?"

I shake my head. "I have no idea."

The questions go on for way too long, until my craving for a cigarette becomes almost unbearable. Flynn gets back into the conversation but is more gentle. Until the end.

"Did the senator's wife know about your affair?"

"He said she probably knew there was someone but not my name."

"And you believed him? That she didn't know your name?"

"I'm not sure. I don't know what she knew. Maybe you should ask her."

"And you never spoke to her, never met her, according to what you told Detective Thompson earlier?"

I feel a chill, sense a trap. "I might have run into her at a function or something like that, but I don't remember being introduced to her."

"And you'd remember if you talked to her, especially if she acted like she suspected something?"

"Yes, I'd remember. That would have been very upsetting."

"But you had to know that having an affair with her husband was risky that way. That there was always a chance she'd find out?"

I don't know what they want me to say so I just shrug.

They look at each other and Flynn shoves a piece of paper in front of me. "What's this?" I ask.

"It's permission to look at your phone records. It's voluntary, but it would help us eliminate you from our inquiry?"

"How?"

"We'd be able to verify some of the facts we're having trouble with."

I feel my head spinning, but I don't think anything in my phone records will be a problem. I can't see the harm and refusing will make me look guilty. I shrug and sign the paper.

They thank me and let me escape.

Wherein New Problems Arise

Sam wakes to three new voicemails. He answers Lisa first and is pleasantly surprised she only wants to talk about their weekend with Betsy and Logan. He can't help feeling good about that. It's the first time she's reached out to him since the separation.

"I'm glad that worked out," she says. "Betsy and Logan were happy to see you, and it was important for Betsy to know you are doing okay. You *are* doing okay, right? You weren't just putting on a strong face for her?"

"I'm working on it. We had a good weekend and I'm grateful for the chance to see them. It was a stroke of brilliance for you to arrange it."

"I did need a dog sitter. And Dodger really misses you. Sometimes she mopes around and then settles in your study as if waiting for you to show up."

Sam hesitates. There is so much he wants to say, but he knows he shouldn't, and especially not on the phone. He wants and needs some indication of how this will play out, and he knows that's impossible for either of them to predict. Still, he'd like a sign. Even a small one. Maybe that's what this call is.

"Logan is growing up fast," Sam says. "He's a smart little boy."

"He needs a sibling. I wish Betsy and Ben would reconsider adoption. She didn't mention that, did she?"

"No," he says. "Logan will be fine. Don't worry."

"He is smart," she says, a smile in her voice. "He made me read him a book on dinosaurs and kept correcting my pronunciation."

They talk a while longer about the visit and then Sam asks about Wasserman. "Have you heard anything more from him?"

"You know I won't answer that."

"But you've taken him on as a client?"

"It's not the kind of law I practice now. I gave him some recommendations, but he says he has no money. I really shouldn't be handling him, but I won't leave him hanging."

The conversation peters out and Lisa says she has to go. He thanks her for calling.

After he hangs up, Sam refills his coffee cup, replaying the conversation, looking for clues to what the future might hold and not finding any, other than the fact that she called. He decides that's good enough, a sure sign of something, a thawing of sorts.

He checks the time, sees he ought to get ready for work, but has to return the other two calls. He punches up Danny next.

"Did you know the police interviewed Kelly again?" Danny asks.

"No, how would I? You're my source. What did they want?"

"I'm not sure. She went alone and won't say much about it. But they really freaked her out. She's in panic mode, worse than ever. She even asked Ariana to take care of her cat if she gets arrested."

"She must have said something about what they wanted?"

"She said the interview was more formal. And they asked for permission to access her phone records. She gave it to them, which I don't think I would have done. Let them get a warrant if they have cause. Sounds too much like a fishing expedition."

The third call was from Molly, who asks what took him so long to get back to her.

"Long story," he says, offering no other details. "What's up?"

She hesitates. "I've really screwed up and need some help. Can we meet?"

"Screwed up how?"

"That's what I want to talk about. In person, somewhere out of the office. It's not so much that I screwed up, but I've gotten myself into a fix, and I'm not sure how to get out of it."

They agree on dinner, and Molly surprises him by inviting him to her apartment.

"I'll cook," she says. "Something easy. Don't expect gourmet."

But when he arrives, she tells him that Uber Eats is bringing Chinese food. He's not surprised. He'd considered bringing wine but decided that might give the wrong impression. And Molly sounded so serious that maybe it'd be best to stay completely sober, though Molly has other ideas.

"I know you like bourbon. I've got Jim Beam, if that's not too pedestrian."

He smiles. "It's fine."

She pours it, along with a glass of white wine for herself, and he sits down at the kitchen table while she collects dishes and utensils and sets the table in front of him. Her apartment is small and furnished in something modern, a step above Ikea but a small step.

"Have you and Kyle figured out where you're going to live?" he asks, knowing Kyle works in Baltimore and the location is a bit of a problem.

She sighs. "No, not yet. Somewhere in between obviously, but we haven't even started looking. Kyle gets free parking at his office, so it makes more sense to live closer to Washington so I can Metro in. But we're way behind. Too much else to do."

"Wedding planning was never my favorite part of being a father, not that I was much involved."

He is about to ask her what she wanted to talk about when the buzzer sounds, and he goes to the door to get the food. "I already paid for it, including a tip," she says.

He gets the food, tips the driver another $5, and they spread their dinner onto the table. She's ordered wonton soup, sesame chicken, moo shoo pork, and Szechuan string beans.

"Don't worry. I'll eat the leftovers for a week."

They sit down with the soup and he asks her what's going on. "You said you were in a jam."

"I'll get to that, but let's eat first."

Over spoons of soup, he tells her that her work on the Morgan murder has been really good, that he's impressed with her scoops. "You've got great sources."

She stares at him for a second and says there'll be no story in the paper tomorrow because she's come up dry today. The FBI is still pursuing several leads and not saying much.

"You said you have multiple sources, but I gather it's one guy mainly?"

"Yeah, and that's kinda what I want to talk to you about. I'm getting everything confirmed—and my first tip on Wasserman came anonymously—but I'm definitely getting the best stuff from one guy at the Park Police. Anyway, he says they're still looking in multiple directions."

"What do you hear about my pen pal?"

"That she's still in the picture and that some things about her story don't check out, but I don't know what they are or how serious. Plus, she has no alibi."

"Most innocent people don't. It's the guilty ones who go to great lengths to set one up."

She gives him a look of doubt. "That's not what you told Wasserman."

Sam smiles at that. He wants to tell her that they questioned Kelly a second time—he knows he promised to keep her informed—but he's decided he can't play both sides of the fence. He'll stick to his plan of not feeding information to the paper unless it comes from a neutral source like Howie. It's a matter of weighing one ethical violation against another.

"Is Morgan's wife a serious suspect?" he asks, mostly so he's not tempted to talk about Kelly.

"Yes, but one of many. They can't believe she didn't care about his affairs. She told them she didn't mind as long as he was discreet, and he was anything but. It was almost as if he rubbed her face in it."

"That's not much. Just speculation."

"Morgan's wife also claims to be ignorant about his private email account or his burner phone."

"So she buried her head in the sand."

"Maybe," Molly says, but he can see she isn't buying it.

Sam pushes his plate aside and finishes his drink. Molly takes the hint and starts clearing the dishes. "Go have a seat in the living room. I'll be there in a second."

Sam does as he's told, stopping to put another splash of Jim Beam in his glass. He takes a sip and wonders whether the Woodford Reserve he prefers is worth the extra money. He decides it is.

He waits while Molly finishes the dishes and then while she goes into the bathroom, he tries to guess what it is she wants to talk about. He can't.

"Well," she says as she settles on the sofa opposite his chair. And then she pauses.

"Well," he prompts.

She bites her lower lip and he senses the tension but doesn't know how to ease it, so he waits.

"It's about this Park Police source I have. I need to tell you about him. And I need some advice on how to handle a problem."

Suddenly he has an inkling, but he stays silent.

"He's in all the briefings, and he knows what's going on. Nobody has challenged anything he's told me."

"Sounds good so far. How'd you meet him?"

"That's the problem. He's a friend of my dad's. A good friend. I've known him since I was a kid. Well, a high school student, anyway."

She hesitates, and he's tempted to wait, but he can't. "So what's the problem?"

"He's always acted not quite right with me. A little too familiar. Too quick to give me a hug and too slow to let go. Letting his hand drift down towards my rear end. That kind of thing."

Sam waits.

"It never went too far. It was uncomfortable, but he was a friend of my father's, and sometimes I thought I might be making too much of nothing."

"You probably weren't."

She sighs. "No, I probably wasn't. But I dealt with it mainly by staying away from him, which I could do. There weren't many times when I had to see him, especially after I went off to college. It wasn't like he was stalking or going after me. So it was no big deal."

"But now it is."

"And it's my fault."

Sam waits, but Molly takes a sip of her wine, stalling, so he asks. "How is it your fault?"

"When I realized he was on this case, which only happened when I saw him at a press conference, I made a point of saying hello. He gave me his card and said I was free to call him. And he winked at me."

She's talking slowly and Sam knows where it's going, so he tries to relax and let her go at her own pace.

"When I got the anonymous tip about Antifa Man, I called him to see if it was true. He said he couldn't comment, but he was at the office then, and when he got free, he called me back to say he'd see me. He suggested my apartment, but I said I was on deadline, and we ended up meeting for coffee. Which we've done a few times now, and he's been very helpful."

"But now he wants something in return?"

She swallows but doesn't say anything, so Sam pushes on. "Did he ask for something explicitly or do you just feel that coming? Have you told him you're not interested?"

She bites her lip again, and this time he notices tears in her eyes. He fears what's coming.

"I have to admit I'm partly to blame. I knew that flirting a little would be effective, so I did it. I haven't done anything overtly sexual, but I guess you could say I led him on."

Sam doesn't know what that means precisely. "Flirting how?"

"Oh, mostly with smiles and compliments, occasionally touching his hand or his arm. But we've never been alone where something could happen."

"Does he know you're about to get married?"

She laughs. "He ought to. My dad invited him. And his wife, of course."

"But he doesn't care. What exactly is he doing? Or asking you to do?"

"He's getting touchy-feely, and I know it's only a matter of time before he shows up at my door some night. I don't know how I'm going to handle that."

Sam needs a second to consider what to say so he asks if he can get a little more bourbon, which he does. When he settles back down, he looks at her.

"You don't have to stare that way," she says. "I know I was wrong. I made a bad mistake leading him on."

"That's not what I was thinking. Reporters use all sorts of less-than-sincere behavior to get sources to cooperate. There's a lot of gray area and it's not always obvious when we cross the line. The important thing is to realize when you have, and then move back to the other side. Sounds like you're doing that."

"But I knew what I was doing. I knew from the start, but I thought I could keep it in check."

"You can and you have."

"So far."

"You're not even sure he'll show up and force a confrontation. But you do need to stay away from him. Don't call him again and don't take his calls. Be firm, with him and with yourself. Isn't that possible?"

She shakes her head. "It might be if he were a stranger, but he's my dad's friend and he's coming to my wedding, for God's sake. I can't ignore him forever."

"That's not what I mean. Just stop asking him for favors and make sure you're never alone with him."

"You make it sound simple."

Sam doesn't say anything. He sees a tear roll down one cheek, though she's not exactly crying, and he doesn't want to embarrass her, so he looks around while she wipes her face with a tissue. He studies the furniture and revises his earlier judgment. It's really no better than Ikea. When he turns back to Molly, he sees her eye makeup has smeared. He looks down and focuses on her boots, odd for this time of year, and expensive looking.

"You think I'm awful," she says.

"No, no," he says, and he means it. "It happens to all of us. We want the story. The goal is a good one and sometimes we go a little too far. And he's more to blame than you are. He's been harassing you for years. Your mistake was taking advantage of a known weakness, but you stopped it before it went too far.

That's what's important, and you know what you need to do going forward."

"If I can stick to it."

"You can, and you told me so that I can hold you to it." He says it with a smile and she can't help returning it.

"Maybe that is why I told you. But I still can't figure out how to handle him next time I see him."

"Which is why you should postpone that as long as you possibly can. Stay away from him."

"If I do, it will mean no more scoops."

"He's not the only source out there. Just work harder, be more imaginative, and if you can't find another way, let someone else break the story. It's more important you do what's right, both what's right journalistically and what's right for you."

"Okay," she says, but he's not sure what she means by it. Maybe just that she's done talking.

"Have you talked at all with Kyle about this?"

"Oh, no. He wouldn't understand. Not in the least. He'd be upset I let it get as far as I did. Or else he'd want to punch the guy out. No, telling him is not a good idea."

Sam accepts that and then offers to help. "I can keep working on my friend with the Capitol Police. He knows more than he's telling me. And let me talk to Peg Morgan again. Maybe I can pry something loose."

"I'd appreciate the help. We've never had a joint byline before."

"Probably not a good idea to put my name on a story no matter what. Truth is, I've been walking a pretty fine line too, mixing reporting with giving advice to suspects. I'm on shakier ground than you've ever been."

They talk about that, and if Sam was hoping for reassurance, he doesn't get it.

"You really are operating on the edge," she tells him. "If

Brenda finds out how much you've been holding back, she's going to have to do something about it."

"I haven't done anything to hurt the paper."

"You're keeping secrets from her, things she has a right to know. You'll lose your column if she finds out, maybe your job."

"So everyone keeps telling me." He knows there's risk to what he's doing. He's just not about to change course now.

He turns the conversation back to Molly's problem and by the time he leaves, he thinks he's helped calm her down, though he knows she's still worried and unsure about what comes next.

But that's a good thing. She should be worried.

And she's not the only one. When he gets to his car, he inspects it carefully, a routine he adopted after the flat tire. And on the way home, he makes a point of checking his rearview mirror repeatedly.

The Problem With Phones

Sam calls Howie first thing and asks for another meeting. He's surprised at how easy it is to arrange, wonders why Howie's being so cooperative, then decides he probably wants another free breakfast. At least this time, Sam hasn't eaten.

They meet in the same café at the same table. "This is getting to be a habit," Howie says with a grin. Howie places the same order, and Sam asks for an egg-white omelet, but with bacon and hash browns on the side. The waitress, who's all business, doesn't bat an eye.

"Any progress?" Sam asks after the coffee is served.

"Too much. Too many leads to follow. I do have a few tidbits for you, though no one knows what they mean."

"Like what?"

The breakfast dishes arrive, and Howie takes his time on the toast, lavishing it with butter and marmalade, making Sam think of a painter carefully preparing a palette. At one point his knife slips and he gets butter on his sleeve. He dips a napkin in water and does his best to clean it.

"So, what's happening?" Sam prompts.

"Something interesting in the woman's phone records—the one who was having an affair with Morgan and who alleges he was harassing her."

"The way you said that sounds like you don't believe her."

He shrugs. "No reason not to."

"So what's in the phone records?"

Howie takes a bite of toast and chews slowly, clearly thinking. "Mostly what you'd expect but with a couple of contradictions."

He takes a sip of his coffee and Sam gets edgy. "What contradictions?"

"As she'd indicated, there were a lot of calls over three months from her phone to the senator's burner—at least the number she says was his burner—and from that phone to her. Then the calls suddenly stop. Until he calls her again eight days before he's killed. They talked for four and a half minutes."

Eight days before he was killed, Sam thinks. That would be two days after Sam's first meeting with Kelly.

"What's suspicious about that?" Sam asks as nonchalantly as he can. "She'd been emailing him to leave her alone. He could have called her to talk about it, to deny it again, or threaten worse."

"Could be, but if so, she forgot to mention it. And there's something else," he adds, then goes back to his coffee before continuing.

"Four days before Morgan was killed, the woman made a call to an unknown number. Turns out it was a burner, but it wasn't the one Morgan had been using."

"Maybe he had more than one."

Howie makes a face that dismisses the thought. "The call was only four seconds long. Four seconds. And here's the thing, when they checked it out, they found it was purchased at a 7-Eleven—with cash of course—only three blocks from where she lives. And she would have walked by the store going and coming from the Metro every day."

"What does that prove?"

"Nothing yet, but they're getting a warrant for the store's security video. It'd be interesting if her face is on it."

Sam ponders that as he bites into a piece of bacon. "That doesn't make sense. Why would she buy a burner and then call herself on it? For four seconds?"

"That's the question alright. Unless she bought a burner and then gave it to someone else. Like a hired killer."

"For a four-second call?"

"Could be a signal. Or to say meet me tomorrow at the usual place. How long does that take?"

Sam doesn't buy it. "A professional killer would buy his own phone. That makes no sense."

Howie doesn't say anything. He's finishing his eggs, with considerable gusto, Sam observes. "Maybe not," Howie says finally. "They want to ask her who she called, but they want to check the video first. Of course, they're also getting a warrant to dump the burner's call records."

"Could be a dead end. If the call only lasted a few seconds, it was probably a wrong number and a coincidence."

"Maybe."

"It's not much," Sam concludes.

"Hey, don't blame me. You asked what was new. Don't shoot the messenger."

"What about the wife? I heard they were taking a harder look at her."

Howie raises his eyebrows. "Who told you that?"

"You know better than to ask."

"Well, I haven't heard that, but I'll ask. Then you can buy me another breakfast." He laughs as he says it, but Sam knows he's not joking.

Howie is still smiling when Sam decides to confide in his old friend. "This is probably nothing," he begins, "but I need to tell someone. Just in case it's not nothing."

Howie's smile evaporates and he looks straight into Sam's eyes.

"I got a warning the other day to back off, presumably meaning the Morgan story. A note on my windshield, with a flat tire for emphasis."

"Did you report it?"

"No, the whole thing seemed amateurish."

"Not to me. Who have you been talking to? Who might consider you a threat?"

"That's just it. I can't think of anyone. It's not like I've uncovered some big clue that is going to reveal the murderer."

"You might have without realizing it. Or you might be so close, someone is afraid you will. You should report this. Maybe even get protection."

Sam hesitates and Howie goes on. "If you don't want to report it officially, I could give you a name. He runs a pretty good agency that protects big-shot CEOs."

"That seems extreme."

"It's not." Howie takes out a notebook, rips out a sheet of paper, and writes down a name. "Give him a call."

Sam takes the paper, though he doesn't commit himself.

Sam calls his office to say he's working on the Hill and won't be in until the afternoon. He then dials Molly to ask how she's doing.

"I'm okay. Talking to you helped. Still not sure how it's going to work out, but at least I have a plan."

"You'll be fine," he assures her. He hangs up without telling her about his conversation with Howie.

Peg is not glad to see him.

"You again?"

But she doesn't send him away, even invites him in for coffee, which he accepts, though he's had his quota for the day.

Sam is surprised that she's willing to talk and even more surprised by the way she looks. Gone is the elegance, the style, the got-it-all-together look. She's wearing casual slacks with what looks like a stain at the knee and a blouse that is rumpled. Both are black, but somewhat different degrees of black, giving her outfit the appearance of a suit that doesn't quite match. He studies her face, concludes she's wearing makeup, but that it's different than the last time he saw her. Not as thick, or maybe too thick. Or maybe just applied hurriedly. He knows none of this matters, that she is a woman in mourning who may not have been expecting guests, but he thinks of her as someone who is always ready for guests.

"How are you holding up?" he asks, then immediately realizes how stupid the question is.

But she doesn't react that way. "I'm doing okay for a grieving widow who's being treated like a suspect. Never mind who my husband is. Was."

"They treat everyone as a suspect at this stage. They must be under a lot of pressure to solve this. It'd make anybody tense. Can't do much for their bedside manner."

She makes a sound like a grumble. "They don't care about the niceties."

"If it makes you feel better, nothing in our reporting indicates they're focused only on you. They're still following all sorts of different leads."

"They do seem to be looking at one of the women Wade was involved with."

"They told you that?"

"They asked if I knew about her. They asked other things—they can't believe I was home alone that night—but they seem obsessed with what Wade did after he dumped her."

"Does the revenge porn sound like something Wade would have done?" he asks.

She pauses before answering. He can't tell whether she's thinking about the question or deciding whether she should share her view.

"Wade always told me the other women weren't important and I believed that, so it's hard to imagine he would be upset if one of them broke it off. But he had an ego. Maybe she pressed the wrong buttons. That kind of behavior is not completely out of the question."

Something about the way she says it keeps him interested. He wants to ask why a man like Morgan, who seemed to have no trouble finding a woman when he wanted one, would get so upset about Kelly's decision. But the question is too impertinent to ask his wife.

"Surely the FBI can figure out whether he did those things," Sam offers.

"So you'd think."

"What about the threatening letters?" he asks. "Has the FBI said anything more about what they're finding?"

She looks at him and shakes her head. "Am I your only source? Aren't you supposed to know these things?"

He guesses the trap in the question. "Well, we know about one man they're looking at, but I'm sure you read that in the paper."

"Yes. And I saw that Lisa is representing him. That was a surprise. Your doing?"

Sam pauses to consider his response, then decides he can't avoid answering and doesn't see any harm. "I passed along her name."

"Then I assume she's told you that he's gone missing?"

Sam doesn't try to hide his surprise. "How do you know that?"

"You're not the only one with sources. Consider that my little tip of the day. Just don't say where you got it."

"Maybe they just don't know where to look for him," he says.

She sighs and he senses the conversation is over. When she stands up, he knows it is. He thanks her and promises to keep in touch.

"Do me a favor," she says at the door.

"Sure."

"Don't come back unless you have something to share."

Peg

Well, I think that went as well as it could, and it was certainly better than my latest encounter with the detectives anyway. Not that it matters. It's amusing to banter with him, but he's a lot smarter. A real threat. He knows more than he's telling me. If I can't get him to mind his own business, I better keep him close. At least he gives me a heads up on what the press is thinking.

The detectives came to fill me in on the investigation, or so they said. "Keep you updated," the Black one said.

The big news was the analysis of Wade's computer, the one he kept hidden in the closet. Like I didn't know. I never planned to let them see it, but somehow they were able to trace the harassment to our address, and when they asked to search the house, I couldn't very well refuse. Why wasn't I smart enough to destroy it? Well, no one's perfect.

"There's no longer any doubt," the White cop said. "Your husband's computer was used for the revenge porn. We thought you ought to know."

The way he said it bothers me. Why did they share that news with me? They didn't have to and there had to be a reason for doing so. What were they hoping to get out of me?

I gave them the appropriate reaction. Utter shock. I should have been an actress. What really pisses me off is that I let Larry fuck me last night just to get the same information. He's still in regular touch with the task force, and I don't have any other sources I can count on. Better to keep him on the string until this is over.

I had been tempted to tell Turner what the FBI found on Wade's secret computer, but they made me promise not to say anything. I could always tip off the other reporter, that Molly-wannabe-famous.

And I have to keep pushing the newspaper to focus on this guy who threatened Wade so they spend less time delving into his personal life. That's the last thing I want to read about. The idiots on Twitter are helping. They call this guy Antifa Man. No matter that it was me who started the hash tag. I've always liked Twitter.

Maybe I should give Lisa a call. She sent a nice note. I know she won't tell me anything about Antifa Man, even if I ask, but I might pick up a clue. Besides, she was always nice to me. Maybe I can talk to her about my playing a more substantive role at KidsPlace. I do think I can do more there.

It's time to move back home. My sister is getting on my nerves. This waiting around for things to happen is maddening. I'm the kind of person who likes to take things in hand, to make things happen. But now I'm left sitting and waiting for the cops to do their thing and worrying about what Turner is going to find. I can try to guide it, but I can't control it.

And control is something I really crave.

Two Disturbing Encounters

Sam doubts he'll get much, but he decides to call Lisa anyway.

"I understand Wasserman has disappeared."

He can hear the surprise in her silence, but he's not sure whether she's surprised at the news or the fact that he knows about it.

"No comment."

"Do the feds want to talk to him again?"

"No comment."

Sam smiles to himself and asks if she can meet for lunch. She hesitates, leaving no doubt that she's reluctant, but then she agrees. The way she says it scares him. There's something else on her mind.

And he is right.

Once they're seated at an almost empty Italian restaurant on Cordell Avenue in Bethesda—she'd been working at home—she gives him the news.

"Sam, there's no easy way to say this, but I'm seeing someone else. It's not serious—only a couple of dates so far–but it might become serious."

He nods, hoping to hide his reaction. It's not exactly shock. More disappointment. Deep disappointment. He tries to think quickly, but his mind is hung up on the word "date," which puts him mentally back in high school. He knows the younger generations don't use the word, and it feels out of place for people in their fifties. He's tempted to ask who it is but has enough sense not to go there.

When his silence continues, she touches his hand. "I don't know what happens next, but I didn't want you to be thinking about us getting back together, and I know you are. I won't say never, but not in the near future. I need some time. And some space."

The waiter comes and takes their order, though Sam has already lost his appetite and chooses a salad he knows he won't eat. When the waiter leaves, Sam tries switching gears and talking about the case, although he knows what she's going to say and he lets her say it.

They somehow get through lunch, quickly and without much talk.

Outside, as they part, he tells her he understands and won't be a nuisance. She shakes it off, says she's not worried about that, she's worried about him.

"I'm okay," he says, trying to reassure her, although he can't even reassure himself.

"Do you want the key back?" he asks, reaching into his pocket.

She shakes her head sharply. "That's not necessary. You keep it."

Then he has a thought. "Do you mind if I go by there now? I'd like to take Dodger for a walk."

She smiles. "She'd love that, I'm sure. I'm headed to the office so let yourself in."

Dodger greets him like he's been away too long, which is exactly the way Sam feels. Her tail wags so vigorously, Sam has to grab it so it doesn't knock something over. He bends down and lets her lick his face, buries his head in her neck, and is suddenly sobbing uncontrollably. Dodger stands still and in her own way shows she's concerned. When Sam gains control, she gives him another lick on his nose. Sam laughs. Dodger knows exactly what he needs.

Sam gets a leash, heads out the front door, and then decides he doesn't want to walk along the residential streets. Instead, he loads Dodger into the back seat and drives to his favorite local park. Dodger, who must have an internal GPS, figures out where they're headed when they're still two blocks away and gives a bark of approval.

They find the park deserted on this weekday afternoon, save for an occasional runner or bike rider. Sam is tempted to let Dodger off her leash but knows that's forbidden, even in the wooded areas. It doesn't seem fair that the deer and rabbits are allowed to roam free, but Sam supposes that's exactly why dogs don't get the privilege. Still, he can't understand the need for a pooper-scooper plastic bag in the middle of a forest.

They walk at a leisurely pace, Dodger bouncing along but stopping to smell everything she can. Sam remembers reading that dogs have three hundred million odor receptors in their noses, compared to a mere six million for humans, and it looks like Dodger is using all of them.

Sam wants nothing more than to enjoy the sunshine, the park, and his dog, but soon his mind returns to his troubles. He's not surprised about Lisa. Somewhere inside, he knew their marriage was over, but he didn't expect the ending to come so soon. He wanted to hang onto the hope, but now he can't. He wonders, only briefly, about the other man, resisting the temptation to guess who it might be. He also wonders how serious it is, and yes, whether they've slept together, but he knows it doesn't matter whether this particular relationship leads to anything. The point is, she's moving on, and so too must he. He's just not ready.

He'll take his time, not that he has a choice. He needs to think of it as a new chapter. He still has the children and the grandchildren, though they are far away. That leaves him with his work. He's always had that. Maybe that was the problem, that he had too much invested in his career, though he doesn't believe he was ever a workaholic or that this was the cause of the strain in his marriage. We grew apart, he thinks, then revolts at the cliché. What does it even mean?

He still hopes they can be friends, but a part of him knows how hard that will be, especially if Lisa is in another relationship. Someday he may be in one too, though he can't imagine that. Not yet anyway.

Sam suddenly feels a sharp pull and before he realizes it, the leash has left his hand and Dodger is racing away. He gives chase, hollering for Dodger to stop, trying to make his voice as loud and stern as he can. But that makes it harder to run, which is more important. When Dodger goes over a hill, he loses her, and when he reaches the top, he looks around but can't find her.

He tells himself not to panic and scans the area, hollering Dodger's name, but the trees are thick and he can't see much.

After what feels like several minutes but is probably only a couple, he hears a crashing sound and turns to see Dodger coming back. When she arrives, she looks sheepish, and when Sam bends down to catch the leash, he gags at the smell.

A skunk. No doubt about it.

Sam laughs, mostly out of relief that they are reunited.

On the walk back, Dodger acts mortified. She keeps stopping and trying to roll in some leaves, though Sam warns her that won't help. "You're in for a bath, girl."

Back at his car, Sam opens his phone and types into Google, "My dog met a skunk." He's lucky enough to find an old towel and some plastic landscaping paper in his trunk. He uses the cloth to wipe off as much of the skunk oil as he can, but it doesn't help. He spreads the plastic over his backseat and

Dodger climbs in for the ride home. Sam has the distinct impression his car will never be the same.

Back at the house, he ties dodger's leash to a fence and goes inside to prepare. The house has a shower downstairs, close to the garage door, that Sam always used when he came in from gardening, but there's no tub, which is what he really needs. The internet recommends a tomato juice bath, which seems out of the question. He follows the second option and prepares a solution of hydrogen peroxide, baking soda, and soap, then fills a couple of buckets and brings Dodger in.

She accepts her fate calmly, standing in the shower while Sam carefully spreads the solution on her and then sprays it off. When they finish, Sam waits while Dodger shakes off as much water as she can, and then he surrounds her in towels and rubs her down. He does the best he can, but when he lets her loose, Dodger races through the house excitedly, rolling on the carpet to finish drying herself. Her new burst of energy is filled again with joy, and despite the lingering smell, Sam can't help feeling happy and content.

He doubts Lisa will feel the same when she comes home to the mess they've made.

Kelly

Danny is insisting I get a lawyer, but I don't know anyone I can trust, and I don't want to go to the strangers that Danny came up with. I consider calling the one person who probably could get me one, but I'm afraid I'm being watched and listened to. And I can't shake the notion that showing up with a lawyer will be an admission of guilt. I tell myself, for what feels like the millionth time, that I am the victim here. I must make them believe that.

It was Latisha who called and asked me to come in for still another interview. "Just to clear up a few things," she said. I was tempted to ask what, but I knew she wouldn't tell me.

Danny and Ariana both offer to go with me, insisting if I don't bring a lawyer, I at least need to bring a witness, but I have a feeling the police wouldn't allow them in. And besides, what good would a witness do?

I spend an inordinate amount of time deciding what to wear, finally choosing a white blouse and gray slacks, my typical work uniform when I was still able to go to work.

Once again I'm escorted upstairs by a uniformed cop, and Latisha greets me at the elevator as she has before. She takes me to Flynn and introduces me to a man wearing a suit, a white shirt, and a too-skinny tie. Latisha identifies him as an FBI agent, and I'm sure my sudden fear is written on my face. All three of them take me into still another interview room, one that's bigger and more imposing than the last.

They invite me (hardly an invitation actually) to take a seat on one side of the table, while Latisha and the guy—Lampack is his name—sit on the other side. There's an empty seat next to me, but Flynn chooses to stand, leaning against the wall. Latisha and Lampack have notebooks, and Lampack also has a plain manilla folder in front of him. For a second, I feel like the kid in school who failed to come prepared because I don't have any writing materials with me. Maybe it would have made sense to bring Danny or Ariana just to take notes.

Latisha turns on the recorder and announces the date and time and the names of everyone present. Then Lampack takes over, which turns out to be an excuse to go over everything again. He says as much.

"I know you've been through it, and Detective Thompson has briefed me, but it would help if you could start at the beginning, when you first met Senator Morgan."

I tell the story again quickly—I know it by heart by now—and I try to show no emotion this time. I look at Latisha more than Lampack, but she's staring down at the table, showing no sense of what she's thinking. Probably bored, having heard it all before. Twice.

When I finish, Lampack asks a few questions about the harassment, focusing a lot on dates that I don't have. I give him the sequence as best I can. It only takes a minute for me to realize they've been examining my phone records, because a lot of the questions are about when I called Wade, especially in the period after the breakup. Fortunately, after the harassment started, I stuck mostly to emails.

I do my best to answer them and Lampack keeps nodding. I can see I'm confirming what he already knows.

Then he opens the folder and pulls out several sheets of paper. "Thank you for letting us look at your phone records," he says, as though I had a choice. "We've been going through them, and for the most part they confirm what you told us."

'For the most part' is all I hear.

"But there are a couple of anomalies," he says, and slides one of the sheets in front of me.

"On March 18th, you received a call from another cell. It lasted for four and a half minutes. Can you tell us who called you?"

What a fool I am. I should have remembered. I try not to show a reaction. "It was from Wade," I say. "It was after my last attempt to get him to leave me alone."

"What did he say?"

"He again denied everything. Then he tried to talk me into seeing him again, but I refused."

Lampack offers no comment on that, but his finger moves further down the list of calls. "On March 21st," he says, "you made a call, highlighted on the sheet, to a number with a 240 area code. Can you identify that call for us?"

I look at it and swallow hard. "The number doesn't ring a bell with me," I say. "Whose number is it?"

"It leads to a prepaid phone. One that was purchased with cash at a 7-Eleven a few blocks from your house."

As hard as it is, I look at him with what I hope is a blank expression.

"Still doesn't ring a bell?" he asks.

"No."

"The call only lasted a few seconds."

I shake my head. "I don't know what it was. Maybe a wrong number."

"Have you ever purchased a prepaid phone? What's commonly referred to as a burner?"

I look at him and then to Latisha. "Wade wanted me to buy one for when we talked, but I could never see the point."

"And after you broke up, you never bought one."

"What would I need one for? I have a phone."

"Indeed," he says.

Lampack reaches across and retrieves the sheet of paper and puts it back in the folder. The silence is deafening and I finally break it.

"You don't know whose phone it is?" I ask.

Lampack makes eye contact. "Not yet. We're working on it. We do know it was used only one other time, the day the senator was killed."

I don't try to speak. I can't. Latisha and Lampack exchange a look, but neither says anything. They wait for me to break the silence and finally I do.

"Can't you trace the numbers and locations of cellphones?" I ask with as much bravery as I can muster. "Won't that help you figure this out?"

Lampack answers without answering. "Sometimes. Depends on the phone, cell towers, that kind of thing." He gives me a look that is meant to be penetrating, and it is.

"Well, I hope you can find out," I say. "You seem to feel it's important."

"Could be," he says.

I wait to see if he has anything else, but Lampack thanks me and says I can go.

Some New Clues

Sam hears the excitement in Molly's voice. "I think the task force is getting close. Two big developments. Get here when you can."

At the office, he finds Brenda, Molly, and Allison Tinh, the paper's police reporter, gathered in a conference room. Brenda brings him up to speed.

"One of Allison's sources told her that the cops got the phone number on a new burner phone that Morgan was using in the weeks before he was killed, and they were able to track it on the night of the murder to the picnic spot in Rock Creek Park where they found his body. They still haven't found the phone, and there was no signal after eight p.m. And Molly was able to confirm that with one of her sources."

Sam glances at Molly. He doesn't need to ask who her source is.

"There's more," Brenda says. "Allison says the FBI found evidence on Morgan's laptop confirming he was harassing the woman he broke up with a few months ago, even posting revenge porn."

"Did they give Allison the name of the woman?" he asks Brenda, not looking at Molly.

"No," she says. "No names."

"Can we use this?" Molly asks.

"I don't see why not," Brenda adds. "We know the woman told police he did it and now they've confirmed it. What's to stop us?"

Sam doesn't object because he can't. "As long as we're careful and just say what we know and attribute it all to FBI and police sources. We have to be careful not to imply it was the motive for his murder. We don't know how or if the two things are connected."

Sam gets up and paces. "So where does that leave us?" he asks. "Morgan sends his security team home and goes to a secluded spot in Rock Creek Park. That all suggests he was planning on meeting someone—maybe a woman—and presumably she kills him."

"Or hired someone to kill him," Molly says.

"But why would Morgan agree to the park instead of the woman's house, which was his usual pattern?"

"Maybe she's married and they didn't have a place," Brenda offers. "And he didn't want to be seen in a hotel where he might be recognized. Or maybe it wasn't a woman."

Sam shakes his head several times, frustration knitting his brow. "Something's not right. Something's missing. It's too farfetched."

They all look at him, but no one says anything.

They spend some time talking about how to frame the story and when to put it on the web so that other papers don't have enough time to catch up before tonight's press run.

Sam wonders if he should contact Kelly, tell her the police have confirmed Morgan's harassment while warning her that someone is leaking information and it won't be long before her name comes out. He can't decide so instead he calls Danny.

"How's Kelly doing?" Sam asks.

"She's terrible. The police called her back for a third interview—this time with the FBI present—and they gave her a very hard time. They've been going through her phone records and she said they asked all sorts of questions. I don't understand it. She'd already told them all about the affair and the harassment. I can't imagine what she's upset about."

Sam can, but he doesn't enlighten Danny with news about the burner phone that was purchased at the 7-Eleven near Kelly's house and the four-second call she made to it. "I'm afraid it's going to get worse before it gets better," he says. He tells him what the paper is going to report in its next story. "We won't use her name, but I'm getting the sense that eventually it's going to come out. You might want to prepare her for that."

"Jesus," Danny says. "She's so fragile. That could push her over the edge."

"Is she getting help?" Sam asks.

"Ariana goes over every day, but Kelly won't let her stay long."

"I meant professional help. Is she still seeing her shrink?"

"She does, but I don't know how that's going. What she really needs is a lawyer, but she won't hear of it. Says that makes her look guilty."

"That's crazy. If you do one thing, make her get a lawyer."

As soon as he hangs up, Sam dials Molly's extension. "You talked to your source? How'd that go?"

"Well enough. He wanted to meet me, but I told him I was on deadline and needed the confirmation. He gave it to me, then hinted he'd have more soon, and we should plan on getting together."

"I know I told you to avoid him, but he's not going to let you. You're going to have to tell him why you won't see him."

"Yeah, I know. But I still need him as a source. I've come this far, and I can't see the harm in postponing it as long as I can."

"If he thinks you're using him, it could get ugly."

"It's already ugly. He just doesn't know it yet."

Sam thinks about that, decides he doesn't know what it means, but doesn't ask. "Be careful with him. Let me know if I can help."

"Don't worry. I'm a big girl."

A Reporter and Her Sources

The school has told Sam that he's obliged to follow the syllabus, but he surprises his seminar—and himself—with a last-minute switch.

"We'll get to privacy in a bit, but I want to start by following up on our discussion earlier this spring on sources and talk about how we balance the need to establish a trusting relationship with a source and the equally important need of keeping a distance. It's tough in a city like Washington, where reporters often mingle with newsmakers, attending private dinner parties at one another's homes, sharing lunch, or playing golf. Given that, how do you stay neutral?"

Danny's hand shoots up. He and Ariana are here this week. "If you're friends with someone, you shouldn't be reporting on that person or any story he's involved in," Danny says. "You have to recuse yourself from anything he tells you."

"Is that realistic?" Sam asks.

Josh answers him before Danny can speak. "How will you ever get a scoop if you're that strict? You have to depend on friendships. Enemies won't help you."

Cynthia Bergman, the class elder, suggests a middle ground. "I think you can't accept information from a friend or good acquaintance if he or she plays a key role in the story—or if you think they did something wrong or is covering up wrongdoing. But you can't have a blanket policy against all friends. You have to take it on a case-by-case basis."

They debate it for a few minutes before Sam interrupts, essentially agreeing with Cynthia without putting it that way. "Let me give you an example," he says. "There's a guy I served with in the Marines. We became close friends and now he's in a position to help me with a story I'm working on. I've used him as a source, letting him decide what he's comfortable sharing. Is that wrong?"

"Aren't you guilty of using him?" Danny asks.

"In a way, but he's a big boy. He knows what I do and why I'm asking him questions. He's free to not answer, and sometimes he won't."

No one responds right away and Sam waits.

"I'll give you an even harder situation," he says to break the silence. "What about when a reporter is married to an administration official or a member of Congress? Maybe even a lawyer representing someone involved in a scandal? Remember when there were questions about Andrea Mitchell, the NBC reporter, who is married to Alan Greenspan, the former Federal Reserve chairman? How do you handle that?"

Cynthia raises her hand, and Sam calls on her. "You have to set ground rules from the start, and probably the best ground rule is not to share anything. The official should never put the spouse in the position of hiding a good story."

"Nice thought," Sam says, "but that can make for a marriage that is less than ideal. In a good relationship, one advantage is sharing problems. And if one spouse is hiding a tough dilemma, it can take a toll."

He looks around and they are all following him closely. "I think you set limits—if one party is a member of Congress, for example, obviously the reporter shouldn't cover Congress. And he or she shouldn't cover any story related to Congress. And anytime you get close to the line, you need to let your editor know."

"It can work the other way too," Eliza says. "Maybe your paper is working on a big story and if you told your Congressman-husband, he'd want to warn his colleagues. You'd have to keep that secret too."

"Absolutely," Sam says.

"Sounds like you shouldn't get married in the first place," Josh says, and several students laugh.

Sam uses the moment to change the equation.

"Here's a related issue. You want to develop a relationship with someone who might be able to give you information on a continuing basis. You chat, you have lunch together, you start to develop trust. But how far can you go? Is it okay to pursue a friendship with someone just so you get information?"

They think about that.

"I think it is," Sam says when no one raises a hand, "but within reason. Like most of the things we talk about here, there are a lot of gray areas. One extreme here is to refuse to be friendly at all, to make no attempt to establish a relationship. That won't allow you to do your job. And at the other extreme is the reporter—male or female—willing to sleep with a source solely to get more information. But where exactly do you draw the line? Is it okay, for example, to flirt with a source as a way to get friendly?"

"What do you mean by flirting?" Ariana asks. It's the first time she's participated and Sam suspects she's having trouble concentrating on anything but Kelly.

"You tell me," Sam says.

She doesn't answer right away and no one pops up to help.

"This is not an uncommon situation," Sam says. "Let me tell you one story. Awhile back, when I was an editor and looking to pick someone to cover the White House, I asked the reporter leaving the post for advice on what to look for. She surprised me by telling me to hire an attractive young woman. 'It makes a difference if you flirt a little bit,' she told me. 'It loosens up the men who run this place.'"

Sam pauses for effect, then continues. "That really caught me by surprise—not because I doubted it—but because I wouldn't have expected her to tell me to take advantage of it. That was twenty years ago, and attitudes have changed for the better, so maybe that would never happen again. Or maybe no one would admit it still happens. I'm afraid it does. And it would do all of you good—no matter your gender—to think about how you would set boundaries. Would you intentionally flirt if you thought your pretended interest would get you more information? And would you put up with flirting to get information? And, as Ariana points out, flirting is a pretty general term. You have to decide on your boundaries."

Sam notices that Cynthia is shaking her head, a grim look on her face, and he asks her what she disagrees with.

"Why are you focusing on sex? That only feeds the stereotype of women sleeping their way to the top. Men are just as guilty of deception that can be just as bad. What about losing a game of golf on purpose or giving a source the impression you're on his side when you're not? Reporters are deceptive all the time."

"Not all the time," Sam says. "That's not true."

But Cynthia is on a roll. "Wasn't there a famous case where a reporter pretended to side with a murderer and then got sued for taking advantage of what he told him?" she asks.

"Yes, that's a good example," Sam says. "How many of you know what she's referring to?"

He sees a lot of blank stares so he explains. "A reporter, Joe McGinniss, was working on a book about Jeffrey MacDonald, who was on trial for murder. MacDonald and his attorneys cooperated with the author, thinking he was sympathetic, but when his book proved to be otherwise, they sued him. The case was ultimately settled, but another reporter, Janet Malcolm, later wrote a couple of *New Yorker* articles, and eventually a book about the whole thing, examining the ethics of source relationships."

Sam takes a minute to rummage through his briefcase and pulls out a copy. "It's become a classic and I almost made it part of our syllabus, but let me read you one quote: 'Every journalist who is not too stupid or too full of himself to notice what is going on knows that what he does is morally indefensible. He is a kind of confidence man, preying on people's vanity, ignorance, or loneliness, gaining their trust and betraying them without remorse.'"

Sam stops and gives the class time to absorb what he's read. "Do you agree?" he asks.

"Yes," Danny answers with a sigh in his voice. "To a degree anyway. Reporters do take advantage of vulnerable people."

"Agreed," Sam says, "but it's not always a one-way street. Sometimes sources take advantage of reporters too, especially here in Washington. Often the source is more sophisticated than the reporter and knows he has the upper hand. The reporter can be desperate for a tip, willing to push the point of view, knowingly or unwittingly, that the source wants to push."

Sam asks if they could cite any examples, but the quote seems to have hit them hard. They sit in silence, and Sam decides to leave it at that.

A Bold Encounter

Out in the parking lot, Sam checks his car for any sign of tampering before climbing in and starting home. He turns on the radio to get the latest news and catches a fortuitous traffic report on WTOP. There's been an accident on the outer loop of the Beltway, a tractor trailer truck has overturned and there's a huge backup.

He checks his navigation system for an alternate route and begins an unfamiliar trek that will allow him to get around the beltway backup. He pulls out, checks carefully to see if anyone is following him, and turns his attention to the GPS.

Within a few minutes he sees a car behind him. He can't tell much in the dark, but he tries to remember the arrangement of the headlights so he can tell if the same car sticks with him.

The road he's on twists more than he expects and, not being familiar with the area, he slows down and concentrates on the turns. He glances at his rear-view mirror and sees what he believes is the same car. When he reaches a wide spot in the road, he pulls over to let it pass. All he can tell is that it is white and going faster than it should.

He starts up again, hits a straightaway of sorts, and picks up his speed. He reaches a small strip mall closed up tight, and as he passes, he sees a car pull out of the parking area and fall in behind him.

Is it the same car? The lights look similar, but he's not really sure. What he is sure of is that it is following too closely.

He picks up his speed and so does the other car. He glances to the left and right, looking for a place to pull over, but it's dark on both sides, and he can see the area to the right of the road slopes down, almost as if there is a creek down there.

He looks in the rear-view mirror and sees nothing. Too tense, he thinks, I'm imagining things. But he picks up his speed and moves toward the middle of the road, a position that will give him more options if he needs them.

Then he sees a shadow in his side mirror and quickly moves to the shoulder.

Thump.

The blow is glancing, thanks to his quick maneuver. He pulls to the side and watches the other car continue down the road, waiting until it's long out of sight.

He starts up slowly, keeping his eyes ahead of him in case the other car comes roaring back.

Within minutes, he sees that somehow it has gotten behind him again, and before he can react, it slams into his rear bumper again, this time sending his car off the side of the road. He feels it tipping and turns the wheel and steps on the gas out of instinct. The car straightens but the air bag has deployed, throwing him back against the seat, while his knee gets hit hard by something.

But he's not hurt seriously. He thinks about climbing out, but then wonders if the other driver will come after him, either to help or try to finish him off. He sees no one. The other car is gone.

He gets out gingerly and surveys the damage, first to himself and then to the car. He feels a sharp pain in his side when he moves and he figures a broken rib or two, but not much more. The car looks far worse.

A part of him would rather not call the police. They're sure to ask questions he'd rather not answer, but that's probably stupid. And not very practical. He can't walk home and leave the car. He dials 911 and sits on the ground to ease the pain and think.

Did someone just try to kill him?

Who?

Why?

He tells the officers who respond that it was a hit and run, leaving out the likelihood that it was intentional. He can't describe the other car and the only evidence is a smearing of white paint on Sam's blue Mazda. He spends the rest of the night in the ER getting checked over. Except for two cracked ribs and a badly bruised knee, the damage is minimal. He considers calling Molly or Lisa, but instead uses Uber to get home.

Back to Work (With a Limp)

Sam gets a few hours of fitful sleep and then gingerly climbs out of bed. Both sides of his chest hurt, and he has trouble standing on his leg but, after taking a painkiller, he finds he can walk well enough. He makes coffee, and as he carries it to the table, his hand shakes and he almost spills it.

He takes a few breaths, surprised at what he's feeling. Shit! He's been in combat, for god's sake. He survived a massive bomb attack on his barracks. Yes, he's been scared before, but that was with reason. This is nothing in comparison.

But then he realizes he's back in combat, at least a form of it. What happened was no accident. It could have been meant as a warning—one that got out of hand—or it could have been attempted murder.

Probably not attempted murder, he tells himself. Running someone off the road is no guarantee of getting your target, but clearly whoever did it was willing to accept his death if it came to that.

He can't see any motive for the attack but one: His investigation hit a nerve.

But where and with whom? It's not like he's figured anything out. He isn't close to a conclusion, but he must have said or done something somewhere along the way that made Morgan's killer think he was getting close. But closer than the police? It doesn't make sense.

He still doesn't want to tell the police any more than he has, but he knows he can't risk another attack, and he knows he can't protect himself without help. He digs around on his desk for the paper that Howie gave him and calls the protection agency he recommended. By using Howie's name, he's able to get through to the head of the agency, who agrees to send someone over to talk to him to see if they can help.

While he waits, Sam adds a little bourbon to his coffee, hoping to calm down. He's still angry at himself for being so rattled.

Who could want him dead? And who has the means to make it happen? It has to be someone who thinks he's close to finding Morgan's killer, and the only ones he's talked to about it are Kelly, Peg Morgan, and Wasserman. He can't see Kelly or Morgan trying to run him off the road, and Wasserman didn't seem that tough either. But it could be someone working with or for one of them.

He wants to talk to them all again, but Wasserman has gone missing and he's put Kelly off limits, at least for now, so he has to start with Peg Morgan.

He decides to change his approach. He needs to be more confrontational with her, if only to provoke another attack. She's been lying to him from the start, and he needs to know what she's hiding. He knows if he goes too far, she'll shut down and throw him out. His best bet is to make it clear he has new information she needs.

He starts to dial and then stops. How should he begin? If she's behind the attack, she'll be surprised to hear from him, though the other car never stopped to find out whether he was seriously hurt. Hard to know what to expect.

It takes a few rings before she answers, and obviously she's looked at the caller ID.

"Sam Turner," she says with something that sounds like sarcasm or mockery. "So good to hear from you."

"Can I see you?" he says. "There are some new developments I need to run by you."

"Such as?"

"Better we do it in person."

She hesitates, but he knows she's too curious to refuse. Still she puts him off until the evening. That's either to plan what she wants to say or to lay a trap.

Sam tries to rest while he waits for the security agency, and within seconds, he's asleep. An hour later, the buzzer wakes him.

Sasha Rudin is not what he expected. She's a couple of inches over five feet and slight, but she moves like she's in good shape, and when he quizzes her, she turns out to be ex-military. She's also been a cop, though she quit after two years. "The bureaucracy was almost as bad as the Army's," she says. "Anyway, how can we help?"

He pours coffee and they sit across from each other at a counter in the kitchen. "I need someone to watch my back," Sam says. "It may be nothing, but it's possible someone wants to kill me."

She raises an eyebrow at that. "You better start from the beginning."

He gives her a rough outline of the situation, leaving out many details and repeatedly downplaying his concern.

But she's not buying it. "If someone's trying to kill you, you should go to the police. This isn't a job for a private firm."

"I can't get them involved. It's not like someone is going to come at me with guns blazing. In fact, they seem fixated on my car. I just need someone to help me keep an eye out."

She keeps at him, probing for details and urging him to take it more seriously, but he's adamant. She asks for a private room to call her office, and he tells her to use the kitchen or the balcony. He's going to take a shower and get dressed.

When he emerges, she lays out the rules. "I'll drive you where you need to go, with backup as needed, but you have to follow my instructions. I'll try not to get in your way, but I won't let you take unnecessary risks. I'll be on twelve hours, with a replacement the other twelve unless you're safely settled in here. What kind of security does the building have?"

Before they finish talking, she makes him sign an agreement that includes a clause saying he declined her recommendation of a higher level of security and police involvement.

With several hours before his appointment with Peg Morgan, Sam decides to go see Howie. As they leave his apartment, he hands Sasha his car keys, then remembers he no longer has a car. He apologizes, but she shakes her head.

"We were going to use my car anyway," she says. "That's a rule."

It's midafternoon when they reach Howie's office, and Sam goes in alone while Sasha loiters outside. The receptionist says Howie is in, calls him, listens for fifteen seconds, and then tells Sam she's sorry, but they have nothing to tell the press. Captain Stone won't see him.

Sam understands. The heat is on and Howie has to feign a cold shoulder, at least officially. Sam goes for a walk, his limp obvious, with Sasha not far behind, and he's not surprised when Howie calls. They agree to meet in a secluded corner of a hotel bar. When Howie arrives, Sam can immediately see he's stressed.

"Who the hell is talking to you guys?" he says by way of a greeting.

It takes Sam a minute to realize that Howie is referring to yesterday's story adding details about the last weeks and minutes of Senator Wade Morgan's life. He finds it hard to believe that was just a day ago.

"You know I can't answer that," Sam says.

"You didn't get that from us."

"No. Everything in the paper came from another source."

"Even so, if they find out I've been talking to you, they'll assume it all came from me."

Sam tries a smile. "So, you had all that stuff and held out on me."

Howie rolls his eyes. "Actually it was mostly news to me. I'm not part of the inner circle. Apart from limited briefings, I get most of my information from the security guys we had on Morgan. They've been assigned to help with the investigation."

"But it's true? We got it right? No mistakes?"

"How would I know?"

"What else is happening? Did they get the security video from the 7-Eleven? Was it the woman who had the problem with Morgan that bought the phone?"

"I can't tell you anything else. This has got to be our last meeting. It's too risky for me to be seen with you."

"We could talk by phone. But you wouldn't get a free drink or breakfast out of it."

Howie doesn't even smile.

"Just tell me if the video shows she bought the phone," Sam says. "Shake your head if it wasn't her."

Howie looks at Sam, then finishes his beer. "I gotta go."

But he doesn't. "This is the last thing I'm giving you. It looks like her, but they can't be a hundred percent sure."

Sam nods. If they're not sure, he doesn't know what to do with the information. "Was the phone used for anything else? Besides the four-second call from Kelly's regular cellphone."

A look of resignation appears on Howie's face. "The day of the murder. Morgan called it from his own burner."

Sam shakes his head. "I'm confused. You're saying she buys this burner a couple of days before the murder, calls it the same day, and then Morgan calls it from his own burner the day he died, each time for a few seconds?"

"Morgan's call lasted several minutes."

"It still makes no sense. What do they make of it?"

"They're still working on it. The obvious guess is that whoever he called led to his being in Rock Creek Park where he got murdered. Could be the woman or someone she gave the phone to."

"You can't prove that. The call may be completely unrelated to what happened later."

"I'm just saying what it looks like. If we knew for sure, someone would probably be behind bars."

Sam tries to come up with another explanation. Morgan could have called Kelly to argue his case and the timing could be a coincidence. No way to tell. "Do they have Morgan's burner?" he asks Howie.

"No. We can't find it. He left his regular cell at the house on the night he died, but there's nothing useful on it."

"Was the 7-Eleven phone the woman supposedly bought tracked to Rock Creek or just Morgan's phone?"

"I don't know if they have that information yet. I haven't heard. Tracking a phone's history, especially when it's dead, isn't as easy as it looks on television."

When Sam doesn't say anything to that, Howie says again that he has to go, but Sam raises a hand to stop him.

"I took your advice," he says. "I hired some private security." Sam goes on to explain, ignoring the look of concern he sees when he gets to the accident.

Howie looks around the bar. "Where are they?"

"She," Sam says. "And she's outside. I told her to stay out of sight. No one's going to attack me in a public place.

Howie spends a few more minutes trying to talk Sam into going to the police but then gives up. "I have to get out of here, and I can't be seen with you again."

Sam watches him walk out, deeply concerned by everything he's heard. It may not be conclusive, but one sure thing is that Kelly is in trouble. Why would she buy a burner phone, then call it from her own phone? And why would Morgan call that phone the day he was killed? He remembers the hit man theory, but why would Morgan call the hit man? Unless he was being blackmailed. Is that possible? He plays with the thought for a few seconds but knows that if Kelly bought a burner and gave it to someone else, it would still make her guilty. Of something.

He considers calling Molly with the news about the phone calls. But he doesn't.

Is It Always the Wife?

Sam's next stop is the Morgan household. He tells Sasha to park in front of the house next door, and he calls Peg, tells her he's fifteen minutes away, and apologizes for being early. He's not surprised when she sounds annoyed and ends the call quickly.

After he hangs up, he and Sasha settle in to wait and watch, for what he's not sure. Sasha doesn't ask any questions. She's obviously used to the whims of her clients.

Sam's reward comes five minutes later when the garage door opens, and a car backs out. He has Sasha follow a few blocks, long enough to get a license plate off the black Acura SUV, the kind rich people, or security details, are likely to drive. Then he asks Sasha to double back to Peg's house. Before he gets out, he hands Sasha a slip of paper with the plate number.

"Can you track this down?"

She takes the paper without answering, and Sam gingerly gets out and walks to Peg Morgan's front door.

"Thanks for seeing me," he says when she opens it.

"You didn't give me much choice." She's dressed even more casually than last time, in jeans and a natty looking sweater, no longer in black.

He starts for the living room, but she stops him and steers him down a hallway. Sam notices that she follows instead of leading the way and tries to walk as normally as he can on his bum knee. If she's surprised that he's survived the accident relatively unscathed, she hides it well.

She directs him into a room off the hall, a study that is clearly hers, not her late husband's. Its walls are filled with certificates of Peg's awards for volunteer work and photos that show her with her sleeves rolled up at soup kitchens or thrift shops. The only picture of Wade Morgan sits by itself on a credenza.

She takes a seat behind the desk and he takes the only other one available, which faces her. A power game, he thinks. It certainly isn't the friendly setting and atmosphere that marked their earlier meetings, although he'd always known that was fake.

"You said you had something for me," she says.

He doesn't respond directly. "Did it surprise you that the FBI traced the revenge porn to his computer?" he asks.

She looks at him, then turns away. "I wasn't surprised. He could be stupid when it came to his little floozies."

"Really? You left me with the impression they were never very important to him." He waits a beat, then adds, "and therefore they were never important to you."

"Don't be so literal. Of course, it hurt. A little, anyway. But I knew he'd never leave me."

"So you said."

She turns back to him and squints in disapproval. "I meant it. Look, you said you had new information. What is it?"

Sam stands up, does his best not to limp, and paces, though the room is too small, and he knows he's being rude by turning his back to her. But what he's about to say needs to sound as if he's reluctant to disclose it. Plus, he knows how risky it is.

"They're looking at the woman who was the target of the revenge porn. Very hard."

"But do they have any evidence against her? What did she tell them?"

"They have some evidence that suggests she wasn't completely honest with them. They're looking very hard at her."

"I suppose they're looking hard at everyone, including me, and including that leftwing nut who made the threats."

"What makes you believe they're looking at you?"

She shrugs. "What about his latest floozy? What makes them so suspicious of her?"

Sam is still pacing, and she tells him it's annoying, asks him to sit. He takes one last look around the room and his eyes settle on her cell phone, which has fallen into the crevice of an easy chair. He lifts it up, surprised that it's an inexpensive one—he would have expected her to have the latest iPhone—and hands it to her as he returns to his chair. She slips it into a drawer.

"It's actually a cellphone that has them looking harder at the other woman," Sam says, gesturing to the phone she just put in the drawer. "They think she bought a burner the week before the senator was killed, and they don't know why."

Peg takes a minute before answering. "Maybe she has a new boyfriend. I'm sure it didn't take her long to find one. Anyway, there's no law against having a phone."

Sam considers telling her about the suspicious phone calls, the four-second call and the longer one from Senator Morgan to the burner on the day he died, but he doesn't.

"I don't know what it means," he says instead, "but they are hoping the phone will eventually tell them what they need to know."

"And that's it? You couldn't have told me that on the telephone."

He shrugs and then gets up. "Well, I won't keep you," he says.

She starts to walk him out, then stumbles and knocks against him. He can't help but utter a sound of pain.

"Are you okay? Did I hurt you?"

"I'm fine, just startled," he says and picks up the pace despite his discomfort.

When they reach the front door, he asks a final question. "Shouldn't you have some security around?"

"No, they've set me free. Just as well. I never liked having those guys around, and I can't see why anyone would want to hurt me. I'm harmless."

He thanks her and leaves, goes straight to the car. His knee is barking and at least one of his ribs feels like it's stabbing him, but he tells Sasha he's fine when she asks.

As soon as he's back in his apartment, he takes a painkiller and chases it with a couple fingers of bourbon, telling himself that it's the best way to get some sleep.

Kelly

I can't go on. There's no point. There's no way out. I can keep pretending I'm innocent, but they know too much. What's the point?

If anyone ever made a mess of her life, it's me. I had everything to live for, every chance to accomplish something useful. Hah! I was going to make a difference. Well, I guess I did. Just not the kind I expected.

I've been so stupid. From day one. From the first time I slept with him. I can't believe I ever thought he loved me. I thought I'd be okay when I finally got up the courage to end it. Until that point, my life was salvageable. But when the attacks began . . .

Those pictures. Oh, I can't even think about what will happen when my name gets out. Everyone with an internet connection will be looking at them.

I should have given up when Wade denied everything. Just quit my job and run to the other side of the country. It would have stopped then. There would have been no point.

But it's too late. Woulda . . . Coulda . . . Shoulda. What difference does it make now? If only I could have it all back. But I can't.

I call out to Lassie and she wanders over, jumps on the couch and onto my lap, almost spilling the bottle of wine. I can't believe I'm drinking out of the bottle. Never did that before. Of course, I'm racking up firsts every day, doing things I never thought I'd do. I wasn't that kind of girl. Or maybe I was.

The email to Turner. Why did I write that? And what made me think I could handle the police? Well, I suppose I had no choice but to try. By then, the die was cast. It probably didn't make any difference what I did at that point. I had already made too many mistakes. It was bound to unravel.

I take another drink, finishing the bottle and putting it on the table, right next to the Ambien and the Xanax. Always good to have my friends nearby. Be prepared, as the Boy Scouts would say. That's another organization that let me down. A once upstanding example for young men that proved to be a bunch of perverted pedophiles. Or is that redundant? Can you have a pedophile who's not perverted?

The wine is taking its effect. Which was the idea. Not enough though. Wish I had something stronger. Liquor is quicker. Isn't there some saying about that?

I add a cigarette to the mix. Usually I go outside on the balcony, but what difference does it make now? Unfortunately, Lassie hates the smoke and goes into the bedroom, leaving me alone with my less affectionate friends.

Is there any way out? Or is it too late? How can I explain the phone calls to dear old Latisha and that nasty Lampack? Talk about good cop/bad cop. They're probably both Democrats.

They'll trace the burner to me. Probably the clerk at the 7-Eleven will identify me. He can't possibly remember me, but they'll get him to say so. They have their ways. I know all about that. Seen it on TV.

I hear a noise and go out on the balcony, half expecting to see the cops, but there's no one. Getting paranoid, though something tells me it's only a matter of time until they arrive.

Is it too late to run? But what will that mean? I can't run forever, and they'll never stop looking for me.

No. There's no way out of this.

ANOTHER DEATH?

Danny wakes Sam up at midnight, just moments after he'd lulled himself into sleep with another painkiller. "It's Kelly," Danny says. "An overdose. She might not make it."

Danny's tone is matter of fact and calm, and Sam's first thought is to wonder why he's not more upset. Or not surprised. But that's silly. He may be in shock or maybe it hasn't hit yet.

"What happened?"

"Looks like she took a bunch of pills, but she must have had second thoughts because she called Ariana. She didn't say anything, just hung up. But Ariana called back and when she got no answer, she called 911. She got there as the police arrived, and they broke down the door, found her unconscious, and rushed her to the hospital, but they're not making any predictions. She's still unconscious."

"A coma?"

"I'm not sure. Ariana's there and I'm going over shortly."

"Had she said anything about suicide? I know she was depressed, but I didn't think it had reached that point."

Danny takes offense. "We've been trying to see her every day, trying to take care of her, but she usually sent us away after a few minutes. We did what we could."

"I didn't mean it that way."

"I should go. I want to get down there."

"Please keep me posted."

Sam hangs up, sits down, and tries to assess his feelings. He gets up and starts pacing the apartment, but his leg feels worse than ever and he goes over to the couch and lies down. Is he partly to blame? What could he have done to prevent this? He feels guilty, no question there, but he's not sure where he went wrong. Would it have helped if he'd gone to see her after she talked to the police? No, it wouldn't. Because he wouldn't have gone to help. He would have gone to get information, asked questions, added to the pressure, and probably made it worse. Is that why he feels guilty?

But that's what journalists do, isn't it? Of course, the real problem is that he tried to walk that line between being of some help to her and being a journalist. He was doomed from the moment he got the email. Maybe he should have gone right to the police. If he had, maybe Morgan would still be alive and Kelly wouldn't be in a hospital bed.

Sam gets up carefully, looks at a clock, and decides it's okay to take another pill. He lies down to think it through again, trying to put the guilt aside and figure out what he should do now.

What does a suicide attempt mean? That she was guilty? Or that she couldn't take the pressure because she knew the affair was about to come out? Could be either, but most people, including the cops, will assume she's guilty. The phone business pointed that way, and if she dies, there may never be a definitive answer. In fact, if she dies, it will be easy to consider the case closed.

He still finds it hard to believe she killed Morgan. She never seemed emotionally strong enough. But desperate people do desperate things, and it was clear from their first meeting that she was desperate, truly desperate.

He closes his eyes and within seconds he's asleep, but the pain returns at dawn, in time to wake him up for another day.

He takes a shower, dresses, and reminds himself he has another decision to make. Should he tell Molly about the suicide attempt? Doing so might trigger the release of Kelly's name, and while he knows that's probably inevitable, he wants to delay it as long as he can. He calls Danny instead and asks what hospital they're at.

"Adventist in White Oak," he tells him.

"Mind if I come out there and wait with you?"

There's a beat before Danny answers. "I can't stop you," he says, "but I don't understand why. It's not like she'll talk to you or any other reporter if she wakes up."

"I'm not coming as a journalist."

"Then why?"

It's a good question and Sam doesn't answer. "See you a little later," is all he says.

Sasha drops Sam off at the entrance to the hospital, and he finds Danny and Ariana huddled in a corner of a waiting room. Danny raises his head in acknowledgment, but Ariana looks away. The room is cold and she's wearing her coat, but Sam senses there's more to the chilly atmosphere than a poorly performing thermostat.

"She's still unconscious," Danny says.

"Where's her family?" Sam asks.

"Michigan. They're on their way. Thank God the doctor called them. I was afraid I was going to have to."

"What about the task force? Have they been notified?"

Danny looks to Ariana, who finally turns to Sam. "Not that I know of. The doctors say they'll do a psychiatric evaluation when they can and decide what happens after that."

Sam nods, but this isn't what he meant. "The police need to know she's here. She's still a suspect in a high-profile murder. Or at least a person of interest. A witness. Whatever. The task force needs to know."

"Then you call them," Ariana says.

Sam doesn't say anything and Ariana gets angry. "What's it any of your business? Why are you even here?"

"Because you talked her into writing to me. You two got me involved. I don't know why you're blaming me."

"When was the last time you talked to her?" she asks.

"Apart from a brief phone call, not since that time at your apartment."

"Ariana," Danny says. "He's right. This is not his fault."

Ariana bursts into tears, then gets up and walks away. Danny looks at Sam and shakes his head. "I'm sorry. She's upset. She blames herself."

Sam tells himself to relax and be patient. "It's natural enough. We're all going to wonder if we did everything we could have done."

Danny keeps his eyes on his hands, which are clasped and resting on his lap, making him look like a schoolboy at church having trouble staying quiet. "Kelly was in a tough spot," he says. "I don't know if I would have handled it any better. But she made some big mistakes."

Sam catches the import. "What are you saying? What don't I know?"

"A lot, but I'm not sure I'm the right one to tell you."

They sit there in silence until Ariana returns. She apologizes for her outburst. "I should have called someone," she says. "I knew she was desperate and how closed-in she was feeling."

"Because of the police?" Sam asks. "Did they really think she was guilty?"

"Who knows? The point is, Kelly *felt* guilty. And maybe she was."

Sam is surprised by the comment. "Guilty of what? I thought she was the victim."

Ariana and Danny exchange a look. "That's not the whole story," he says, which is already obvious.

"So tell me," Sam says. "How can it hurt?"

Danny turns to Ariana and she sighs and begins. "I don't know the whole story. In fact, until two days ago, I didn't know a lot of it. But then Kelly told me that after she met you, she got angry at herself, and at us, for bringing you into it. She didn't think the police would do anything about a senator, and she didn't think the newspaper could do anything. So she tried one more time to plead with Morgan."

"She went to see him?" Sam asks.

"I'm not sure how much of this to believe. She was very upset and had been drinking when she told me this. But she said she went and surprised Morgan one day when he was coming back to his office after a Senate vote. He denied harassing her, as he always did, but later he sent her an email saying he'd figured out who was behind it and would make sure it stopped. Kelly said she was relieved at first. She didn't know exactly what he meant, but figured it was his way of promising he'd stop bothering her. But then she got another photo by email, the worst one yet, and she knew it wasn't going to end."

Ariana stops and Sam is afraid that this is the end of the story. "And then what?" he prompts.

"We don't know," Ariana says, "but I think she went to see Morgan's wife. She'd threatened to do that. She wanted to confront her, get her to make him leave her alone."

"But did she actually do it?" Sam asks.

"This will sound bad, but Kelly passed out before finishing the story. But she must have gone to see her."

"She passed out?" Sam asks. "From drinking?"

"Yes, and probably that was on top of too many pills. And that's partly my fault. I gave her some of them, though I didn't know she had access to others."

Sam waits to see if there is more, but neither Danny nor Ariana says anything. He tries to process it all, but he's overwhelmed. He wonders what he would have done if he'd known, what he could have done, and he can't think of anything. But he still can't figure out how the situation went from A to B to C.

"So you don't know whether she actually confronted his wife?"

"Not for sure," Ariana says. "But in hindsight, the way her behavior changed—she must have."

"How did her behavior change?"

"Less depressed. More confident her problem would go away."

Sam thinks about that. "If she went to Morgan's wife, when would that have been?"

"It couldn't have been long before the murder," Danny says. "There wasn't that much time between when she threatened to go and Morgan's death."

"Could Kelly have killed him?"

"No," Ariana says. "She had plenty of motive, but she was falling apart. If he'd attacked her or something, maybe, but to plan and then actually shoot him, no, I'll never believe that."

Sam doesn't know why, but he agrees. Still, it took a lot of courage to confront Morgan's wife if she did, and he can't understand where that strength came from either, though he keeps the thought to himself. One thing he does know is that if she did meet with Peg Morgan, Kelly held back that information when he met with her after the murder. And Peg lied about it too, although he's beginning to realize she lied about almost everything.

"The police need to know what you've told me," he tells them. "It changes the whole course of their investigation. If Kelly had told them, everything might have been different."

"So why didn't she?" Danny asks, with an edge to his voice. "Why didn't she tell them? That's what I can't get my head around. She told them about the affair, about the pictures. If Morgan—or his wife—was threatening her or blackmailing her, why wouldn't she tell them that? It doesn't make sense unless she had something else to hide, unless she really did kill him."

Ariana shakes her head while Danny is speaking, and Sam can see they've already had this discussion. "You don't know her the way I do," Ariana says. "I know with every bone in my body that she didn't kill him. I just do."

She stands and walks away, leaving Sam and Danny in silence, with Sam thinking that what Danny said makes sense if you're trying to be logical, but there's so much emotion and pain involved in this situation, logic doesn't seem to have a place. Still, there's a lot that he can't make sense of, including what the police have learned about the phones.

He stands up, ready to go, but just then the doctor comes out. He mistakenly assumes Sam is Kelly's father, but Sam corrects him, says Kelly's parents haven't arrived, though they're on the way. Danny asks how Kelly is and the doctor gives an uncertain look. "The next few hours will be crucial," he says. "That's all I can tell you."

Before he leaves, Sam pulls Danny aside and asks him if he's going to call the police and tell them about Kelly's overdose. "If you don't, I will," Sam warns. "They need to know, and they'll find out sooner or later. No point in getting you or Ariana in any trouble."

Danny shakes his head. "Ariana would kill me."

He leaves it at that, and Sam understands he's asking too much. As soon as he settles in Sasha's car, he calls Howie and gives him the word. He then calls Molly. Within an hour, the story is on the newspaper's internet site. It says the woman who accused Morgan of posting revenge porn may have attempted suicide, but they still aren't using Kelly's name. It's a small victory, but he'll take it.

PEG

Damn! Just when I thought I'd succeeded, everything goes haywire. Isn't that the way it always is? Well, it's only a temporary setback, and maybe not even that.

Larry wants to come over tonight, but I won't let him. Truth is, Larry always wants to come over. He's another problem I have to deal with. Not sure how yet. He's easy to control—and easy to keep an eye on—as long as I let him think I care about him, but I'm running out of acting skills. I suppose I can always let his wife find out and let her rein him in. That seems to be the new go-to method for keeping a guy away. Or maybe I'll join the #MeToo thing. I'm sure Larry won't want to lose his job.

No, better to let his wife find out, without it being traced back to me. That's a whole lot safer. I can't afford to have him mad at me. I'd rather have things to hold over his head than the other way around.

I'm dying to call the hospital and find out what's going on, but I don't dare. The stories on the web say she's fighting for her life. Larry tells me cops are outside her room. Not sure what that means. I guess they want to talk to her in case she wakes up. If she knows what's good for her, she won't. Doesn't sound like she will.

That should put an end to it all and get me out of their sights. They have to see suicide as an admission of guilt. I know how badly they want to wrap this up, and a solution has been handed to them on a platter—or a gurney, as the case may be.

She better not wake up, although if she does, I bet she's no more than a vegetable. Even if she tells them about me, they'll never believe it. She certainly can't prove anything. Any roads that lead back to this house will lead to Wade.

What an idiot he was. Did he think I'd never find out? Did he think I didn't know about the burners and check them regularly? You'd think he could have found a better place to hide them, but he was always too cocky, assuming I was too dumb or didn't care. The first time I stumbled across one, he was right there, and he made up some cockamamie explanation as to why he needed a private phone for top-secret calls. Right, as though the cheap thing he had could be confused with something encrypted for secret information.

He was right about one thing. I was willing to put up with his cheap whores, as long as he was discreet and changed them out often enough. Not that I didn't regularly check and keep tabs on them. That's how I found the texts. And the pictures. So disgusting. As though it was all worth documenting for posterity. Or what? To assure their silence?

It took all my willpower not to confront him, but I still believed his other women were no real threat. Until Kelly Lancaster came along. That got too serious too quickly. The texts with her were different, too much like when we first were dating. He even used some of the same lines. I had to put a stop to that.

And his carelessness made it so easy. I just sent the pictures from his phone to the laptop and then pretended I was him. And it wasn't hard to intercept most of her emails to him. The only surprise was that it took so long for him to figure out that I was the one making the bitch's life hell and blaming it on him.

Ha! I got the last laugh there.

I admit he surprised me when he finally confronted me and said he was going to divorce me because of it. Really? It was over between them by then anyway, but he said he could never forgive me. What I had done was too awful and he didn't care what the political ramifications were. Our marriage was over.

The gall. What *I* did was awful? Who was he kidding? I didn't believe him for a minute, and I told him so. And then to prove I wasn't intimidated, I sent that last photo. The most disgusting of all. She actually looked like she was enjoying herself. Remembering it almost makes me sick.

The real surprise was her coming to see me. I didn't expect that. She tried to be all tough and intimidating, but what a joke. I could see right through her. Her voice trembled, her hands shook, the blood drained out of her face as she recited her rehearsed speech. I almost felt sorry for her.

Well, not really, but it did make it easier to sit her down and pretend she was a sister—both victims of the same cruel man. I was so consoling. Even made her a cup of tea. Took less than an hour to turn her from foe to ally, albeit an unwitting one. And it worked out fine. For a while. But nothing good lasts forever, does it? I probably should have seen that coming. Well, I did, but I needed her. Until I didn't.

Antifa Man

I had to run. Absolutely no choice. But it looks bad. I know that. Can they arrest me just for that? They have no evidence I committed a crime, so I should be safe. Although they did tell me to stay in town, and the lawyer warned me they were serious about that.

But here's the thing. Andy and Stevie were going berserk. Absolutely berserk. They convinced themselves that Ethics man had set a trap and I'd fallen into it. Their crazy solution was to go to New Jersey and fake an attack on a Democratic congressman. "We won't hurt him," Stevie said, "just rough him up so it looks like whoever killed Morgan is an equal opportunity menace."

Like that would work. Unless they killed him, or at least shot him, preferably with his own gun, it wouldn't look at all the same. Of course, with Andy along, who's to say it wouldn't get out of hand and that's exactly what would happen? So I had to come with them to make sure they behaved themselves. Without me, who knows what they might do? I learned that in Virginia when they blew a hole in the wall of that right-wing think tank. Thankfully, the cops could never trace it to us.

Not that it did much good. Somehow nothing ever does any good. The Arctic is turning into pure mush, the whole western half of the country burns every summer, and the Gulf Coast keeps getting hit with huge hurricanes—and no one cares. The stupid Republicans insist climate change is a hoax, and the Democrats can't get their act together. They'd rather trip over themselves racing to the center so they can win over the suburban moms, or whatever they call the swing voters these days.

As if the ballot box is the answer. It might be if elections made any difference, but Congress is so broken, nothing ever gets done, no matter who's in charge.

No, elections don't do it. Never have. And we're way past the point where nonviolence is any use. But figuring out how to use violence effectively is tough. And the risk of it backfiring is huge.

Stevie and Andy want to get more aggressive, but neither is the smartest guy in the world. They need constant watching. Every time I let them out of my sight, they get in trouble. So I had to go with them.

But now comes the hard part. I've got to find a new identity and I don't know anything about how to try. Carl Wasserman must disappear, at least for now. But how to latch onto someone new? Andy and Stevie can help short term—they can do the driving and use their credit cards and be the front men so I can stay under the radar. But that won't last forever.

And for some reason, Andy insisted we take my car. His is bigger and it's usually what we use, but he said it needed a brake job and we didn't have time. That means if we ever get stopped, the cop will see my name on the registration. How's that going to work?

My fear is that somewhere along the line all of our names were connected. I don't think so, but if they are, the feds can find them and that will take them to me. And then I'm dead. They'll find some way to convict me for Morgan's killing. I suppose that's what I get for not thinking things through.

A lesson to remember and live by.

What About Larry?

Sam is annoyed and frustrated. He knows he's taking too many painkillers, but he won't let his injuries slow him down. As it is, he's boxed himself in by telling Molly not to lean on her Park Police source, and Howie says he has nothing new. It doesn't leave him with an easy way to get answers. His only other sources are Peg, who is completely unreliable, and Kelly, who at last report is still unconscious. He considers going around to the hospital but then remembers the police are there and unlikely to let him in. He settles for calling Danny.

"They won't let me or Ariana near her. Only her parents are allowed on the floor, and her dad keeps asking questions I can't answer."

"'Why?' being the biggest, I presume?"

"I'm not even sure they've gotten that far. They can't understand the police presence. Cops are all over the place, with one in the room at all times. Sounds like overkill, doesn't it?"

"She is a suspect in the murder of a senator," Sam points out.

"But she's unconscious. She's not about to get up and run away, and her father said something that's strange. He said they are there for her protection. That's what the cops told him."

"Might just be what they said to get him to stop asking questions."

"If they did, it didn't work."

Sam thinks about that for a few seconds. "Danny," he says. "It was a suicide attempt, right? No suggestion of foul play?"

"None that I know of. But it's not like they've gone out of their way to tell us anything. I guess we just assumed. How could it be foul play? Who would want to murder her?"

Sam doesn't bother stating the obvious. If Kelly committed suicide, everyone would assume she's guilty and they'd close the case. Which could mean the real killer goes free.

"Ariana still believes it was suicide, right?" Sam asks. "She said Kelly was distraught and didn't see a way out. Ariana knows her better than anyone and she believes it was suicide."

"As far as I know. We both thought suicide. It fits her mood, and when Ariana and the police found her, she didn't notice anything amiss."

"Apart from an unconscious body, you mean."

Danny sighs. "Yeah, apart from that. Obviously."

"Is she there? Can I talk to her?"

When Ariana takes the phone, Sam asks her to try to remember as much as she can and describe the scene in detail.

He hears her take a breath and waits. Sam hopes she's trying to remember. "Well, it was almost like on TV. She was sprawled on the floor next to the couch, lying on her back, one arm kinda twisted under her, like she'd fallen without any time to brace the fall. The cops surrounded her quickly so I didn't really see that much."

"The pill bottles were where?"

"They were spread out on the coffee table. The caps were off and most of the pills were gone. A few remained, like she'd passed out before she finished or thought she'd already taken enough."

"But you don't know the bottles were full to begin with, and you said she was using pills regularly. Were there any on the floor?"

"None that I noticed."

"Had she vomited?"

"No, nothing like that. She looked kinda peaceful. Like she was finally at rest."

"What was she wearing?"

"Why does that matter?" But she tries to remember. "The usual. Jeans and a T-shirt."

Sam keeps pushing for anything unusual. "Think hard about the room," he says. "Can you think of anything that was different from the usual?"

He waits while Ariana tries, but she doesn't come up with anything. "Do me a favor," he says. "After we hang up, draw yourself a picture of everything you can remember. It might help. If you come up with something, call me back."

"What are you getting at? Do you think someone else was there that night, someone who pushed her over the edge?"

"I don't know what I'm getting at, but try to remember everything you can that might have been different from what you normally saw when you visited."

Sam has no idea how long it will take to hear back from Ariana, so he decides to go to his office and check in there.

Sasha is waiting out front and the drive takes about twenty minutes, but just as they're approaching the paper, Sasha takes an unexpected turn and asks Sam to get down on the floor, or as close to it as he can.

"What's happening?" he asks.

"Not sure, but there's a white car that's been following us. Maybe a coincidence, but maybe not."

Sasha takes two more random turns and then ducks through an alley, just ahead of a delivery truck, whose driver honks angrily. Sasha drives by the newspaper building and when Sam asks where she is going, she tells him they can't go in.

"It was probably just a coincidence, but if it was real, they'll know you were headed to the newspaper."

"I can't let them control me."

"You have to take this seriously."

They eventually agree on a compromise. Sasha drives around aimlessly for twenty minutes, long enough to be sure they aren't being followed. She still doesn't like it—someone could just be waiting in front of the newspaper building—but they both doubt an attack in broad daylight.

When they pull up at the building, Sasha gets out first and looks around, before opening the door and escorting Sam into the lobby. She wants to go upstairs with him, but he refuses to let her.

"Call me when you're ready to leave," she says as he enters the elevator.

Sam sits behind his desk and collects himself, wishing for the first time that he kept a bottle of bourbon in his desk. When he feels sufficiently calm, he goes out to find Brenda and asks if there's any news.

"No, the police still won't say anything. Everyone else is trying to chase our story, but they're being forced to cite us as the source of the link between Morgan and the woman who attempted suicide. They're outside the hospital—everyone is outside the hospital—but no one has her name. The cable networks are going wild with speculation, but they don't have a clue and their theories are all over the place."

"If they had her name, they'd use it," Sam says.

"So far they haven't."

"What about her parents? Has anyone talked to them?"

"Molly tried, but the police aren't letting anyone near, and I doubt her parents want to talk to the media."

"We probably know more than they do anyway."

"So what's next? Any thoughts?"

"One. Has Allison picked up any hints from the cops that it might not be suicide?"

Brenda is silent. "What makes you ask that?"

"Nothing, really. I'm grasping a bit, but I gather the police presence is huge."

"That may be our fault for doing a story. They need to keep the media away."

"Maybe, but one of the girl's friends says the cops were there even before our story ran, and they told the parents it was for her protection."

Brenda waits a beat before responding. "How do you know that?"

Caught, Sam gives a sheepish grin, but tries to keep it out of his voice. "One of her friends is in my ethics seminar."

"And you found that out how?"

"Long story, not important."

Brenda doesn't push it. "I'll get Allison and Molly on it right away," she says. "You think someone tried to kill her?"

"I don't think anything yet. Hopefully, she'll pull through and tell us."

"The medical experts say the longer she lives, the better her chances. The question is whether she'll have brain damage."

Sam shudders. They talk a bit more about possible avenues of investigation but can't come up with any.

Back in his office Sam sits down to figure out who might know something to advance the story. He can only come up with two options: Howie, who's made it clear he doesn't want to be approached at work, or Peg Morgan, who he wants to confront to find out if Kelly really did go to see her.

While he's considering that, Sasha calls. She's outside in her car, her home away from home. Sam can't imagine how she whiles away the time. But she's calling with information. She'd gotten someone to check the license plate on the SUV they'd seen leaving Peg Morgan's house, and now she has a name,

Larry Coleman, and an address. He asks her if she can find out who he is, but after he hangs up, Sam plays a hunch and calls the Capitol Police office and just asks for Larry Coleman. He's not available, but the receptionist transfers him to his voicemail. Sam hangs up without leaving a message.

He knows that Coleman is not likely to talk to him, but a surprise visit will give him a chance to gauge his reaction and maybe take the measure of the man. He calls Sasha to tell her he's coming down, but before he gets to the door, his cell rings. It's Ariana.

"There's only one thing and it's probably meaningless."

"What?"

"Lassie, Kelly's cat. She adores it. I could never understand why, but then I'm not a cat person. I didn't think of it at the time, but Lassie was there when we broke in and almost escaped from the apartment. It's the kind of thing Kelly would have worried about. If she were going to commit suicide, she would have put Lassie in the cat carrier rather than leave her behind like that."

"Maybe she had bigger things on her mind."

"No, she loved that cat too much. She probably also would have made some kind of arrangement for someone to take Lassie instead of leaving it to chance, knowing that might mean they'd put her down. She would have left a note asking me to take care of her."

"But she asked you earlier, when she thought she might get arrested."

"Yeah, but that was more a throwaway comment, not really serious. If she planned to kill herself, she would have left a reminder and done everything she could to make me feel guilty if I didn't take Lassie. She wouldn't leave her like that."

Coleman lives on Capitol Hill in a modest row house in a borderline section off Maryland Avenue. It's taken Sam and Sasha forty-five minutes to fight through the evening rush hour to get there, and when they do, he directs her to pull into an illegal parking space a house away, and they settle in to wait.

"What exactly are we waiting for?" Sasha asks. "You think this is the guy who tried to kill you?"

Sam thinks about that. He's not sure. "He's involved in something he shouldn't be involved in. I'm not sure what."

"He drives a black car."

"He could still have access to a white one," Sam says. "Can you check?"

"Probably."

"While you're at it, could you check the cars of the others—Peg Morgan, Kelly Lancaster, and Carl Wasserman?"

"None of them are white. Not as far as we can tell. It was the first thing I did when you hired us."

Twenty minutes pass and Sasha asks if he wants her to go ring the bell. "We should at least find out whether he's home."

Sam doesn't answer and she asks again what they are waiting for, but Sam isn't sure. He'd like to confront Coleman and see how he reacts, but confront him with what? He wants to know why he was at the Morgan house the other night, but Coleman could ask him how he knows that or say he was there to make sure she was okay. Even if he's not assigned to her, it's not unreasonable that he'd look in on her. Sam doubts that's the case, but he can't prove anything else.

Sam is still contemplating the options when they see the door open and Coleman exits. He goes to the black SUV and drives away. Sasha follows at a distance, but Sam doesn't care where he's going unless it's to Peg Morgan. He wants to see her anyway, so he gives up on trying to stay with Coleman and tells Sasha to just drive to the house in Georgetown.

And lo and behold, the SUV is parked in the driveway.

They find an almost legal parking place a short distance away, and once again Sam ponders his options. As he watches, he notices a light come on upstairs and wonders what that means. He considers asking Sasha to go to the door, but then decides to do it himself.

He rings the bell, but no one answers. He rings it twice more and looks up to the room where he'd seen the light. He catches a man looking down at him. The man pulls back and turns away as soon as he sees Sam, but not in time.

Sam rings one more time to no avail and then leaves.

Kelly

Where am I?

I try sitting up, but shooting pains force me to curl up in bed. But it's not my bed. The sheets don't feel right.

Someone is calling to me. I must be dreaming because it sounds almost like Mom. Then I feel a hand on my shoulder and I open my eyes. It is Mom. And Dad's here too.

"What happened?" I say.

"She's awake," my mother says and within seconds, there's another person. She's dressed like a nurse. I'm in a hospital. How did that happen? I try to remember.

The nurse starts asking questions, and soon another woman joins her, elbowing my parents to the side.

"I'm Dr. Simone," she says. "Can you hear me? Can you understand me okay?"

I nod, but that brings the shooting pains back and I cry out.

"Lie still," Simone says. "Where does it hurt?"

"My head. It's killing me."

"Lie still," she says again. "Does it hurt anywhere else."

"No," I whisper, remembering to keep my head still.

"We're giving you something to help. It will only take a minute."

I hold out my hand for a pill, but she tells me to stay still, the medicine will come through the IV. I see my mother crying and I wonder what's happened to me. I can't remember how I got here.

The doctor pries open my eyes and shines a light in them. It's uncomfortable, but I'm beginning to feel better. The pain isn't nearly so bad, but I still don't know how I got here.

"What happened?" I ask.

"What's the last thing you remember?" Simone says.

I try to think. Gradually images come back to me, but they're vague and incomplete. I'm in my apartment. Lassie is there on my lap. I'm drinking wine. But it's a blurry recollection, and it hurts to try to bring it into focus.

"It's okay," Simone says. "It may take some time until it comes back to you."

"But what happened?"

"Don't worry about it. Try to rest." She starts to leave and tells my parents to do the same.

But they linger. "Kelly, you're going to be okay," my mother says.

"What happened?" I ask again.

"You took an overdose," my father says. "Don't worry about it now. We'll talk about it when you're better."

Simone turns sharply and literally pulls my parents out of the room.

I lie there, thinking about what my father said. An overdose? I don't do drugs. Well, only the kind that are prescribed. Maybe a bit more than I'm supposed to, but an overdose? That can't be right.

I try to remember again, but I can't. Instead I think of what I've become. I've made such a mess of my life. I used to be a good person. But it all went wrong.

For some reason I start listing my mistakes. I've never been that great at picking men—not that there were many—but having an affair with a married man was the worst of my sins. My parents will disown me if they find out, and I have a feeling they're going to find out. That thought brings back the headache, though not the shooting pain kind.

And the pictures. Definitely mistake number two. If I hadn't agreed to those, it wouldn't have been so bad. I cringe when I think of them and how many men might have seen them. And what they did when they looked at them.

I begin to drift and can't concentrate. It must be the drugs they're giving me.

Wait, did my father say I took an overdose? How did that happen?

Lassie. Where's Lassie? Is someone taking care of her? I roll toward the bedside table to look for a phone. I need to make sure someone is feeding her, and she hates it when her litterbox is full. I might need more litter. I was running low. I meant to go shopping, but there was no time.

I should get up and go check on her. I slowly lift myself and look around the room. Definitely a hospital. It's only then I notice the policewoman sitting in the corner reading a magazine. Has she been there the whole time?

"Who are you?" I ask, then realize how obvious the answer is. "Why are you here?" I ask, the real question on my mind.

"Pay me no mind," she says. "Forget about me. The doctor said you should rest. Try to sleep."

I suddenly realize how tired I am and put my head back down on the pillow.

Howie and the Donuts

Sam calls Howie at seven a.m., unable to wait any longer. "I know you said not to call, but I really have to tell you what I learned, and I'd rather not do it on the phone. You won't regret it."

Howie suggests his usual breakfast haunt, but Sam rejects it. "You don't want to be seen with me, and it can't wait that long." They agree to meet at eight at a Dunkin' Donuts near Howie's home.

Gordon (call me Gord-O) Yardley is filling in for Sasha today, and he drives Sam to his destination without comment. He's not the talkative type. He's all business and his eyes are constantly scanning their surroundings.

"Dunkin' Donuts?" Sam says as soon as he sits down opposite Howie. "You're proving the cop stereotype."

Howie is sitting with a large black coffee and a honey-dipped donut. "Why do you think it's a stereotype?"

Sam has no answer.

"So what's so important?" Howie asks.

"Larry Coleman. You know him?"

Howie nods, his mouth busy chewing, so Sam continues.

"I gather he was part of Morgan's security team."

"Speaking of security, where's yours? Don't tell me you let them go."

"Outside. No one's going to attack me in here. Besides, I have you. But you're changing the subject. Was Coleman part of Morgan's security team?"

"Yeah, and he's been helping the task force. I don't think he's been assigned to anything else yet."

"I think he's assigned himself."

"Meaning?"

"I've seen him at Peg Morgan's house twice in the last two days. The second time he was in an upstairs bedroom. It doesn't take a detective to figure it out."

Howie looks up and meets Sam's eyes. "Maybe she needed him to change a light bulb."

Sam uses his eyes to say he's in no mood for jokes.

Howie takes another bite of donut. Then another. "It happens. Guys get close to their subjects."

"His subject was Morgan, not his wife."

Howie stares off in the distance, avoiding eye contact. "I don't know what Coleman was up to, but what he does on his own time isn't relevant. Not that I won't look into it, but what significance does it have to the case?"

"You don't really have to ask that, do you?"

Howie sighs. "No."

But Sam tells him anyway. "Chances are the affair was going on while he was working for the senator. It gives him motive for the murder. Gives her motive too."

"I don't buy that. They might have been playing around, but I can't believe either of them was serious enough to think it would lead to more than that."

Sam tells Howie to wait while he goes for coffee. When he gets up, his feels a stab in his side but tries not to show it.

"Bring me another donut," Howie says. "Boston cream." When Sam makes a face, he adds, "Hey, you got me before breakfast and the only thing decent here is the donuts."

When Sam returns, Howie has a more serious expression. "It looks bad. I'll give you that, but don't jump to conclusions. I'll talk to Coleman. He may have taken advantage, but he'd never let himself get involved in Morgan's murder. Never. But I'll talk to him. You won't put any of this in the paper, will you?"

"No, not unless it proves relevant. I don't have anything hard. But let me know what you find out."

They sit in silence for a bit, drinking their coffees, Sam watching Howie finish his donut. "You got cream on your chin," he says.

When Howie wipes it off, Sam asks if there's any other news, glad they've gotten beyond Howie's earlier vow not to talk about the case.

"Did you know she woke up?" Howie asks.

"Kelly? No, I hadn't heard."

Howie catches the slip. "You know her name?"

Sam nods without offering any explanation. "What is she telling you?"

"Nada. Nothing useful."

"She won't talk?"

"She says she doesn't remember anything."

"How can you not remember a suicide attempt?"

Howie looks away and Sam realizes there's more. "What? Tell me."

But Howie goes back to his coffee and looks over at the counter. Sam can't tell whether he's considering another donut or just stalling. Probably both. He waits.

"The docs don't believe it was suicide. They called in the Medical Examiner, and a number of things don't quite fit. They found almost empty Xanax and Ambien pill bottles, but only low levels of those substances were found in her bloodstream. What almost killed her was OxyContin."

"Did she have a prescription for that?"

"No and none in the apartment."

"She could have gotten it from a friend or bought it on the street."

Howie shakes his head. "They don't think she got it that way. Her friends admit she was a drinker. Wine, according to them, not hard stuff. And there was a full wine rack to back that up. We found a glass in the sink. It had been washed pretty well, but not well enough. There were traces of Oxy on it."

Sam is confused. "Meaning what? She could have had traces in her mouth and transferred it to the glass."

"Very unlikely."

Sam remembers his conversation with Ariana about the cat. "So it wasn't suicide," he says.

Howie shrugs. "Anyway, that's why there'll be cops in and around her room until further notice in case whoever wants her dead tries to finish the job when they find out she survived."

"Does that mean she's no longer a suspect in Morgan's murder?"

"Too early to rule out other possibilities."

"Like?"

"It's possible she hired someone to kill Morgan and that person began to worry she'd lead us to him and wanted to foreclose the possibility."

"You've checked her finances? Any payments to someone she might have hired?"

"No, but she could have found a way to hide it. I'm not saying anybody thinks that, only that we can't rule it out."

Sam takes a sip from his coffee, which is already cold. Then he asks Howie one more question. "Why are you telling me all of this?"

Howie smiles. "Because now you're going to explain how you know her name and what the officer in her room heard her say when she was coming to."

"What was that?"

"All she could make out was the phrase "Mr. Ethics."

Sam smiles and then leans back, trying to weigh his obligations to Kelly against his obligation to reciprocate with Howie. The decision doesn't take long.

"Let me get another cup of coffee and I'll start from the beginning."

"I'll try a cinnamon donut this time," Howie says with a smile.

Howie listens to Sam's story without saying much, though he shakes his head a lot and swears repeatedly under his breath, obviously angry at Sam for holding back so much for so long.

"I'm sorry I wasn't more forthcoming," Sam offers. "At first, I felt I couldn't say anything if she didn't want me to, and after a while, it all got too complicated."

Howie shakes his head and frowns. "No wonder someone wants you out of the way," he says. "You're conducting your own investigation."

"For all the good it's done me."

Howie picks up the last crumb of his donut and looks longingly at the counter and the lush donuts piled up behind it, but then he pushes his plate aside.

"Have you figured out who it could be?" he asks. "Who has reason enough to try to kill you?"

"I can't see that I'm a threat to anyone."

"Clearly you are. Go over every conversation. You must have said or done something to make the killer think you're on to him. Or her."

"I don't think it's Kelly. She would have known I was teaching the night of the car attack, but I don't see she had a motive. I was trying to help her, not that I was very successful."

"Still, if she was working with someone, that someone might have been worried about you."

"It seems farfetched."

"Maybe," Howie says. "I'm not so sure. What about Antifa Man?"

Sam frowns. "I don't think so. I don't think he killed Morgan, and if he's not guilty, he won't be worried about me."

"No one's ruled him out yet."

"The only one I've offended is Peg Morgan. And maybe Larry Coleman. It could be he doesn't want me revealing their affair. It could have nothing to do with the murder."

Howie seems to think about that, but the expression on his face is doubtful. "The timing doesn't fit. The attack was before you saw Coleman at her house."

Sam tilts his head. "True, but he could have worried I'd find out about them eventually Maybe he wanted to stop me from hanging around."

"So he was more concerned about you than the task force?"

"You said he was helping them. So he knew they were getting nowhere."

"I don't buy it."

"Or maybe Peg Morgan put him up to it," Sam tries. "Do you think Coleman could have helped her kill Morgan? Or maybe acted on his own so he could have her for himself."

"People have killed for less, but you're assuming a lot."

"It's worth looking at Coleman, though. How long have they been having an affair? What if Morgan found out and threatened to get Coleman fired?" Sam is talking faster, his mind working, excited at the new theory he's developing on the fly.

But then Howie puts up a hand to stop him.

"You're stretching," he says.

"Maybe. Can you find out whether Coleman has access to a white car? I know he drives a black SUV, but maybe his wife has one? Or is there a pool of unmarked white police cars he can use?"

"I'll look into it, but I can't believe he's involved."

Sam won't be deterred. "I need to think it through. It's possible."

Sam checks his phone when he reaches the car and finds a voicemail from Lisa asking him to call back as soon as possible.

Concerned, he dials right away. "Is everything okay?"

"I need a big favor," she says. "I have to go out of town right away. A work problem, and I wondered if you could take care of Dodger. I wouldn't ask—I know you're in crisis mode too—but if you can't do it, I have to board her somewhere."

It's hardly convenient, but he isn't about to refuse. "Of course," he says, grateful that she's let him keep a key. "I can grab my stuff and be there by midafternoon."

"Thanks," she says. "I thank you, and Dodger thanks you."

"No problem. What's the crisis?"

"It would take longer to explain than it's worth. I'm not sure how long I'll be. I'll call you when I can."

Sam hangs up feeling uneasy. Lisa's corporate work rarely involves emergencies, and he doubts she'd leave town to help Wasserman. He wonders if it's personal. Maybe having to do with her new boyfriend. None of his business. He is grateful she called on him. It suggests her relationship with the new guy hasn't progressed to living together.

He calls the paper, asks for Molly, and tells her that Kelly is awake. Molly listens but not with the interest he expects. She tells him she already has that from other sources and is putting together a story now. But then she asks if she can see him after she finishes.

He gives her the address of his old house, Lisa's house, and says he'll meet her there. He knows the location is an inconvenience for her, but she agrees. He's afraid to guess what's so important she can't talk about it on the phone.

Gordon drives Sam to his apartment, he packs an overnight bag, and they head to Bethesda. Gordon insists on walking around the house before they enter, a move Sam finds unnecessary and annoying, and then they go inside together. Dodger greets Sam with his usual enthusiasm and then gives a more subdued welcome to Gordon. Sam only has twenty minutes until Molly arrives, and he asks Gordon to move his car and stay out of sight. He knows Dodger needs to go out, so he drops his stuff, grabs a leash, and they go for a short walk, barely long enough for Dodger to take care of business. It makes Sam wonder how she gets through the long days.

Molly at Risk

Molly is a little late and more than a little upset. Dodger is abnormally restrained in her greeting, again showing her uncanny ability to sense the mood and react accordingly.

"Do you have something to drink?" Molly asks as she rubs Dodger's head.

Sam opens the bar and shouts out the options. "Plus wine or beer," he adds.

"A gin and tonic would be great. Make it strong."

"Sure. I'll see if I can find a lime."

He makes the drink, pours himself a bourbon, and they sit in the great room. Dodger joins them, but after going over to Sam to check for food, she settles in a corner.

"What's up?" Sam asks, though he already has a pretty good idea, at least of the subject.

"That source I told you about?"

"The family friend," he says.

"I kept putting him off, but last night he showed up at my apartment unannounced. I nearly freaked out."

Sam waits. He's getting better at that.

Molly continues. "I should've told him I wasn't alone and asked him to leave, but I didn't think fast enough and I let him in. He started casually enough and as a peace offering—more like a bribe, I guess—he asked if I was still working on the story and needed some help. He knew of course that I'm always desperate for help and wouldn't say no."

"So you said 'yes.'"

"Actually, I don't think I said anything, though I'm not sure. I froze, that much I know. I could tell I was in trouble."

Molly sighs and closes her eyes. Sam watches until she goes on.

"He asked for a drink and I poured us both a glass of wine. And then he started talking about the case and how they're looking pretty closely at what happened to your pen pal."

"Did they say whether it was attempted suicide or something else?"

"He said they're not sure and when I asked him why there were so many cops at the hospital, he said it's normal procedure."

"So he starts with a lie. What new information did he offer to explain why he came?"

"The name. Kelly Lancaster."

So it's out, Sam thinks. "Anything else?" he asks.

"Only that they'd been going over all the records with the phones and they have no doubt that she was the one who purchased the burner at the 7-Eleven. They also traced the location of the phone, and it never left her apartment. Besides the four-second call, she used it one other time, to accept a call from Morgan the day he was murdered. After that it goes dead."

This confirms what Howie had said, but Sam hasn't told Molly any of it.

"I was able to get Lancaster's address," Molly adds. "If she gets released from the hospital—as opposed to arrested—I'll be able to find her and try to interview her."

Sam doesn't like that. Not one bit. But there's not much he can do.

"You didn't use her name in your story today?"

"No. I told Brenda that I had it, but we both knew it would be wrong to use it until we know more."

She tells him a little more about what she wrote, none of which is new to him. When she finishes, he gives her an understanding smile. "But the story isn't why you're here," he says. "It's not why you're upset."

She lets out a big sigh. "After he gave me the information, he sat back with this shit-eating grin on his face, like he'd done me the biggest favor in the world. Then he moved over to the couch, so he was right next to me, brushing up against my leg, and asked if I had any questions. I said no and started to get up, but he grabbed my hand, and said he'd saved the most important information for last. That I needed to know one more thing. I looked at him and shook free and got up and moved to the other side of the room."

She stops at that point, finishes her drink, asks for another.

"Are you sure?" Sam asks. "You drank that pretty quickly. Maybe you should tell me the rest first."

"It'll be easier with another drink."

Sam gets up and makes it, but he goes very easy on the gin. Dodger follows him out of the room and when she's again disappointed, she goes back to her corner. Sam brings the drink to Molly and waits for her to go on.

"When I moved away from him, he asked me what was wrong. I didn't know what to say. Finally, I told him that I valued his friendship, but I wasn't interested in that kind of relationship. He didn't say anything for a minute and then made some stupid comment about how he knew I was getting married and with the age difference, he knew a relationship couldn't last."

Molly stops there, starts to chew on her lower lip, then catches herself and takes another gulp of her drink. Sam waits until she's ready to continue.

"But then he said getting married didn't mean I shouldn't have some fun and this was probably my last chance. That's all he wanted." She shakes her head. "Some fun."

She closes her eyes and leans back against the couch. "I was stunned. I'd always known what he wanted, but I didn't believe he'd say it out loud. I told him no, and I didn't say it very nicely. I told him I had no interest, that there was no attraction. *That* was a mistake."

She stops again and this time Sam can see the tears. Dodger notices as well, and she comes over to Molly and licks her hand. Molly laughs and pets her, then gets on the floor to give her a hug. When she gets up, Dodger heads back to her corner, but she stops before she gets there and turns around and leaves the room. It's like she wants to allow them some privacy.

"That's when he got angry," Molly says. "Asked why I thought he was giving me such great stories. 'Did I think it was a one-way street?' I tried to tell him I appreciated his help, but he was angry and I got scared. He said I had led him on, implied I was interested, taken him for a fool. That kind of thing."

She finishes her drink and holds up the empty glass to Sam, but he shakes his head. "What happened then?"

"He called me a bitch. And a few other things. Then he came over to me and grabbed my arm. Fortunately, it was the left one and I slapped him with the other. Then he lost it and punched me in the stomach. It knocked the wind out of me and I fell on the floor. He came over to me and I really thought he was going to rape me."

She stops to compose herself, and Sam takes her glass and goes into the kitchen to give her a moment. He comes back with plain tonic water and hands it to her. She makes a face when she tastes it.

"You don't have to go on if this is difficult," he says, but she ignores him.

"Nothing happened. It would have, but I started yelling at him. Told him I'd tell my father and write a story about him in the newspaper, that it would kill his career. He stopped then, seemed to realize what was at stake. He called me some more names, but he had regained control. We both had. But he warned me that if I ever told anyone he'd ruin me, that he'd say I tried to bribe him for information with sex. And then he stalked out."

"You stopped him," Sam says after a moment. "That's what's important."

"I can't believe I threatened to tell my father. Like a little girl."

"You said he's an old family friend. It's a natural response under the circumstances."

She laughs at that. And then she starts crying, loud sobs that shake her whole body. He comes over by the couch, hesitant to touch her, but finally he puts a hand on her back and then she leans into him and they hug.

"Don't say you told me so," she says when she's able to wipe away the tears. "I know you told me to stay away from him. I shouldn't have let him in. But at least he advanced the story. Assuming he was telling the truth."

Her words surprise Sam. All this and she's thinking about her scoop.

Then he realizes he's not much different. He's bent all the rules, made more stupid decisions in the last month than in his whole career. Which he's put at risk, much as Molly has. No, she'll be alright. She may have flirted with the guy, but that's as far as it went. He, on the other hand, has crossed some lines, and he has a feeling that he's not done doing so.

It's almost six and Sam asks her if she's hungry. Neither of them is, but he doesn't want her to be on her own right now. He asks about Kyle, but he's away on business. Sam considers options for keeping her in his company, but all he can come up with is talking about the case. He's smart enough to understand what this says about his life, and maybe hers.

"I'm going to order a pizza. You'll be hungry by the time it comes, and whatever's left over can be my breakfast."

"Breakfast?" she asks with a grin.

"In the meantime, why don't we figure out everything we know about Morgan's murder and see if we can come up with some new insights."

The idea cheers her, and she pulls out her notebook. He places the order and then gets a yellow legal pad, preferring the larger palette. He still hasn't told her about the attack on him, and he doesn't intend to. She doesn't seem to notice that he's walking stiffly and protecting his chest.

"I have a feeling the phones are the key," he says when they begin, "but let's go back to the beginning and start with the basics."

Morgan was found in his car in Rock Creek Park, after giving his security team the night off. He was killed with a bullet to the brain that came from his own gun, which was found in his hand. What's not clear is how the killer got the gun. He or she could have surprised Morgan and taken it away when the senator tried to protect himself. Or it could be someone close enough to the senator to know about and steal the weapon and then use it to kill him.

Morgan was a showy conservative politician who took pleasure in making enemies, of which there was no shortage. In particular was one Carl Wasserman, who'd made threats against the senator. Wasserman denies having anything to do with his death, and after meeting him, Molly and Sam are both inclined to believe him. But he's disappeared, which keeps him squarely in the suspect pool.

Also threatening the senator is Kelly Lancaster, but her threat came in an email to Mr. Ethics, and everything they know about her, including what her close friends say, suggests she's not the kind of person to hurt anyone. Still, they know anybody is capable of murder under the right conditions, and Kelly certainly had a motive. If she felt backed into a corner—truly desperate, in her words—then maybe she felt she had no choice. But that goes out the window, or at least as far as the windowsill, if it's true that someone tried to kill her and make it look like suicide. And that's what the evidence points to.

That leaves the senator's wife. She knew about Morgan's affairs, but claims not to have cared that much, but if Kelly confronted her, that could have changed everything, and it would mean she lied about never meeting Kelly.

And then there's Larry Coleman, the Capitol Hill officer assigned to Senator Morgan. They don't know enough to put him in any category yet. He's probably having an affair with Peg Morgan, but they don't have any proof. All they know is that he's been hanging around her in his free time.

"Where's that pizza?" Molly asks. "I'm hungry after all."

Sam ignores her. "Let's go through the phones next," he says. But then the doorbell rings and they take a break to eat. Dodger suddenly appears and Sam makes her dinner. "No pizza for you, young lady."

While Dodger eats, Sam sets the table with plates and flatware but serves the pizza out of the box.

"I can't believe you like anchovies," Molly says.

"I only got them on half. It's my way of making sure you don't eat more than your share."

She asks for a beer and he gets two Amstel Lights. He's worried about how much she's drinking.

"When is she coming back?"

"She didn't say. I don't know what the problem is, but it probably won't be more than a couple of days." Dodger seems to hear that and wags her tail. Sam tries not to take it personally.

Sam gets Molly talking about the wedding plans and her mood brightens, even though she's worried about how far behind she is. "I've had to delegate a lot to my mom. It's easier that way, but I know there will be some surprises I won't like."

"It's your day," Sam says. "And Kyle's, of course, but it's hers too. Will she really plan anything you'll hate?"

Molly takes a bite of pizza. "Probably not. I mostly care about the ceremony, and Kyle and I are on top of that."

"Then you'll be fine."

"You're coming, right?"

"Didn't you get my RSVP?"

"My mom's in charge of those."

When they finish eating and cleaning up, Sam lets Dodger finish the scraps in the box, mostly crusts. He's already put the leftovers in the refrigerator.

They settle back onto the sofa and resume their work. "Let's get back to what we know about the phones," Sam says.

They know that Morgan had a prepaid phone, in addition to his regular cellphone, and he used it to communicate with Kelly during their affair. But then a few days before he was killed, Kelly bought a burner of her own. And she apparently called it that day, just for four seconds, probably by mistake.

"Unless she wanted to test the burner," Sam says. "She'd never had one before. Maybe she needed to try it out."

"Maybe," Molly says, "but more important is the fact that Kelly—or someone—used it to accept a call from Morgan the day he was killed. They don't know why she gave Morgan the number or what was discussed on the call, but it's possible that the purpose was to set up a meeting between them, which would mean Kelly really did kill Morgan, and that it might have been premeditated."

"We also know something about the phones from the GPS tracking," Sam says. "We know Morgan had no phone when he was found. His regular cell was at home and his burner was missing. It can be tracked to the Rock Creek Park site, but then it dies, presumably because the battery was removed."

"And Kelly's burner never left her house, from the day it was purchased to the day of the murder, when it also went off the grid, according to our sources," Molly says. "That doesn't look good."

Sam concedes the point and puts his pad down. Dodger reappears, almost as if she'd been waiting for that signal. It's time for her evening walk. Sam tells her to wait a little longer, then asks Molly if that's everything.

"I think so. My brain's fried. I better go home and crash."

"But we haven't figured it out."

"No," Molly says, "but it helps to organize it this way. I think the evidence points to Kelly. You sure she didn't do it?"

"Not sure, but it's more likely to be whoever tried to kill her, if in fact someone did."

"Let's sleep on it. Can you send me a copy of your notes?"

"If you can read my handwriting, I'll just run it through my copier," he says and goes off to do that, while Molly calls for a car. He can see she is feeling better, or at least has her mind on something that's easier to handle, but he still worries how she'll do home alone.

"Don't worry, I'll be fine," she says, reading his mind. "He won't bother me anymore."

A Walk and a Reckoning

The day is perfect. Sunny, warm enough to get by without a coat. The tulips and daffodils and forsythia are still in bloom, and the big lilac bush by the driveway has begun to break out.

Dodger picks up on the plan. She's waiting by the front door, eager for Sam to finish the paper and turn off the TV.

Sam has been up for a while catching up on the story. The cable news stations are struggling. Congress is out of town and the president's abroad, so they've returned to the Morgan murder. The "Breaking News" signs are again flashing—do they ever stop?—on CNN, Fox, and MSNBC, although all they are doing is rehashing what Molly reported. The screens are filled with talking heads who pretty much agree that the FBI has had more than enough time to solve this case. The commentators attack the FBI for incompetence or, in the case of one Fox analyst, for not caring about the murder because of Morgan's conservative leanings.

Sam turns off the TV, gets the leash, and goes out with Dodger. He goes over to Sasha, who is back on duty and tells her he's going for a walk. She agrees to walk a hundred yards behind them, but no further.

He stays in the neighborhood, turning left, right for a few blocks, left, right, wandering aimlessly. He doesn't have to worry about where they are. He knows the streets well, having lived here for years and walked Dodger, or her predecessor, Penny, twice a day for nearly twenty years. With no need to think about where they're going, Sam has plenty of time to let his mind play with the two big problems he faces: what to do about the murder investigation and what to do about his life.

He hasn't heard from Lisa today, which surprises him. He would have thought she'd call to say when she'll be back. She must be busy, but she didn't tell him where she was going or what hotel she's in, which seems odd. Of course, he can always call her cell, but he doesn't want to.

He figures it's another way of her sending a message that the marriage is over. No need, he thinks. He's gotten that message. Time to move on. It will be hard. No one can take Lisa's place.

But he'll always have the kids, and now the grandkids. He'll have to start taking more of his vacation time, making a much stronger effort to connect with them, developing a real relationship with the grandchildren. He thinks of Logan's visit and smiles.

Still, he can't spend *that* much time with the kids. He knows that grandparents, especially single grandfathers, can easily wear out their welcome. He'll visit more, but not too much. Try to be useful, but there will have to be limits. Which means a lot of time alone. And lonely. He'll throw himself into his work, assuming the mistakes he's made in this case don't put him out of his job.

Funny that he thinks of it as a case rather than a story. It shows he's gone too far and is acting too much like a detective instead of a reporter. He can't stop, though. He's too involved to step back. He has to figure it out.

But he can't.

They reach an intersection with one of the larger estates in Bethesda, one with a huge expanse of lawn and the house far from the road atop a hill. The owner has a little garden near the street and has kindly placed a bench right next to it. Sam takes a seat, and Dodger looks at him, wondering why, but then she lies down at his feet. Actually, on his feet.

Sasha walks by them and Sam is tempted to invite her to sit down, but he really wants to be alone with his thoughts.

Sam reaches down and scratches the top of Dodger's head between her ears, and she leans into it. Sam can't help but feel they belong together and wonders why Lisa no longer feels that way about him. Suddenly he finds himself weeping, silently but with tears running down his cheeks. Dodger presses harder against his legs.

Sam knows he must stop feeling sorry for himself. He forces himself to consider the case. Something keeps nagging at him and he thinks it's the phones. The key is in there somewhere. The four-second call that Kelly made to her burner is part of it, but it's the other call that is more troubling. Morgan's call to the burner Kelly bought. He'd always called her on her regular cellphone, so why use a burner now unless one of them was trying to hide something. He knows that's what Molly believes, but he doesn't see it.

He can't imagine Kelly killing Morgan. He did entertain the thought briefly when it looked like she attempted suicide, but if someone was trying to kill her, that changes everything. It had to be the real killer, and not a hitman. How would Kelly know where to find one? If anything, Kelly was a pawn who unknowingly set Morgan up. But how could that happen?

So who?

Certainly not Antifa Man. He looked suspicious for a while—and may well be guilty of something—but not Morgan's murder. Could his friends have been involved? They've always been a mystery.

Sam thinks again of the four-second call from Kelly's phone

to the burner she purchased. A mistake, he knows, isn't likely because Kelly would never have entered it in her contacts. It can't be a matter of hitting the wrong button.

No, it had to be that she was testing the new phone she'd bought from the 7-Eleven. But why buy a burner when she'd resisted doing so for so long?

The secret is in the phones, he keeps telling himself. There's something he's missing.

And then he remembers.

Soon a plan forms in his head. He'll need Molly's help, and he'll have to get her to give it without asking too many questions. And he'll need to time everything perfectly.

Can he pull it off?

Peg

Larry wants to come by, but I tell him no, it's too dangerous, though that's not the real reason. I just don't want to see him, and there's no longer any need to. His sources have dried up abruptly, and he admits that his boss asked him about me. He assures me his excuse for coming here—that he thought I still needed protecting even though he'd been officially taken off assignment—was enough to satisfy his supervisor. I'm not sure, but that's the least of my problems.

It must have been Turner who reported Larry's visits, but why was Turner even here? Why does he keep coming back? Why has it been so hard to get him to go away?

I made a mistake in talking to him, but after that whore told me about the email she sent him, it seemed best to find out what he knew and keep track of what he was up to. Not that he ever gave much away. But then, neither did I.

None of the networks has any news. The paper said she's awake, but what does that mean? Is she able to talk or will she forever be damaged goods? She won't tell them anything—she's as guilty as I am—but having her around is awfully risky.

The phone rings for the third time today and for some reason I get up to look at the caller ID. Turner. What could he want now? The ringing stops and I sit back down. He hasn't left a message. I guess he wants the element of surprise. It occurs to me that he might just show up. Should I let him in?

I could use a drink, but it's too early.

He's going to come, try to trick me into a mistake. I shouldn't answer the door, but he might know something useful. Maybe an update on her condition. I'll let him in if he shows up and see where it goes. Avoiding him is risky too.

I think I will have that drink.

I sit and wait for the knock on the door, but it doesn't come. Might as well get it over with. When I call, he answers with his name. I don't understand why people do that with their own cellphone. As if I don't know who I'm calling.

"I see you called me earlier," I begin.

"I did. I was wondering if I could come by to see you."

"About what?"

"It'd be better if we talk in person."

I give in to that and he says it will take him half an hour to get here. That leaves me time to make a plan. I want to get information, not give anything away, but it's always a tradeoff. The trick is to give something he already knows, or thinks he knows, without letting on.

I go over various scenarios in my head, rehearsing different ways the conversation can go, but it's hard. I don't know what to expect.

Something about Larry, for sure. He's going to say something about that, want to know why he was here. I can ask the same question of him. Plus, I can ask why he thought it was his business to report Larry to his supervisors.

I check my phone. An hour has passed, and I'm still waiting. Bad traffic? Or some kind of game he's playing to make me nervous? I ought to call him, tell him I have to go out and he's missed his chance. But that will only put off the inevitable.

I hear the car before I see it and move away from the window. No point in letting him know how anxious I feel. The alcohol didn't help at all.

I greet him at the door as nonchalantly as I can, and he comes in saying he appreciates my making time for him.

"Time is something I have plenty of these days," I say. It's a silly comment and I regret it as soon as the words come out. I better be more careful.

He asks how I am, and I tell him fine, how is he? Also fine.

Then I decide to get right to it. "So, I gather she woke up."

"Yes, she's awake."

"Has she told them why she tried to kill herself?"

He shakes his head. "I don't know what she's told them, if anything. I only know she's awake."

"I suppose I should say something nice at this point, like 'poor girl' or something, but having never met her and knowing she was screwing my husband, kind words escape me."

He looks at me oddly, as though I've said something that surprises him. Did he expect me to weep for her? I try to mollify him. "I suppose anybody who tries to kill herself is very troubled. By definition. In need of help."

"If it really was a suicide attempt," he says.

I hear it, but I don't acknowledge it.

"Would you like something to drink?"

He glances at his watch and then asks for water. I get up to get a glass for each of us, happy for a chance to collect my thoughts.

"What do you mean?" I ask when I get back. "The TV networks all said it was a suicide attempt."

He shrugs and I can see he's playing with me. "I don't know if the FBI has drawn any conclusions yet," he says. "It looks like suicide, but I hear they're not ruling out foul play."

"Foul play?" I say, not sure what expression I'm showing him or how he'll interpret it. Why didn't Larry know this? "You mean someone tried to kill her?"

He doesn't say anything, just looks around the room. Then my phone rings. I pull it out of my purse and glance at it, but I don't recognize the number and decline the call.

"New phone?" he asks.

I shake my head, confused. "No, I've had it for ages." Then suddenly I remember, and I feel a bad sensation in my stomach. Another mistake.

"You had another phone when I visited earlier," he says. "The one I found in your couch wasn't an iPhone."

My head starts spinning and for a minute I worry I'm going to faint. "It must have been one of Wade's. He had several phones. What difference does it make?"

"The police never found Wade's burner. It wasn't with him and you didn't turn any in."

"It was probably buried in the couch for eons. I can't see that it matters."

"Why did you tell me you didn't know Kelly Lancaster?"

"I beg your pardon?"

"That's her name. Kelly Lancaster. The girl in the hospital. But you knew that, didn't you? Because she confronted you."

"Why would she confront me? I'm the last person she would want to tell about her affair with my husband."

"Because of the abuse she was taking after she broke up with him. The stolen identity, the revenge porn. She thought it was your husband's doing and she came to believe that telling you was the only way to put a stop to it."

"It was my husband's doing. The FBI found it on his computer."

"But you had access to the computer."

"What are you implying? I told you I didn't know the girl or what was going on. I didn't care about his little one-offs."

He smiles. "This wasn't a one-off, though, was it? It was a bigger threat."

Now I know it was foolish to let him come here. Nothing to gain and everything to lose.

"I don't know what you're talking about, but I think you better leave before you make a bigger fool of yourself than you already have."

"So how did you work it? Did you and Kelly kill him together? And then you got worried she wasn't strong enough and would tell the police, so you tried to kill her? Or did you get your friend Larry to help do that?"

I'm on my feet now, steadying myself as best I can. I walk to the front door and he follows me, and when I open the door and point, he leaves without another word.

Kelly

I told the police everything. I couldn't hold it in any longer. They already knew enough to put me away, and I was too weak to fight them off. My lawyer says they had no right to question me when I was so sick, but I waived that right before he got here. I just wanted it to be over. It would have been better if I had died.

I think of the email I sent to Mr. Ethics. Would it have been any different if I had let him go to the police then? Probably not. He never really understood my problem. Wade had destroyed my life. I was justified in doing whatever I had to do.

Too bad it all turned out so wrong.

There are so many moments when I could have stopped. If only I'd been strong enough to keep my wits about me and figure out how I was being used. I could have blown the whistle on all of them.

When Wade told me he'd figured out who was making my life unbearable, I wanted to believe it was someone else. But then the other picture came. It always came back to the pictures and the fact that Wade was the only one with access to them.

Except that's not what the detectives say. The photos were on his computer, sent there from one of his burner phones.

And maybe not by him. They say his wife must have found the phone with the pictures and taken it from there.

How could a person do that?

Why didn't I believe Wade? I wanted to. That's why I confronted his wife, but she was so convincing. I believed her when she said she'd had enough, that she was ready to divorce him and would make sure he left me alone. But she needed one favor from me. She needed proof of his affair.

She had it all worked out. I just had to arrange to meet him, and she'd have a private detective there to snap pictures.

More pictures. I wish they'd never invented photography.

It seemed like a simple enough request. She was so convincing. If you had told me back then, that she was behind all the harassment, I would have laughed at you. I really believed her.

I didn't question it when she called at the last minute and told me I didn't have to show up at the park. Just having him there waiting for me would be enough to get what she needed to force a divorce on her terms, and that would keep my name out of it.

And I believed her.

How stupid was that?

But I was so relieved that I didn't have to face him again, I would have believed anything.

I should have told the police everything after Wade was killed. I knew it had to be her. She would have known where he kept his gun. But I also knew I'd set him up, that I was guilty too, even if I did it unwittingly.

They haven't arrested me yet, but I'm sure that will come. In the meantime, there's a cop in my room and one outside the door. I suppose the one staring at me as I lie here is supposed to make sure I don't try to kill myself. I certainly can't get away.

I wish I had killed myself. I would have if I'd had the courage. And I still don't remember much about that night. I thought it was strange—and risky—when she came to my apartment. After that, everything's a blank. The doctor says it may come back to me in time.

But I'm not sure I want it to.

A Sort of Ending

Sam is waiting for Molly in the front yard, tossing a ball to Dodger, who is beginning to tire, though she'll be the last to admit it. She probably knows Sam will quit first, and anyway, he doesn't get this chance often.

Lisa has finally called. She'll be back this afternoon, so Sam's time with Dodger is running out. He wants to make the most of it.

Dodger is a terrific tight end. If Sam can throw the tennis ball with the right amount of height and speed, Dodger will put her head down, run hard, and somehow look up and turn just in time to grab the ball in her mouth. His ribs and sore leg make it hard for Sam, and in the instances when Dodger misses, she manages to make it clear it's Sam's fault. And every time Dodger brings the ball back and drops it at Sam's feet, challenging him to go again.

They're so busy with their game that Sam doesn't realize Molly has arrived until he hears the car door slam. Dodger gives her a glance, stares at the ball she just dropped at Sam's feet, then runs to greet her visitor. Chalk one up for Molly.

They go inside to make a pitcher of iced tea and while he's brewing it, his phone rings. It's Howie.

"Something you should know. The task force is still looking for Carl Wasserman, and they've been going around to his known associates. One of them is a guy named Andrew Varner. The name mean anything to you?"

Sam remembers that Wasserman's first alibi, the one he gave to Sam and Molly, involved a couple of anonymous friends, but he has a clear conscience in telling Howie he's never heard the name.

"Well, there was an outstanding arrest warrant on him, so they were able to get into his place and look around. I've just been looking over the report and it says there was a white Forrester in the driveway, registered to Varnum."

"And?" Sam asks, though he knows what's coming.

"Damage to the front right headlight and fender. When I saw the report, I asked them to look more closely and now they say there are traces of blue paint, consistent with a Mazda 3. We can do more tests if you let us go over your car."

Sam agrees and tells him where to find the car.

"So what does that tell you about Wasserman?" Howie asks.

He thinks about it. Wasserman is gone and running away always implies guilt, though in this case, he thinks Antifa Man just worried about getting blamed. Or maybe he worried about his friend getting caught. Sam can't see how he was a threat to Wasserman. In fact, he helped him get a lawyer, but maybe Wasserman decided that was a trick. Or maybe he couldn't control his friends.

"Very little about this case makes sense," Sam tells Howie. "Let me know what you find."

Molly comes looking for him just as he hangs up and pours the iced tea. They take a seat on the screened porch, and Dodger picks a corner to lie down in.

Sam's exhausted and in pain, and when Molly asks why, given that Dodger did all the running, he doesn't try to explain. He still hasn't told anyone but Howie about getting run off the road. But the pain is only part of it. The whole case has been exhausting, and he still has the burden of deciding what life's next chapter holds in store for him.

When they're comfortably settled, Molly tells him that she still hasn't been allowed to interview Kelly. "I think she's willing, but her lawyer won't let her. I did get to speak to him a bit, and Allison's sources have confirmed enough of what you figured out. The story's set to go online in a couple of hours." She looks at her phone instinctively, knowing that as editors and lawyers pore through it, she's likely to get calls and questions.

"Have they charged her?" Sam asks.

"Who? The wife or your pen pal?"

"She has a name."

"You feel sorry for her, don't you?"

He considers that, though he doesn't really have to. "I have from the start. I always thought of her as a victim."

"But there's no denying she made some bad decisions."

"No, I guess not. Have they charged her?"

"Not yet," Molly says. "She's not going anywhere, and the doctors aren't sure yet whether she'll have any lasting damage."

"But she remembers?"

"A lot of it. She remembers what led up to Morgan's murder, but I don't know if she remembers what happened to her with the overdose. No one will tell me."

"What would they charge her with?" Sam asks. "Conspiracy to commit murder? Impeding an investigation? Obstruction of justice?"

"I talked to one of the prosecutors and he doesn't think she'll ever go to jail. Not if her story holds up. They'll take a plea bargain to keep her out of prison in exchange for her testimony against Peg Morgan."

"I thought Larry Coleman would testify against Morgan."

"Apparently he doesn't know that much," Molly says. "Enough to put her in deep shit, but there are too many gaps in what he saw."

"Why is he talking at all? To save his job?"

"I'm not sure he can, but he turned against Morgan when she tried to blame him for killing her husband. Kind of a dumb move, but I guess she was desperate. She didn't know he had an ironclad alibi. I would have thought she was smarter than that."

Sam looks out the window and wonders about that. "You figure out the timeline?" he asks after a minute.

"Yeah. Kelly's story tracks with the data. After she first sent you that email, she made one last attempt to convince Morgan to stop harassing her. He denied it again, but she told him the photos meant it had to be him. She hadn't mentioned those before."

"They were always the hardest part for her," Sam says. "She couldn't talk about them, even to him."

"Anyway, he finally figured out it was his wife. She'd been aware of his burner phones all along and regularly tracked his dalliances. She sent the pictures from his phone to the computer and made them part of her attacks on Kelly. When he confronted her, he said he was getting a divorce. She couldn't let that happen."

"So that was his death warrant."

"It was part of it," Molly says. "She got her opportunity when Kelly decided to confront her. Kelly didn't believe Morgan, so she went to his wife. And Peg Morgan convinced her they were both victims. She claimed she was the one who wanted a divorce and had hired a private detective to catch her husband in the act. She had Kelly set up the meeting. He wanted to meet at her apartment like they always did, and he called her on her new burner—Peg Morgan told her to buy one and make sure Morgan had the number—but Kelly insisted on more neutral ground, told him they needed to talk, not have sex."

"But she wasn't there when he was killed."

"No. At the last minute, Peg Morgan told Kelly she didn't need to go, that she'd figured a way to get what she needed without her. Kelly was so relieved she didn't question it."

"So she had no idea what Peg had in mind?" Sam asks.

"Not according to my source. They believe her."

At the mention of a source, Sam looks at her and Molly gives a sheepish grin. "He called to apologize. Said he never meant any harm and hoped I could understand he was just a dinosaur—as opposed to evil, I guess."

"He's afraid you'll tell your dad."

"Most likely. It's okay. My dad doesn't need to know. Not as long as his friend behaves himself from here on out."

"You handled it."

She nods. "With your help."

"I didn't do anything. Though I would have beaten him up if you wanted me to."

She can't help but laugh. "He's bigger than you and he carries a gun."

"Yeah, there's that."

His mind drifts back to the case. "But do they really have enough to convict Morgan on murder?"

"Not clear. Kelly's testimony is a big part of their case, and Coleman saw the two of them together the day before the murder."

"Sounds circumstantial."

"Well, they're still looking," Molly says. There's also the matter of her lying repeatedly, to say nothing of attempting to murder Kelly."

"But Kelly has no memory of it?"

"No, but Peg Morgan doesn't know that, and they're keeping her guessing. And they found she recently talked her doctor into giving her a prescription for OxyContin. Not conclusive, but it's one more thing."

"Not sure a jury would feel that's enough."

"My source says it won't get that far. They'll reach some kind of plea bargain with Kelly so she'll tell them everything Peg did. Then they'll have at least enough evidence to reach some agreement with Peg. The truth is, they're not dying to go to trial and admit that the security team went home every time Morgan asked them to. Nobody would come out looking good."

"What about the four-second call?" Sam asks. "Do we know why Kelly called her own burner?"

"As you guessed. To test it. She'd been so nervous, she wrote down the number and then destroyed all the literature that came with the phone. Then she worried she had the number wrong and wanted to check. At least that's my source's version, and it makes sense."

"A natural criminal. How specific is your story going to be?"

"Pretty much everything we know, with a feature Sunday completely recapping how it all went down. I'm still hoping to talk to Kelly before then, but it's a long shot."

"Good work. You did a terrific job on this one."

"With your help. It's going to be boring to go back to covering a dysfunctional Congress again."

"As opposed to a dysfunctional family."

She raises her glass in an approving toast. "But I get a break before then."

"Right," he says, remembering. "You're getting married. How are the plans going?"

"My mother says not to worry, she's got it all in hand, which is exactly why I am worried."

"It'll be great. And if it's not, it won't really matter. The wedding may seem all-important now, but it's what comes after that you care about. Kyle's a great guy. You make a great couple."

She looks at him and he knows she knows what he's thinking.

"Lisa really has her mind made up?" she asks.

"Yeah, I'm afraid so. A new guy in the picture too. That kind of seals the deal."

"You never know."

"Better to accept it and try to move on."

They sit for a bit without saying anything, and then Molly gets up to leave. He walks her to the door, and she thanks him again.

"You're a good man, Mr. Ethics."

That bothers him. "Not sure I'll go back to that. I made some bad choices over the last several weeks. It wouldn't feel right. In fact, I think it might be time to kill the column. I'm not sure it was ever a good idea. The short letters and answers tend to oversimplify complex situations. If ethics is about doing the right thing, you can't always rely on a cookie-cutter list of rules. The situation matters."

She doesn't argue. "Then you'll do something else. Did you hear that Brenda's moving over to the editorial page? You'd be a great replacement for her."

He shrugs at that, walks her to her car, and just as she drives away, Lisa drives up. Dodger insists on greeting her first, but when the greeting is over, Sam gives her a careful hug and asks how the trip was.

"Fine," she says. "I appreciate your coming to the rescue that way."

"I was glad to do it," he says, really meaning it. Lisa hasn't given him any explanation for the trip and he's not about to ask.

He goes upstairs to gather his things, trying not to make anything of the fact that she doesn't ask him to stay for a drink or dinner. It's only on the way out that he realizes the one thing he would like from her.

"Lisa," he says, in a tone that gets her to look at him seriously. "I've decided not to stay in that apartment I rented. It's giving me claustrophobia. I'm going to get a real house."

"Great," she says, and he can tell she's relieved that's all he wanted to say.

But it isn't.

"I was wondering," he adds, and their eyes meet again. "Can I have Dodger?"

He can tell she's surprised, and she looks down at the dog, who's watching their every move. When she looks back at Sam, Lisa's smiling.

"As long as I get visitation rights."

Don't miss The Jonas Hawke Series By Mark Willen!

HAWKE'S POINT

BY MARK WILLEN

Is there such a thing as a second chance?

Jonas Hawke, a recovering alcoholic with bouts of crankiness and unmitigated orneriness, may be past his prime but he's still a damned good lawyer. That's why everyone in Beacon Junction turns to him for advice as soon as something goes wrong. And plenty does—murder, adultery, corporate conspiracy—everything you'd expect from a sleepy Vermont town.

A mysterious stranger arrives in town to question Jonas's handling of a decades-old murder trial, forcing him to confront an ethical lapse in his past. When evidence surfaces that a heart stent made by a local company may be deadly, he is drawn into an ethical quagmire that will determine how he'll be remembered.

Hawke's Point is the story of a broken man who gets a second chance to do the right thing, a novel with a potent mix of complex characters, life-and-death problems to keep them busy, and a page-turning plot.

Praise for Hawke's Point

"As Mark Willen explores life in a small Vermont community, he addresses large themes: guilt, forgiveness, familial loss, love, ethical dilemmas of many kinds. Vivid, complex characters like Jonas Hawke, retired lawyer and repository of many of the community's secrets, engage the reader and move the narrative along at an energetic pace. This is a novel so rich in humanity and situation that the world of *Hawke's Point* will continue to beguile long after the reader has turned the last page."
– Margaret Meyers, author of *Dislocation* and *Swimming in the Congo*

"Every town has its secrets and almost all hold such confidences close to the heart. It takes a determined, resourceful storyteller to bring such tales to the surface and that's what Mark Willen has done with his new novel set in the star-crossed town of Beacon Junction."
– Tim Wendel, author of *Red Rain, Habana Libre,* and *Summer of '68*

HAWKE'S RETURN

WINNER OF THE
MARYLAND WRITERS' ASSOCIATION
2017 BEST BOOK AWARD

It's his word against hers, and the stakes couldn't be higher.

When a teenager accuses a key official of a local charity of blackmailing her for sex—and then abruptly disappears—a mystery turns into a crisis, raising concerns about the girl's safety, the charity's survival, and the career and reputation of a man who says he is innocent.

Enter Jonas Hawke, retired lawyer and sage of Beacon Junction. Jonas has just agreed to oversee the charitable group, a friend's attempt to help Jonas move past his grief over the death of his wife. It's his job to uncover the facts and ensure that justice will be done.

Jonas is helped—and hindered—by the arrival of Dylan Walker and his eight-year-old son. Why a single dad has chosen to move to a small town in Vermont to start a new life is a mystery that tugs at Jonas, especially when Dylan develops an amorous interest in Jonas's married daughter.

Hawke's Return is the tale of a man groping his way back from the loss of his beloved soul mate, even as he struggles with an intractable dilemma.

PRAISE FOR HAWKE'S RETURN

"The characters in *Hawke's Return* are flawed and sometimes fragile, but their strength lies in their search for what they believe is the truth. An unassuming, character-driven novel that makes you think long after you have turned the last page."
– CINDY YOUNG-TURNER, author of *Thief of Hope*

"The pleasure of *Hawke's Return* lies in the details of human interaction and in the author's restraint, which keeps life in this small town both more real and more civil than life as we see it . . . immune from madman Tweets and random mass murders. Instead, decent but faulty people struggle with ambiguity."
– Gary Garth McCann, author of *The Man Who Asked to Be Killed*

"This second in Willen's "Hawke" series is a winner. By the time you come to the conclusion, the main characters . . . have become your friends. New characters, Dylan and Max, a widower and his young son, bring a lot of interpersonal drama to a story that deals with the problem of sexual harassment."
– Henry A. Zoob, author of *A Lifetime of Genesis*

HAWKE'S DISCOVERY

BY MARK WILLEN

A violent felon unexpectedly set free. An anonymous tip to a newspaper reporter. An ugly scandal that threatens a gubernatorial candidate. Together, they amount to another high-stakes crisis for Jonas Hawke—especially since the newspaper reporter is his son and the violent felon a former client.

With the election drawing close and his son eager to run with a story he can't verify, it's up to Jonas to unwrap the mystery, protect his son, and see that justice is done. What he discovers tests his loyalties and thrusts him squarely into the middle of a political campaign.

Hawke's Discovery, a stand-alone third novel in Mark Willen's Jonas Hawke series, has everything readers have come to expect—a page-turning plot with true-to-life characters confronting ethical dilemmas that have no easy solutions.

Praise for Hawke's Discovery

"In his third novel, Mark Willen continues to explore how and why characters make the critical decisions that shape their lives. With a controversy that pits individuals' rights to privacy against the people's right to know, Willen proves he's a master of creating compelling circumstances and pushing readers to decide what the characters should do about them. Hawke's Discovery is outstanding fiction. It kept me guessing and made me think."
– Sally Whitney, author of *Surface and Shadow*

Acknowledgments

Writing is, at its core, a solitary experience for me, because it inevitably involves my being holed up in a room for days on end with nothing but my imagination, my computer, and whatever experiences and skills I can call upon to put words on paper. It is both a relief and a blessing when that first draft is done, in part because that's when the rest of the team comes into play.

No book can ever make the trip from idea to publication without a lot of support from others, and I am grateful for all those who pitched in to help me.

First and foremost, thanks to the heart and soul of Pen-L Publishing: Duke Pennell, whose skillful editing included lots of creative ideas, and Kimberly Pennell, for all she did to turn the words into a finished product.

I am deeply indebted to those who generously offered their law enforcement expertise, and though they asked to remain anonymous, they were instrumental in helping work through the scenarios that might follow the death of a senator. As always, I took some dramatic liberties in how an investigation would play out, and any errors in procedure are all mine.

Writers, colleagues, and friends who were willing to read various early drafts of the manuscript also helped catch problems and offer insights to improve the manuscript. They include: David Kaplan, Millie Mack, Julia Marx, Andrew Mayeda, Eileen Haavak McIntire, Hank Parker, James Roby, Debra Willen, and Diane Willen.

Thanks also to Jessica Slater for the cover design, Kelsey Rice for the interior design and formatting, and Heather Wallace for advice on how to reach the people who might most enjoy the book.

And, most of all, thanks to my wife, Janet, who talked it through with me (hundreds of times), read every draft, and gave the love and support that made the whole venture possible.

About Mark Willen

Mark Willen, author of the Jonas Hawke series of novels, received a BA in political science from Dartmouth and an MA in creative writing from Johns Hopkins.

After almost 40 years as a Washington journalist, writing and editing stories about government and politics, he now divides his time between writing fiction and volunteer work. As a former graduate-level teacher of journalism ethics, he also tries to help people figure out the right thing to do in difficult situations through his blog, www.TalkingEthics.com.

Visit Mark's website at **www.MarkWillen.com** to learn more about his books, to read his reviews of other contemporary novels, and to sign up for his newsletter.

Thank you for reading *The Question Is Murder*! I hope you enjoyed it and will consider sharing a review on Amazon and/or Goodreads. Reviews needn't be long, and you can use the same review on both sites if you like. I also hope you'll visit my website at MarkWillen.com and sign up for email notifications when my own book reviews are posted.

Mark

CPSIA information can be obtained
at www.ICGtesting.com
Printed in the USA
LVHW041559220621
690863LV00001B/163